ೞ൸

RUST ON THE ALLEGHENY
COREY MCCULLOUGH

ೞ൸

Rust on the Allegheny
First Paperback Edition
Copyright © 2021

All rights reserved. No part of this book may be reproduced in any form. In accordance with the U.S. Copyright Act of 1976, the scanning, uploading, and electronic sharing of any part of this book without the permission of the publisher is unlawful piracy and theft of the author's intellectual property.

Printed in the United States of America

ISBN: 978-0-9966902-4-9
Published by Corey McCullough
10 9 8 7 6 5 4 3 2 1

Dedication

For my family.

A Note to the Reader

This is a work of fiction. Names, characters, businesses, events, and incidents in this book are the products of the author's imagination. Any resemblance to actual persons, living or dead, or actual events is purely coincidental.

Prologue

Latonia City, Pennsylvania
August 1964

NAT MACCULLOCH WAS halfway down the hallway before he realized the significance of where he was. The red-and-cream paisley print wallpaper. The light gray carpeting that looked like it would feel so soft between your toes. And the paintings on the wall. As a boy, he hadn't recognized the faces in those portraits looking down at him. But now he knew them as Edwin Drake, William Penn, and Chief Cornplanter of the Seneca.

The hallway was exactly the same. Neither the decor nor the paintings had changed, despite how much everything in the outside world had. Some of it, for the better. But most, not so much.

The first time he'd been here, twenty-five years prior, he could hardly have imagined himself as the man he was today: business suit, wallet full of cash, polished shoes. Back then, he'd just been a poor boy in short pants from the wrong side of the tracks (literally), with bottle caps and lint in his pockets, and shoes that didn't fit right. A boy who had come to this riverside cathedral of culture with nothing but foolish hope and a healthy dose of childish determination.

Well, thought Nat, *that, and a stolen rope. And a flour bag full of sand.*

"I hope we didn't miss him," the woman in front of Nat said over her shoulder as she walked.

"It's all right," said Nat. "You really don't have to—"

"No, no, I don't think he's left yet," she insisted. "Just up here."

Nat swallowed hard against his dry throat. He usually didn't let himself get so nervous. But the sense of deja vu already had him flashing back through the years, and his nerves seemed to respond in kind, filling him with jittery, anxious energy. The kind of energy that made you want to just up and bolt in a random direction—like a boy being led down the hall to the principal's office, clinging to the fading chance that there might still be some way out of this.

For God's sake, he had been to war. Yet here he was, nervous beyond reason at the prospect of a meeting with this man.

Nat's gaze wandered toward a particular door, and this time, the deja vu made him smile. For he knew that beyond that door was a small office. An office with a window that, on summer nights, the staff left open.

ᏨᏍᎬ

PART ONE
BOOM-TOWN SWING

ᏨᏍᎬ

Chapter One

Latonia City, Pennsylvania
July 2019

WHAT STRUCK OWEN about the lobby of the *Oildom Morning–Herald* was its stunning incongruity. Bite-sized chunks were missing from the yellowed panels of the drop-ceiling overhead. The peeling paint on the walls reminded him of the back corner of his old third-grade classroom. And a NO SMOKING sign hung above the reception desk. This last feature was the most telling of all. Indoor smoking had long gone the way of milkmen and payphones, and Owen suspected that if the lobby had received a fresh coat of paint at some point in the last twenty or thirty years, it might have occurred to someone that the sign really didn't need to be hung back up again.

The whole place had an out-of-time sort of feeling to it. And yet, amid the outdated elements was a magnificent, polished marble floor made of stylishly asymmetrical blocks and shiny copper dividers set down to form a giant mosaic in the shape of a keystone.

In scale and artistry alike, it was undeniably impressive. But all Owen could think about was how misplaced it seemed. To think that enough money had ever flowed through this nickel-and-dime operation to have merited such a *floor*.

And now, they couldn't even afford a fresh coat of paint?

Owen sat quietly, alone, in a chair with squared, stainless steel legs and an embroidered seat whose original color was impossible to discern. It was the kind of chair that reminded him of waiting for his mother to finish talking to the little man at the bank who always gave him a Werther's candy. Funny, thought Owen, how something like a chair could make you feel closer to the five-year-old, legs-swinging, fresh-off-the-assembly-line version of yourself than the thirty-two-year-old, hair-thinning, bargain-basement edition.

There was no risk of anyone sneaking up on you in here; the sound of approaching footsteps against the inexplicable marble floor came echoing down the adjoining hallway long before the source emerged from around the corner: a goateed middle-aged gentleman wearing a polo shirt, cargo shorts, and white tennis shoes. He stopped at the end of the hallway and looked at Owen with an expression that could only be described as distracted bewilderment.

"Mr. Albaugh?" Owen said, rising from his chair. He tried not to wince as the waistband of his khaki pants, which were about two inches too small, pushed into his belly. He'd gained a bit of weight since the last time he'd worn them, but he hadn't thought of that until this morning.

Owen extended his hand as he crossed the room, and Dave Albaugh, senior editor of the *Oildom Morning–Herald*, accepted the handshake . . . apprehensively. His mouth formed a tiny, suspicious *o* as he eyed Owen from behind a pair of wire-rimmed glasses.

"Owen, was it?" said Dave.

"Yes, sir," said Owen. He couldn't help but notice that Dave was squinting at him with the look of someone trying to figure out a magic trick who doesn't particularly like magic tricks.

"O-*kay*," said Dave. "Owen, I think you're a little early." He took an exaggerated look at the gold watch on his hairy wrist. "By about twenty-four hours."

"Twenty-four. . . ?" said Owen. "Didn't we say 10:30 on Wednesday?"

Dave tilted his head to look up at the ceiling while pushing out his lower lip and furrowing his brow, as if in genuine deliberation for all of one-quarter of a second.

"No," he concluded. "We said 10:30 on Thursday."

"Oh," said Owen.

A moment passed. Long enough for Dave to get a good look at Owen, and long enough for Owen to conclude that Dave Albaugh was a man not perturbed by awkward silences. The older gentleman's shorts-and-polo attire had Owen feeling self-conscious about his dress shirt and necktie, making him feel less like a job applicant and more like a waiter about to take a vacationer's drink order. But he also wondered if it was possible that Dave was the one with the ill-advised wardrobe. He seemed woefully underdressed for the elaborate marble floor upon which his New Balances trod.

They *had* agreed to meet on Wednesday. Owen was certain of this. It wasn't worth arguing the point, of course, but neither was he about to defer to Dave's mistake by pretending he was the one who'd gotten it wrong. So Owen just said, "Well. I hope I didn't call you away from anything important. It was nice to meet you, and I'll see you tomorrow."

"No, no, no. You're here," Dave said benevolently— and loudly. He checked his gold watch again. "I can move some things around and make it work, if you can give me five more minutes to finish something up first."

"Only if it isn't any trouble," said Owen.

"No trouble," Dave said, and turned back the way he'd come. "Be back in a minute."

Dave's walk was a bit like a vacationer's, too. An unhurried stride, a slight bend in his upper spine, and hands that swung low and heavy at his sides. More of a wander than a hurry.

No sooner had Dave's bare calves disappeared back down the hall than a sudden *thud* drew Owen's attention to the double doors at the front of the lobby. He looked up in time to see a small bird drop motionless to the sidewalk outside, rebounding from a hard collision with the blurred glass of the door.

Owen blinked. He wasn't one to believe in omens. But if he had been, that surely wouldn't have been a good one. At least, he *tried* not to believe in omens. But it wasn't always easy to cultivate a pragmatic, no-nonsense mindset when you came from a family like the MacCullochs.

A dark bit of movement flashed at the bottom of the door. The flapping of a wing.

Owen looked around. There was no sign of Dave Albaugh or anyone else, other than the top of the receptionist's head behind a bulky, very outdated computer monitor, so Owen crossed the lobby and opened the door. On the ground outside, a common American robin was flapping one wing and kicking one foot as its head rested, unmoving, against the ground. The result was a sort of stationary, pinwheeling motion that reminded Owen of Curly from the Three Stooges and might have even been funny under different circumstances.

He knelt down and cupped his hand, allowing the robin to spin itself into his palm by way of its own momentum. There, it twitched, kicked, and flapped. Maybe it would recover if he put it somewhere it wouldn't get stepped on.

Owen carried the robin to some nearby bushes and was preparing to place it in the grass when it suddenly stood up in his hand, its tiny, claw-like toes gripping the webbing between his fingers.

The bird looked at Owen, and Owen looked back at it. Then it tilted its head back and forth, hunkered down, and took off, stunned but apparently none the worse for wear. Owen watched it vanish between the low branches of a maple tree, and told himself once again that he did not believe in omens. Of any kind. Because if you started believing in the good ones, you had to put equal stock in the bad ones, and that was a slippery slope.

He caught the receptionist, who had very long hair that was dyed silvery-purple, peeking at him from around the bulk of her computer monitor as he reentered the lobby. She hastened to duck back behind it and resume typing. She did not reemerge, not even after Owen had returned to his chair and sat down, rubbing the hand that had held the robin against his pant leg. Moments later, the sound of approaching footfalls against marble announced Dave's return.

"Owen," Dave called before he'd fully turned the corner.

Owen stood and crossed the lobby, smoothing his hair with his hand—*not* the hand that had touched the bird. Although neatly trimmed, his dark, curly hair was a little longer than the current style.

"Sorry about the mix-up," he said as he matched Dave's stride down the hallway.

"Oh, don't worry about it," said Dave. There was a sheet of paper in his hand, and he held it at arm's length so as to examine it through his wire-rimmed glasses as he walked.

After a few steps, Dave came to a sudden stop. Owen stopped, too, and waited while Dave read something on the sheet of paper that Owen could now see was his resume. Dave mouthed a sentence to himself, made a curious face, and then looked up as if suddenly remembering where he was.

"Right in here," Dave said and gestured to the first door on the right.

A large window in the far wall of the conference room offered an impressive view of the confluence of the Allegheny River and Rock-Oil Creek. The table, which very nearly filled the interior of the room, was a definite contender for the newest thing in the building, except maybe for Dave's New Balances, which were as white as a toddler's baby teeth.

Owen waited to see where Dave would sit, then took a chair across the table from him. All the while, Dave continued to hold Owen's resume at arm's length and squint at it. It did not take a keen student of the human condition to infer that this was the first time he had looked at it.

Dave propped his elbows on the conference table and leaned forward. There was a fresh-looking Band-Aid on the back of his wrist. "So, help me understand this," he said without looking up from the resume. "You are a 'freelance copy editor'?"

"Yes, sir," said Owen. "For about a year now. It started as something I did on the side for a little extra money, but after I left my last job, I started doing it full-time."

Dave made a noncommittal sort of noise in his throat and rubbed at his goatee. He put the resume down, then favored Owen with a flat, unconvinced-looking smile. "I think you're the first person I've ever met who does something like that. Full-time, anyway."

"That's why the job opening caught my eye," said Owen.

"MacCulloch, eh? Any relation to Nat?"

"Nat was my grandfather," said Owen. And although he broadcasted no outward indication of it, he mentally braced himself for what was sure to come next. In this town, he had learned to expect one of two reactions to the news that he was the grandson of Nathaniel MacCulloch. If prior experience had taught him anything, there was about a fifty-fifty chance that this interview was already over.

Dave grinned and leaned back in his chair. "My dad was friends with Nat. He used to tell this crazy story about the two of them sneaking into the Derrick Theatre when they were kids."

Owen chuckled. "Really?" he said.

"Oh yeah!" Dave said. "Dad used to tell all kinds of stories about running around the South Side with Nat MacCulloch. Amazing, the stuff he remembers. Some of it may have even happened!"

"Huh," said Owen. "I'll have to meet him sometime and ask."

"You might regret it. If you're ever in the same room with my dad and he hears you're related to Nat, he'll talk your ear off. Boy, I bet *your* dad can tell some stories. He was a hell of a ballplayer. I used to watch him in high school. Probably could've turned pro."

"He tells some stories, all right," said Owen.

This was not very true. It had, in fact, been a long time since Owen and his father had talked about anything at all.

"I'm trying to remember," said Dave, scratching his chin in thought. "Who was it that Dad said they saw at the Derrick. . . ? It was a big-name guy. Eh, can't remember. Dad told all kinds of stories when I was young. I wish I'd written some of them down. But I think every son, up to a certain age, thinks his father is just there to be a supporting character in his *own* story, and now, I'm trying to play catch-up, because when he goes, his stories go, too." He glanced down at Owen's resume again. "And I see you're a veteran."

"Yes, sir," said Owen. "Army National Guard."

"Weekend warrior, huh?" said Dave.

"Sure," Owen said politely.

"You see any action?"

"Iraq, 2008 to 2009."

"No kidding?"

Owen could tell by the look on Dave's face that he was waiting for him to say more on the subject. He usually managed to be patient with people like this, but he preferred not to be asked any more questions about it, so he said, "Even the weekend warriors did full weeks there."

"Of course," Dave said. "Thank you for your service."

Owen nodded.

Then Dave took a deep breath and said, in the span of one long, world-weary exhale, "So, seeing as you've got some experience in this line of work, I'll go ahead and level with you." He removed his wire-rimmed glasses and placed them on the table in front of him. "This paper has historically asked employees to take on multiple roles. Staff writers proofing other staff writers, contributing editors taking their own photos, that sort of thing. The reason I advertised for a copy editor, specifically, is because what we really need is a dedicated copy desk. Full disclosure, the pay is not spectacular, but the benefits make up for it. Our health benefits are some of the best I've ever seen at a small organization like this. Dental and vision. And a 401k-match, which is getting hard to find these days."

He took another glance at Owen's resume, then shook his head and mumbled to himself, "A *freelance* copy editor, I'll be darned. . . ." He sucked his teeth, looked back up at Owen. "The hours are what turn some people off to this work. You'll always have your Saturdays, which is nice, but every other day of the week, it's six to twelve."

"Six in the. . . ?" said Owen.

"Evening," said Dave.

"So," said Owen, "Sunday through Friday, six to midnight."

"Yup," said Dave. "You'll get all federal holidays off, too. Not everyone here does, but we'll make sure you do. You have a family?"

"A wife and a daughter, fourteen months old."

"Ah. Congratulations. I have an eleven-month-old granddaughter. Love that age. You'll see, the older she gets, the more grateful you'll be for those Saturdays."

"I'll bet," said Owen. "I, uh, didn't see the wage listed. Is the position salaried?"

"No," said Dave. "It's hourly."

Then Dave told Owen the hourly wage. And not for the first time since entering the offices of the *Oildom*

Morning–Herald (Owen had no idea why the publication's name was hyphenated), he had to force himself not to visibly react.

"That's our standard entry-level rate, and I don't have any say in the matter," Dave was quick to clarify. "But, like I said, good benefits and lots of opportunity for advancement. When I started here in 1984, I took home $3.35 an hour. You work your way up, that's just how it goes. People don't seem to understand that anymore. I talk to these kids fresh out of college, never had a real job, and they expect someone to hand them $50,000 a year. It's like, 'Wake up,' right? Welcome to the real world, kid!"

"Right," said Owen. "Well, the benefits do sound pretty good."

"Right," agreed Dave. He held the resume up again. "And, remind me, what was it you did before your freelance work?"

"Archaeological field technician," said Owen.

Dave made a face.

"I know," said Owen. "My bachelor's degree is actually in anthropology. I enjoyed the work, but it was a lot of traveling, and. . . . Well, it just didn't work out."

Dave snorted a small laugh. "A veteran archaeologist copy editor. I'm not sure if I should be impressed by your range or nervous that this paper is just your next jumping-off point."

"Family comes first, and I've got a little one now," said Owen. "My jumping around days are over."

"I'll have to take your word on that one." Then Dave patted Owen's resume on the table twice—hard and flat-handed, like he was dribbling a basketball. "Okay, good enough for me. I've got a written skills test around here somewhere. I'd like you to take it, just to make sure you know your stuff. Grammar basics, writing mechanics, that sort of thing. But, hell, I don't think that's gonna be a problem, do you? Mr. Archaeologist?"

"Guess we'll see," said Owen.

"Guess so," said Dave. "Sit tight. I'll be right back as soon as I find the damn thing."

Dave exited the room with sneakers squeaking against the marble, and Owen leaned back in the chair, sighing.

Standard entry-level rate. For who? A busboy?

Chapter Two

IT TOOK FOUR failed attempts at laying the baby down in her crib before Owen finally decided it was time to try the front porch swing. It was a muggy midsummer night and too hot and humid for his liking, but there was something about the sound of intermittent traffic on Route 322 in front of the tiny rented house that seemed to calm Emma.

"Do you know that the only thing I want to do right now is sleep?" Owen whispered to Emma as he took a seat on the swing. He held the fourteen-month-old with a degree of ease he never would have imagined himself capable of fifteen months before. And he was using his baby-voice. Which, it should be made clear, does not mean a voice like a baby, but the voice one uses only when one talks to a baby. Everyone has one of these.

"Someday," Owen continued in standard baby-inflection, "all *you'll* want to do is sleep, and you won't be able to, because you'll have somebody around like *you* who won't let you. Yes, you will."

He leaned in, bringing his face close to Emma's. Her eyes lit up when their noses touched. Everybody had told him about dirty diapers and temper tantrums and the terrible twos. But nobody had told him about things like how present a baby was. Or the way a baby looked at you—as if you were their whole world, all that was, had been, or ever would be. And maybe it was the way Emma's deep-brown eyes caught the light from the lone, dirty bulb hanging from the ceiling of the covered porch, or some deep-seated sense of deja vu, but for a second, Owen almost remembered what it felt like to be so present.

Almost. Then a pickup truck went flying by on 322 with bass notes from its stereo thumping so loudly that Owen could feel the beats vibrating his guts. With that, the feeling of contentment evaporated like a stale smell, replaced by thoughts of the *Oildom Morning–Herald*, Dave Albaugh's New Balances, and a standard entry-level rate that made Owen feel a little sick.

Maybe it was Thursday we agreed to after all, he thought as he pushed with his heels to set the porch swing moving. *Maybe I really did get the day wrong.*

He didn't think so. But he could have made a mistake. Or done it on purpose, as some sort of subconscious self-sabotage. God knew he didn't want the job. The copy editor position paid a fraction of what he'd made as a field tech, but there was a reason he wasn't doing that anymore. And a specialized degree like his didn't allow for a lot of lateral movement. He'd been searching for a steady job for months. And despite the low pay, the newspaper was his best lead so far. He'd had to purchase a newspaper the day before to re-familiarize himself with the format and writing style; it was the first time he'd gotten his daily news somewhere other than a backlit screen in about five years.

By the time Owen had left, Dave had been talking about "getting him set up at the *nice* desk." As if the job not only already belonged to Owen, but that Owen accepting the offer was a foregone conclusion.

If they offered him the job, he would take it, and that gave him the kind of empty feeling in his stomach he'd always gotten as a kid while balancing on the edge of a tall rock or standing at the end of the dock at the river, just before he jumped. Low pay. Odd hours. And as far as Dave's insistence on opportunity for advancement, well, it fell a bit flat, given the less than electrifying prospects for small, local print outlets in the Digital Age.

So why am I doing this to myself? Owen wondered.

Emma made a cooing sound and kicked a foot for no particular reason, and Owen took out his phone. He had opened YouTube and was typing in the title of one of her favorite lullaby videos when something flashed in the corner of his eye.

On their side of the road, the houses sat practically shoulder-to-shoulder, with only narrow concrete sidewalks serving as dividers between them and the adjacent homes. The result was that Owen could have touched his next-door neighbor's outdated wood siding just by leaning out his kitchen window, not that he wanted to. The big white house across the road, on the other hand, had a small front yard and a few trees, including a too-tall spruce that had lived through a hack-job to its lower branches to create enough clearance for a riding lawnmower, and a dogwood that was so pretty when it blossomed in the spring that it was darn near out of place.

As Owen watched, the event that had caught his attention recurred: A dot of warm yellowish green blinked into existence beneath the too-tall spruce for a count of one-Mississippi, then burned out.

Owen's phone made an emulated *click* sound as he locked the screen and placed it on the wooden armrest of the porch swing. With Emma in his arms, he straightened up in his seat, keeping his eyes trained on the location in the yard across the road. Another dot winked on and off again. Then another.

"Fireflies," Owen told Emma in a whisper. "First of the year. Emma Lee, you are going to love catching fireflies. Do you think you'll like that?"

He was always asking her questions like that. One day, she would answer.

"I used to love catching fireflies with your grandpa and grandma," said Owen. "Of course, your grandpa called them 'lightning bugs, not 'fireflies.' I always wanted to keep them in my room like a nightlight. I think I got the idea from a book I had. But he said that was no way to treat Pennsylvania's State Insect."

There were at least three of them, maybe more, talking to each other in their lazy midair waltzes. When Owen thought of fireflies, or lightning bugs or whatever you called them, he always pictured them from a child's-eye view, hovering three or four feet above the grass, within reach. He tended to forget how high they were willing to fly. Presently, one was all the way in the upper branches of the too-tall spruce.

Owen's phone, face-down on the arm of the swing, vibrated to indicate a new message. He started to reach for it but was stopped in mid-reach by a tiny hand touching his wrist. He looked down and noticed that Emma's gaze was no longer on him. Her focus had drifted toward the ceiling of the covered porch, a good sign that sleep was not far off.

Why beg for a job you don't want? thought Owen.

He touched Emma's face. Without breaking her focus on the ceiling, she blinked once. Slowly.

This is why. Remember that.

He adjusted his arm to hold her hand in his. Still without looking, she clamped a tiny, dimple-knuckled fist around his thumb.

"You won't be like me," Owen told Emma, "looking for an entry-level job at this age. You'll probably be a doctor or a lawyer or a businesswoman. Maybe a mom, too. If you want. With your own kids to catch fireflies with. You won't have time for this little town, I bet. You'll be out there, making something of yourself, a long way from rented houses that are too small, and roads that are too noisy, and neighbors that are too close."

The idea made Owen proud. And a little sad.

There were people who claimed that the whole MacCulloch family was "cursed." And the topic was not spoken of like a sneaking suspicion or a theory. Rather, it was discussed as one might inform another of the time of day or the score of the Monday night game. But Owen didn't believe in curses. He didn't want to. Couldn't afford to.

"You're going to be so amazing," he whispered to Emma. "But until then, Mommy and I get you all to ourselves. And I get to show you all kinds of things for the first time. Like catching fireflies."

He looked down. Emma's eyes were closed. Her head was tilted sideways—toward the noisy road instead of away from it. Her grip on his thumb had in no way relaxed.

Owen pushed a lock of her dark curly hair back off her forehead. The same kind of curly hair that he had spent most of his life trying to keep short enough that it *couldn't* curl. Hair that, now that it was becoming noticeably thin in the front, Owen wondered if he ought to have appreciated a bit more while he'd still had the chance.

"You might be the one thing I've done right," Owen told his sleeping daughter. "You'll be better than me. You'll *do* better than me."

He picked up his phone to check the message he'd missed. It was from his mother.

First of all, EVERYONE IS OK, read the text's preview line.

Owen stopped rocking the porch swing. A message from his mother that started like that almost never meant that everyone was okay. He opened it to continue reading, quietly reminding himself of his feelings about things like omens and family curses and such.

Chapter Three

LOU MACCULLOCH WAS the name handwritten on the dry erase board on the hospital room wall. Never Louis. Always Lou.

The name of the attending nurse, which had also been written on the dry erase board, was the same name as a girl Owen had gone to high school with. Not someone he'd *known*, exactly, but someone he had at least been aware of and who had probably, to some degree, been aware of him. He found himself feeling bad for her and anyone else who had to take care of his father. Lou MacCulloch was not an altogether unpleasant person, but he had no love for hospitals. Especially not for this one. The MacCulloch family's relationship with this hospital was ... complicated.

On the television on the wall, a rerun of a 90s sitcom played that no one was watching. "You didn't have to rush over here," said Owen's mother, seated beside the bed with her hands clasped over her knees, smiling, and sounding for all the world as if she might have been waiting to hear from the mechanic about the funny noise her car was making, that's all. "Everything's probably fine."

In the bed beside Deb McCulloch's chair, her husband grunted in annoyance. "I feel fine *now*, of course," said Lou. His dark, curly hair was askew, and despite the circumstances, Owen couldn't help but take note of the location of his hairline. Was that how far back he should expect his to go?

It was beyond strange to see his father like this, in a hospital gown and with an uncharacteristic five o'clock shadow. Mentally, Owen tried to count the weeks since the last time he'd seen Lou, and realized that the time that had elapsed since their last argument was now, in fact, enough to be counted in months.

"Probably nothing, but you know how these places are," said Lou. "They get you in the door, they want to do every check they can think of."

Owen—who, after reading his mother's message, had quickly handed Emma off to Kayla and raced straight over here—could only think to say, "Yeah, that's how they get you." Which was not a statement he particularly believed, but it was usually easier to mirror his father's cynical attitude than it was to contradict it.

It was now 11:45 p.m., and to say that this day hadn't gone as Owen had expected would have been an understatement. By the time he'd made it to the ER, his dad had already been transferred to an upstairs room for observation overnight. His mother and father hadn't offered much in the way of details yet. And one did not "pry" in the MacCulloch family. The unspoken agreement was that anything a person wanted to tell you, they would tell you on their own time. At a time like this, it was a pretty annoying policy.

Owen wanted to say that, with a family history like theirs, chest pains and shortness of breath were about as far from "probably nothing" as it got. And that any category of "probably nothing" that had been bad enough for a man like Lou MacCulloch to have allowed his wife to bring him *here* was probably serious enough for the doctors to be doing a little more than checking to make sure everything was "fine."

You'd probably be acting the same way, thought Owen, *if it was you in the bed and Emma standing here.*

He wasn't sure he liked that idea.

"Probably good to get things checked out anyway," Owen added.

He distracted himself by glancing toward the television. He couldn't remember the old show's name, but he recognized the actors. Other than the TV, there were none of the hospital-noises that Owen would have expected to hear. No whir of machinery. No rhythmic beeping. There was a monitor beside the bed reporting a series of numbers, but he wouldn't have known how to tell if what they were reporting was good or bad. Kayla would have known. She would have known all the right questions to ask, too, and just how to ask them.

"Has anything like this ever happened before?" was all Owen managed to come up with.

Lou tilted his head to the side, eyeing Owen as he might eye a price at the supermarket he didn't much approve of. "Not like *this*, obviously."

Deb cleared her throat again, and the room was silent except for one of those it's-funny-because-it's-so-stupid car insurance commercials on the TV.

Mercifully, a quick knock came from the open door. The doctor entered without waiting for a response.

"Louis? Are you free to talk? Everybody in the room okay to hear this?" Three questions asked all at once. Doctors were nothing if not efficient about their time. Lou answered all three questions with an equally efficient, "Yes."

"Louis, you did not have a heart attack," said the doctor, "we've ruled that out. My question for you is, are you currently taking anything to manage your blood sugar?"

"No," Lou answered.

"Nothing," she said. "Okay. Has anybody ever talked to you about managing your blood sugar?"

"A few times," said Lou.

"Okay. I think it'd be best to keep you overnight and keep an eye on things, but what I'm seeing is that you're right on the line between what we consider pre-diabetic and diabetic. A sudden jump could have caused your chest pains and could account for the shortness of breath, too. We'll monitor your levels for a while, but assuming nothing changes, the steps for you moving forward will be to follow up with your primary physician and get you started on something to manage your levels. Okay? Do you have any questions for me?"

She was already inching back out into the hallway.

"Blood sugar," said Lou. "Huh."

"Can that cause a heart attack?" asked Deb.

"Unmanaged diabetes can absolutely lead to heart disease," said the doctor, "so getting this under control is critical. Okay?"

"All right, I guess," said Lou.

"Okay," the doctor said and flashed her first smile so far. "You need anything, just hit the call button."

And with that, she was gone.

"Not a heart attack," said Deb. "Thank God."

"See?" said Lou. "Told you I was fine."

Fine? thought Owen. "But it could be diabetes," he said.

"*Pre*-diabetic, the doctor said," said Deb.

"Part of getting older," said Lou, "more little plastic bottles with your name on them."

"Well, yeah, but . . ." said Owen. "Kayla's dad had diabetes. It doesn't just go away with the right medicine."

"We know that," said Deb before Lou could say anything regrettable. She spoke to Owen in the same soothing, patient voice she'd always used to calm him down when he couldn't understand his geometry homework. "I thought it might be something like that, and I've been reading up on it. We'll get it under control."

Owen's phone vibrated in his pocket, and he quickly checked it. The text from Kayla read, *How is he? If you need me, let me know. I'll put Emma in the car, or I can have Mom come over and watch her.*

Owen had started to reply that everything was "fine"—maybe the apple hadn't fallen so far from the tree—when his mother said, "I'm just glad we know what it is now. And that it's manageable."

"It's also genetic," said Owen. "It killed Kayla's father. Who knows? It could be what killed Grandpa, too."

At this, Lou sat up a little straighter in his bed. The 90s sitcom was back on. He grabbed the television remote, which was attached to the bed by a long, thick cable, and said without looking at Owen, "Everybody knows what killed your grandfather." Then he gestured around the room, indicating his surroundings. "Here more than anywhere, they ought to know good and damn well."

Deb MacCulloch cleared her throat. Owen MacCulloch moistened his lips. And Lou MacCulloch said, "Dumb show," and pressed a button on the remote to change the channel.

Chapter Four

"OH MY GOD, she's on the roof," said Owen.

"She's not on the roof," said Kayla. "She's on a ladder."

"Gee, sorry," said Owen, leaning forward over the steering wheel to get a better look at the seventy-six-year-old woman two stories up. Admittedly, she *was* on a ladder. Or, at least, a pair of long wooden poles with crossbeams that had once been marketed and sold as a ladder.

Gravel crunched beneath the tires as Owen brought the red Ford Focus to a stop in front of the detached garage. At the top of the ladder, meanwhile, Ruth Lee Woodford paused her work to wave cheerfully down at them with one dripping, grime-covered glove. Then she scooped a final handful of semi-putrefied leaves out of the gutter and dropped the load into the bucket that hung from the top of the ladder by its wire handle. With that, she removed the gloves and began her descent. Kayla had been at work all day at the long-term care facility, and Owen had spent the afternoon finishing up some freelance projects at home. Ruth Lee, meanwhile, had taken Emma for the day to watch her. Or at least, that had been the plan. Owen wasn't sure watching from the top of a ladder counted.

He put the car into park. "What if she falls and breaks her leg, or worse?" He punctuated this thought with a gesture toward the apple tree in the front yard. "While our daughter watches from a swing."

Baby Emma, in a faded pink swing hanging from the lowest branch of the apple tree, sat motionless, with her eyes closed in the sun and her head resting against her shoulder, in the kind of deep sleep that must have inspired some anonymous and long-dead wordsmith to first add the noun "baby" to the phrase "to sleep like a."

By now, it shouldn't have surprised Owen to find his mother-in-law up a ladder. Or soldering the cracked joint of an ancient copper pipe in the basement. Or mowing the lawn on the hill behind her house by means of a push-mower suspended by a length of rope. But no matter how many times he witnessed it, the woman's seemingly age-defying stamina and hardiness never ceased to amaze him. Neither heights, nor electrical wiring, nor high-powered machinery could slow her down.

"Don't you think she's a little old to be doing something like this?" said Owen. "I'd be happy to do it for her if she asked."

Kayla, with an amused grin, cocked one dark eyebrow at him. He'd picked her up from work, and she was still in her scrubs, teal ones. "Except that you're afraid of heights," she said.

Owen made a face. He'd fought insurgents in the streets of Ramadi. He'd manned a .50 caliber heavy machine gun at the top of a Stryker by hand when the RWS controls failed. Hell, during airborne school at Benning, he'd jumped C-130s at 1,250 feet. But as long as he lived, Kayla was never going to let him forget that one time on the Ferris wheel. To be fair, it hadn't just been the height. But it wouldn't have been so bad if they hadn't been right at the tippy-top when that teeth-jarring stop had caused their car to swing practically horizontal. As far as Owen was concerned, it was one thing to take your own life in your hands and another to put it in the hands of a pizza-faced carnival ride operator with an eighth-grade education and an itchy trigger finger.

"I'm not afraid of heights," said Owen. "They're just not my favorite."

"Being active is what keeps her healthy," said Kayla.

"Until she falls," said Owen.

Beside him, Kayla said nothing, and when he finally glanced at her, she was giving him a look. Not necessarily a *bad* look; she wore a perfectly unflustered expression, with a relaxed brow line over her very round hazel eyes and a gentle, forgiving sort of smile. But that sort of look was sometimes even worse than a bad one. It was downright convicting.

"Sorry," said Owen. "I'm a little stressed out."

"I know you are," said Kayla. She flipped open the passenger-side vanity mirror, glanced at herself, and pulled her dark ponytail a bit tighter. "You're stressed about your dad, and you're stressed about the job offer, on top of all the usual things. If you ask me, the last thing you need is to climb a ladder and try to clean a rain spout when Mom's perfectly capable of doing it herself."

"I'm just saying," said Owen, "I'm only a phone call away. I could help her with some of these jobs around the house once in a while. Can't imagine *my* mom doing anything like that, that's all."

"Well, you have to remember how long my dad's been gone," said Kayla. Ruth Lee was now halfway down the ladder, taking the rungs with stunning ease. "And for all that time, Mom has had to rely on herself to climb ladders and clean gutters and provide for me. She doesn't see it as a job she needs to find someone to handle for her. She sees it as a normal part of life. And if you've got a baby to take care of, you put her in the swing and get it done just the same."

"I know," said Owen. "I just. . . . You know I worry about stuff like this."

Kayla smiled, then patted him reassuringly on the leg. "And you have the right to. If you feel strongly about it, you can try talking to her. But so far, nobody's been able to keep my mother from climbing ladders. Just try not to be short with her."

Kayla opened the door and stepped out, but Owen remained sitting a moment longer, watching Ruth Lee step spryly down onto the lawn. Kayla was an only child who had come into the world as a *blessing*, which was what you called a *surprise* when you didn't want to be rude, when Ruth Lee had been forty-four years old. That made Ruth Lee Woodford, whom no one ever called anything but "Ruth Lee," closer in age to Owen's grandparents than she was to his parents. And Kayla appeared to have inherited a great deal of the old woman's unassuming independence. Owen wondered if she would someday be scaling buildings long after he was gone.

Making his way toward the plastic swing in the apple tree, Owen looked around at the thick woods that ran alongside Ruth Lee's house, and the grown-over field on the garage-side of the property, and down the long, gravel drive in front, ending at a country road with little traffic. What he'd decided not to say to Kayla was that *if*, God forbid, Ruth Lee ever did one day fall off a ladder or have anything else happen to her, there were no neighbors within shouting distance to hear her and come help. And although Ruth Lee had turned out to be a whiz on her cell phone once she'd finally decided to adopt the technology—these days, she sent and received more text messages per billing cycle than Owen and Kayla combined—she didn't always carry it on her. Too worried about "running the battery low."

Owen decided he would say nothing else on the subject today. He knew he wouldn't have been able to avoid "being short" with his comments. He couldn't remember if it was him or Kayla who'd first started using that term, "being short," but there was by now an understanding between them that it was the code-phrase reserved for the times when Owen was acting like an ass.

In the swing, Emma slept with her full lips smooshed together in a pout and the lower lip sticking out extra far, just like Kayla when she slept. Emma looked so much like

Kayla's baby pictures. Except for that dark, thick, curly Irish hair. That was all MacCulloch.

"*This* is where we'll come to catch your first fireflies," Owen whispered to Emma, looking around again at the yard and the woods.

This is why, he reminded himself again. *And don't forget it.*

"Your dad feeling any better?" Ruth Lee called to Owen as she crossed the yard, brushing her hands on her jeans. She wore a look of deep, genuine concern, but it somehow still did not disrupt her perpetual smile. Her wiry hair, mostly deep brown but white at the roots where the natural color was starting to grow back in, was plastered flat with sweat above her ears.

"Mom texted me to say he's home and feels normal," said Owen.

"I hope it's not the diabetes," said Ruth Lee, pronouncing it the way Wilford Brimley always had in those old commercials.

"Was Emma good for you today?" asked Kayla.

"Oh, she's always good, you know that," said Ruth Lee. "If youns have anything else you need to get done, go and do it now. You can come back around dinner. Stay for dinner, if you want. . . . I meant to ask you, what did Lou and Deb say about you buying the house?"

Owen cleared his throat. But before he was forced to reveal that he hadn't told his parents about the house yet, something caught Ruth Lee's eye. Owen watched as she walked to the driveway and got down on one knee in the gravel in front of the driver's side of the Focus.

Owen braced himself.

What is it this time? he wondered.

She whistled through her teeth and announced, "My, this tire is *looooo*-ow."

"Is it," said Owen.

He felt Kayla touch his back—a quiet, gentle reminder. About shortness.

"I didn't realize," he quickly added in his friendliest-sounding voice.

"Don't you have a warning light?" asked Ruth Lee.

"Yes," said Owen, "but it started displaying a 'Sensor Fault' message a while back, so it's just always on. I keep meaning to have that looked at."

"Well, easy enough to take care of," said Ruth Lee. And before Owen could say anything to dissuade her, she was entering the detached garage through its side door. He tried to suppress a sigh, but Kayla noticed. (Owen was a sigher, and Kayla was a noticer.)

"She's just trying to help," said Kayla.

Ruth Lee returned from the garage lugging an air compressor. Behind her came a small brown-and-white dog that, by Ruth Lee's speculation, was mostly beagle. Her name was Wilma. Owen wasn't sure where Wilma had come from just now—the dog seemed to come and go and do as it pleased—and wasn't sure where it had come from to begin with, either. The story was that Ruth Lee had picked her up off the side of the road, and no one had come forward to claim her. A veterinarian had once estimated Wilma to be probably eight or ten years old, and that had been ten years ago. So either the vet had guessed rather poorly, or the little mystery mutt was as great a wonder of age-defiance as her owner.

Wilma, with all the grace of a walking sausage link, lumbered over to greet Owen and Kayla. After Kayla had bent low to nuzzle Wilma's head, she stood back up with a groan and stretched her back, producing a series of audible pops. She noticed something on the front of her teal scrubs and brushed it off.

"Do you want to go out somewhere for dinner, or do you want me to make something?" she asked.

"It's up to you—" was all Owen got out before he was cut off by the air compressor roaring to life, shattering the silence of an otherwise serene country summer afternoon. Wilma the mostly-beagle barked enthusiastically at the noise. But Emma, to Owen's surprise, not only didn't wake up but hardly so much as stirred in her pink plastic swing. Little wonder. Spending her days around here, she was probably used to sleeping through the din of power tools.

Chapter Five

"I TOOK IT," Owen whispered to himself as he drove. "I can't believe I actually took it."

The digital display on the car's dash read 6:55 p.m. Beside him, still in her teal scrubs, Kayla sat with her eyes closed and a bag of dinner's leftovers in her lap. She worked long hours and had become highly skilled at power-napping whenever she could, however she could, and as often as possible. Meanwhile, in the back, Emma sat in her rear-facing car seat, visible to Owen thanks to a mirror hanging from the headrest, wide awake and staring quietly out the window.

It had all happened so fast: The email had come through from Dave Albaugh offering him the job during dinner. And Owen, knowing that if he thought about it too long he would surely psych himself out, had shot off a single-lined reply, "See you Monday!" and promptly returned to his bacon cheeseburger, extra tomatoes, no onions. He hadn't even told Kayla yet.

Ahead, a PennDOT worker on the side of the road turned her sign to the STOP position, forcing Owen to ease on the Focus's brakes to comply. He flexed his fingers over the steering wheel in annoyance, producing little squeaky noises against the pleather. "So close," he said.

On the other side of the construction zone, the flag-turner's counterpart turned his sign, allowing the traffic coming from the opposite direction to slowly navigate the temporarily one-lane road beside the final remnants of a monumental cement foundation. A bulldozer was currently in the process of pushing some broken, castle-like blocks from one side of the site to the other.

Owen looked up into the sky, at the freshly unobstructed view where the parking garage had previously stood, and found himself trying to imagine a version of this town busy enough to require multiple vertical levels of vehicular accommodations. The tear-down was long overdue, of course, but that didn't make the resulting disruption to one's commute any less inconvenient.

Oh man, I'm going to have a commute, thought Owen.

At this hour, in this part of town, the surrounding sidewalks were all but deserted. The few exceptions were some pedestrians who looked more like they were wandering aimlessly than moving from one place to another with any real intention. Darkened storefront windows looked in on empty shop floors that had been out of business for so long that even the style of font used on the CLOSED signs looked vintage. The establishments that had managed to hold on until more recently didn't even bother with signs. The windows were just dark. The same lack of signage was the standard at the local shopping mall, too; when the number of stores with their gates down outnumbered those that were open, notices like CLOSED and FOR RENT just felt redundant.

Ahead, the woman from PennDOT stood, staring at nothing, pretending that Owen was not there. It must have been part of their training.

Out of curiosity, Owen attempted to follow her blank stare. She seemed to be studying the mural across the street, painted on the side of what had previously been a bare brick surface. The scene depicted a train yard, with men carrying oil barrels on their backs, preparing to load them onto locomotive cars. They featured various logos: Wolf's Head, Esso, Quaker State, Pennzoil. More than one of those companies had once had their headquarters right here in Latonia City. But those glory days were gone. And so were the oil companies. Along with most of the industry.

No one liked to think of this little town as a sinking ship, but even the sturdiest of vessels could withstand only so great a burden. After its industrial peak in the 1930s, the area had been hit by one economic setback after another. Enough so that when the Great Recession of 2008 hit, the people of Latonia City and Seneca County as a whole hardly noticed; if anything, it leveled the playing field a little.

The money just wasn't here anymore. The big Victorian mansions on First Street that had once been the homes of titans of industry were now rental properties owned by absentee landlords, their once spacious interiors cordoned off into as many apartments as possible, with tacked-on staircases clinging to the exteriors to reach second-floor walk-ups. Other properties just sat empty. There were entire streets of Latonia City where barely anyone lived. *Blight* was what people called it. And every once in a while, an abandoned home that had once been a stately manor would start to fall in on itself, and the city would come and bulldoze it, and by the next summer, it would be a grassy lot overgrown with brush. But the worst was when one would burn down. Which, due to old wiring and poor maintenance, happened more often than one might think. Just the previous summer, a rental had gone up, and one little boy hadn't made it out.

The radio in the PennDOT worker's hand buzzed, jolting her from her hypnosis, and she turned her sign to SLOW. Etiquette compelled Owen to give her the standard salute-wave for the sake of politeness. She performed her part of the exchange flawlessly in response, continuing to pretend that Owen did not exist.

At the intersection of Venango and Center Street, Owen passed beneath the Latonia National Bank Building. It was one of the tallest buildings in the county—a rectangle of gray granite that looked, rather appropriately, like a massive standing vault. But the vault was empty both in the figurative and literal sense. Latonia National Bank had been bought by a larger bank out of Pittsburgh in the 1970s and had been closed sometime in the 80s during a period of consolidation.

Latonia City was a Rust Belt town, plain and simple. One of hundreds like it dotting the Northeast and Midwest. Places that had once been centers of industry but were now languishing—boom-towns turning to ghost towns in agonizing slow-motion. It was no one's fault, really. Over time, Main Streets had turned into empty galleries and shopping malls into ossuaries. And amid the ruins lived a generation of people like Owen, who saw nothing but the bad, and grew cynical. He had to admit that he was guilty of unfair condemnation of this place. Part of him still thought that it had been a mistake to move back here from Ohio after quitting archaeology and leaving the environmental consulting firm. But there was another part of him that was hopeful. Maybe the decline was over. Maybe this was where things leveled out before making an ascent. The infrastructure was all here, after all. All that was needed was for something to happen (he didn't know what, but *something*) for all the latent greatness echoing through this valley to be resurrected. And maybe it was partially his responsibility to make that happen. But how he was going to do that at the *Oildom Morning-Herald*, bringing home their standard entry-level rate, he had less than a single clue.

"Can't believe I actually took the job," he whispered to himself again.

Even the name of the town newspaper was a callback to the area's prime. The original name for Latonia City had been Oildom Centre, back before it and a second town called Lay's Bend had been incorporated to form the combined entity of Latonia City. The fact that locals pronounced "Latonia" with a long *a* sound, as in *Lay*, was a linguistic remnant of this fact. You could always tell you were dealing with an out-of-towner when they pronounced the city's name with a short *a*, as in *lateral.*

After crossing the bridge that spanned the wide, shallow elbow of the Allegheny River, Owen turned up the divided section of Central Avenue. Here, an overly cautious motorist in a white Lincoln cost him his chance at making the turn onto East Front Street before the light turned red. And that was how Owen found himself sitting at a standstill beneath the shadow of the old Derrick Theatre.

Owen looked up at the Derrick. He *always* looked up at the Derrick, could hardly help it.

Much like the majestic keystone mosaic on the floor of the *Oildom Morning–Herald* lobby, the towering art deco design of the Derrick Theatre felt strikingly out of place. The decorative architectural elements at the heights of its facade were painted in bold shades of green and gold. At the front corners were two larger-than-life sculptures of theatrical masks representing the dual personifications of drama—a smiling face to symbolize comedy, and a frowning, slightly terrified-looking face to symbolize tragedy. Both looked down at the street with pitted, crumbling eyes. A green blanket of creeping ivy covered most of the western wall. And on the roof, almost inconceivably, there grew a small, gnarled tree.

The Derrick maintained its theatrical aesthetic even though it hadn't been a theater in decades. Owen recalled a minor public outcry some years prior in response to the decision to gut the historic building and remodel its interior into a cluster of retail spaces. It had been touted as an initiative to help revitalize the local economy, but nowadays, even the relatively new retail spaces inside were mostly empty. The only thing the initiative had accomplished was to ensure that the Derrick would never be a theater again. But the building was so iconic that there was a movement by citizens to have it submitted as an entry into the National Register of Historic Places. There was also a proposal, however, initiated by a group of highly motivated people (with more money and greater influence) to have the building demolished (for reasons that involved the pursuit of still more money and still greater influence).

As Owen looked at the building's old, blank marquee, he wondered if there was any stock to Dave Albaugh's claim about his grandfather sneaking in as a kid. Supposedly, this theater had been one of the major stops for jazz bands and vaudeville shows and such, back when Latonia City had been among the major commercial centers in the Northeast and New England. Owen had never known his grandfather. But it was kind of fun to imagine him sneaking in there, maybe to catch a wartime serial or something. But who knew if the story was true? That was how it was in small towns. Everybody knew everybody, and there was no shortage of tall tales. Or dirty laundry. And God knew there was plenty of both when it came to Nathaniel MacCulloch.

In the dull orange glow of a summer evening, Owen MacCulloch stared up at the frowning mask, symbolizing tragedy, carved on the side of the Derrick Theatre. Then

the traffic light turned green, and Owen continued on his
way.

Chapter Six

BENEATH THE RELENTLESS sun of a cloudless summer morning, nine-year-old Nathaniel MacCulloch stared up at the smiling stone mask carved into the high corner of the Derrick Theatre. It was supposed to represent comedy. But to Nat, the beaming, slack-jawed face looked more like it'd been thumped over the head with a billy club one too many times.

At the tweet of the traffic officer's whistle, Nat took off. He was quite practiced in the art of cutting a path of least resistance through a throng of foot traffic. His run was all business, save for a series of customary hops to clear the silver seams of the old streetcar rails. One couldn't be too cautious about observing such rituals. His hopping, however, proved too rambunctious for the liking of a few fellow pedestrians.

"Slow down, you little cuss, or I'll—!"

The source of the oath—a clean-shaven, gentlemanly-looking fellow in a derby hat—was carrying an umbrella despite the fact that there hadn't been a drop of rain in weeks and today's weather wasn't looking any different.

And that umbrella, previously employed as a walking stick, was now raised off the ground and poised to strike or poke at Nat. But Nat sidestepped the objector, ducked behind a heftier wayfarer, and weaved a slalom-course through the rest of the men in suits and hats mass-migrating across the brick-laid street.

Arriving on the theater-side of East First, Nat stopped and closed his eyes, savoring the momentary respite from the heat that was provided by the shade of the cathedral-like Derrick at this time of the morning. When he reopened his eyes, the sad-looking face carved on the *other* side of the Derrick seemed to be looking straight down, right at him. He would have been lying if he'd said he didn't find that one a little off-putting. The comedy face may have looked smacked-silly, but there was nothing amusing about the tragedy face's elongated, inhuman proportions, creating an expression of horror the likes of which Nat had only ever seen on the faces of innocent bystanders in comic books just before a mad scientist pulled the lever.

Behind him, the traffic cop blew his whistle again to order foot traffic to come to a halt. Then came a second, longer whistle, this one followed by the chugging pops of countless miniature explosions, powering hundreds of pistons in dozens of internal combustion engines, and the street traffic resumed.

It was at this point that Nat realized Dick was no longer behind him. Looking back, he spotted his partner in crime standing on the curb. He had his hands folded behind his back and his head bowed in deference, receiving a firm scolding from the same umbrella-wielding gentleman who'd reprimanded Nat. Dick, evidently, hadn't had the heart to ignore the man, who was presently spiking the tip of his umbrella against the bricks with a *clack* to punctuate an impassioned point. Dick took his tongue-lashing like a good soldier. And when the seminar was complete and the umbrella-wielding defender of justice satisfied, Dick responded with a quick, "Yes, sir," and jogged over to join Nat in front of the theater (a building that was only a few years older than they were).

Dick paused to push a handful of perspiration from his forehead up and over his scalp—an unsophisticated but effective means of styling his straight, brown hair—then jabbed a thumb toward the double doors of the Derrick building. "How early you think Gid shows up for a show?" he said, the brief inconvenience in the crosswalk already forgotten. "You think he's in town already?"

Nat made a face. "Course not. The show isn't for two days. Big stars don't arrive *early*. Some of them do a different show every night. In a different *city* every night. Or even two shows in one day."

"*Two* shows in the same day?" said Dick, doubtfully.

"Yeah," said Nat. "Probably. I bet."

Nat, too, ran a hand over his head to try to flatten a mass of unruly, curly dark hair that was in dire need of shearing. It was so thick that once, several hours into a school day, Nat had scratched his head and felt something hard, which had turned out to be a comb from that morning. Something had distracted him halfway through tending what his mother sometimes called his "rat's nest," and he'd abandoned the task mid-stroke, tool and all. He had extricated the comb, like King Arthur, and slipped it into his back pocket in the middle of a math lesson. To his knowledge, not a soul had noticed.

"He'll pull up in a big private car," said Nat, "right before the show starts. Not a minute sooner than he needs to."

"What if the car breaks down?" said Dick.

"What, do you think they'd start the show without him?" Nat scoffed. "Gid Rust *is* the show. People would wait for him all night if they had to."

Dick nodded. Although he was a nervous boy and a few inches short for his age, Dick was not submissive by nature. Far from it. Around the schoolyard, it was generally regarded as unwise to challenge this barrel-chested, thickly forearmed youth. Nevertheless, Dick usually deferred to Nat, as most of the boys did. In fact, it was only recently that Nat had noticed how other boys in class seemed to gravitate around him almost automatically. A teacher had once referred to Nat as having "born leadership qualities," although Nat didn't quite know what this meant. It was not something that he sought after. But for some reason, situations just seemed to fall into place with him at the center, and when the time came for decisions to be made or judgments to be passed, the heads always seemed to turn toward him. Which was never a good time to discover an errant comb in your hair.

In this case, however, it was only prudent for Dick to take Nat's word for it. Because when it came to Gid Rust, Nat was the known authority on the subject.

"You think he'll play 'When the Saints Go Marching In'?" said Dick.

"Yeah, but I bet he plays 'Down by the Riverside' first," said Nat, "on account of the theater being so close to the riverfront and all."

Dick crinkled his nose. "Isn't that a church song?"

"Not when Gid the Great plays it," said Nat, proudly.

"If you had it your way," said Dick, "he'd play 'Happy Birthday To You.'"

Nat chose to neither confirm nor deny this claim, and stepped forward to get a closer look at the display case outside the Derrick's doors. Secured under glass was a black and white paper playbill. It read:

> GIDEON RUST — IN PERSON
> THE GREAT TRUMPETER AND HIS WORLD-
> FAMOUS JAZZ BAND
> ONE NIGHT ONLY AT THE LUXURIOUS
> DERRICK THEATRE
> LATONIA CITY, PENNSYLVANIA
> SATURDAY, JULY 23, 1939

In person, thought Nat. *Here. . . !*

His stomach did jumping-jacks at the thought. He'd just about worn the needle clean through the grooves of the 78 up at Pastel Records of Gid playing "The Tiger Rag." More than once, old Brozeski had had to remind his employees to "kick that durned MacCulloch kid out of the durned listening booth if there's a queue!" And at home, one of Nat's prized possessions was a pamphlet of sheet music for "Dinah" as played by Gid—swinging, quick-stepping, and blisteringly fast. Nat's sisters had long tired of hearing him clumsily attempt to nail down the intro on his secondhand cornet.

And now, the legend himself would be here. The Rust Man. Gid the Great. Coming to play a show at the Derrick. And on Nat's birthday, no less.

What if Gid really did play "Happy Birthday To You"? He wouldn't, Nat quickly reminded himself, but just as quickly cracked a grin, imagining what those notes would sound like coming out of Gid Rust's horn. . . . End on a high-C and blow the roof off the joint, probably. It was a crazy idea.

And then, Nat got an even crazier one.

He turned to Dick. "Think we could get in there?"

Dick shoved his thumbs into his pants pockets and rocked back on his heels, shaking his head—an amused man-of-the-world addressing some foolish young dreamer. "Your old man got some money squirreled away that I don't know about? Cause I hear the tickets ain't cheap."

"Hey, brainless, can't you read?" Nat pointed toward the red paper banner that had been supplemented to the signage, slapped over the lower portion of the playbill: SOLD OUT.

Nat lowered his voice to a conspiratorial whisper, leaned in close, and said, "I didn't mean with a ticket."

Any lingering traces of amusement were quickly drained from Dick's face.

Dick started to say something, but Nat cupped a hand over the boy's mouth before he could get a word out. Cautiously, Nat glanced up and down the sidewalk, as if expecting to find a cop, a PI, or J. Edgar Hoover himself eavesdropping on two ten-year-olds on a Thursday morning on a street corner in mid-western Pennsylvania.

"Not here," Nat hissed below his breath. "Follow me."

And he took off running.

Chapter Seven

WITH NAT IN the lead, the two boys raced down the First Street sidewalk. They darted through the intersection, turning down Oil Street and sprinting toward the bridge.

Nat cursed beneath his breath at the sound of the bells at the railroad crossing and, a moment later, the wail of a locomotive's whistle. Judging by the timing of the bells and the whistle, there was no chance of them getting stopped at the crossing. But the trick would be making it over the next bridge—the one that spanned the point where Rock-Oil Creek flowed into the Allegheny—and across Venango Street before the signal turned and street traffic resumed. The traffic officers always allowed the automobiles a long time without a stop after a train went through town, and if you didn't get across the street before that, you'd be waiting on the corner for a while.

Gid Rust, live and in person, here in our city, thought Nat as he ran. *Who knows if he'll ever be back this way again? I've got to see him!*

At Front Street, Nat turned on the speed in earnest, racing in front of a slow-moving truck with *Quaker State* emblazoned across its side. He glanced over his shoulder to make sure Dick made it across. He did, although he was chastised by a honk of the truck's horn. Satisfied that he wouldn't lose his friend, Nat proceeded across the bridge and toward the tracks.

The summer of 1939 had been hot and dry, and conditions were getting darn near what most people would have considered an honest-to-goodness drought. Nat had already heard from several of his friends who lived outside the city that their water wells had run dry, and the corn in the fields was noticeably short for this time of year. But most telling of all, the Allegheny River—which ran shallow in this area even in normal conditions—was so low that sections of the riverbed that no one could remember seeing before had been laid bare, creating small islands of rock and sand.

On the plus side, the low river had made for some good treasure hunting. Nat, Dick, their friend Art, and the more adventurous of Nat's sisters had spent most of the past week excavating the banks near Nat's house out in the Silvern Row neighborhood. According to a schoolyard rumor, that was the very stretch of water where, back in the 1850s, a casino riverboat had gone down—run aground on Tobeco Island after being chased by the feds all the way downriver from Drake's Landing. If the story was true, then it stood to reason that any fortunes lost on that ill-fated voyage might still be there, waiting to be dredged up from the deep by ten-year-olds with borrowed garden spades. Stranger things had happened.

When he'd reached the opposite side of the bridge, Nat hurried toward Main Street to cross the tracks. There, the signalman was standing in his box, preparing to lower the gate.

Nat threw a glance west. A dark plume rose in the wake of the locomotive as it crept along the curve of the river. Whether it was the sight of a boxcar or the sound of a distant whistle, Nat's father never failed to remind him that his grandfather had been among the honored few to have served as a driver on board one of those noble Pennsylvania Railroad marvels, back at the turn of the century . . . before that same grandfather had died a death that nobody liked to speak about, the details of which remained foggy to Nat to this day.

Nat paused a moment to let Dick catch up.

"Where are we running to, anyway?" Dick demanded as he crossed the tracks and came to a stop, hands on his knees and gasping for breath. Behind them, the signalman began lowering the gate.

"Need to ask Art something," was all Nat said.

This proved to be all the explanation that Dick required. He thought about it for a moment, and then his eyes glinted mischievously.

"Hurry up!" said Nat and resumed his run just as the locomotive approached the crossing.

Latonia was a city of many bridges, and the next one that Nat and Dick crossed was possibly its smallest, at a narrow point in the appropriately named Rock-Oil Creek. Here and there, the shimmer of rainbows flashed in the waters below, where the summer sun was reflected in a skim of petroleum. Back in the heyday of production, it was said an enterprising individual could practically make a living as an oil dipper, skimming the stuff right off the creek's surface by the bucketful and pouring it into secondhand barrels to sell back to the same refineries upstream that had lost it in the first place.

The boys continued down Main with the train moving right alongside them. The locomotive was forced to limit itself to a plodding rate of speed while traveling through the center of town, and the boys were nearly able to keep pace with it as they ran. Odds were good that this very train was on its way to the Germania Oil Well Supply Company, where Nat's father would have a hand in unloading its freight. It finally veered away from them as they passed the Latonia National Bank Building, where every door and window of the great granite fortress was wide open to combat the heat. Even from street level, Nat could hear some of the yelling from the upstairs windows, where stock prices were communicated by wire from New York City for the brokers to buy and sell. The bank's gray-white facade sparkled in the sun, a monument to the wealth of what Nat's father called "the Biggest Little City in the nation, in the Valley that Changed the World."

Nat and Dick kept chugging along, rushing past so many first- and second-floor shops on Venango Street and its adjoining avenues that a rich lady would have been hard-pressed to visit them all on a Friday night. Dick was struggling but managed to keep up, swinging wide around a group of men standing outside the service station, each with a newspaper and some form of tobacco in hand. A block later, the smell of their cigarettes and cigars gave way to the rich aroma of cinnamon from one of the sweet shops where the owners made their own penny candy.

Finally, Nat skidded to a halt in front of his destination: the little music shop run by his friend Art's parents.

HartSounds was one of several music emporiums in the city, and while it didn't have a fancy soundproof listening booth for sampling the new 78s like they had up at Pastel's, it was the only shop in town that dealt in records, sheet music, *and* new and used instruments. It was here that Nat had purchased his cherished cornet, almost certainly at a price too generous to have done the owners any good to their bottom line. Usually, Nat was not one to accept such charity. He had been taught not to feel sorry for himself, even when others felt that way for him. No matter how poor his family was, he tried to never let it show. Not in his clothes, not in his things, and certainly not in his attitude. But when it had come to a bargain on a cornet—the same instrument Gid Rust had started on before switching to the trumpet—well, he hadn't been too proud to make a small concession.

Naturally, a Gid Rust record was playing on the sound system as Nat and Dick entered through the open front door. It was his recording of "Big Bad Bill Is Sweet William Now." All week, everybody in town had been spinning nothing but Gid Rust in anticipation for Saturday night's show.

"Hey, Art!" Nat called.

At the front of the store, near the register, a thin, serious-looking boy with wispy yellow hair looked up from his broom but did not stop sweeping. "Can't come out till later," Art said. "And Poppy says you can only hang around here if you help out."

Poppy was not a familial term; everyone in town, kids and adults alike, called Art's dad "Poppy" without a trace of irony. Nat had never known why.

"Just need to ask a quick question," said Nat.

As Nat and Dick passed beneath a wall of mounted guitars, Art paused his sweeping. It was clear that Nat and Dick had come calling with a matter of great secrecy and, therefore, great importance. And since the only customers in the store were currently occupied, browsing through the sheet music, he leaned his broom against the counter for a moment. The fact that this spindly preteen's name, "Art Hart," sounded like something out of a superhero's origin story was lost on no one. But he didn't like to be called "Arthur," and "Artie" sounded too kiddish. So, there stood Art Hart. Son of Poppy.

"Make it quick," said Art, adjusting his shopkeep's apron.

Nat leaned in close. "Your uncle—Poppy's brother Chuck. Does he still do deliveries for the shop sometimes?"

"Yeah," said Art.

Nat double-checked that the coast was clear. Then he said, "Does he ever deliver to the Derrick?"

CROSO

PART TWO
SUMMERTIME STOMP

CROSO

Chapter Eight

IT WAS THE golden hour before sunset, and the *bump-bump-bump* of a pump barker reverberated over the face of the water.

Nat MacCulloch's father, barefoot and knee-deep among the reeds, leaned to the side to let a trail of tobacco-brewed saliva fall from his lips into the lake. Nat, watching from his old man's opposite side, also barefoot but more like hip-deep, turned and spat out a clear line. His aim was not as practiced as his father's, but it was the effort that counted.

"They're smarter than they look," said Grant MacCulloch, pretending not to notice as his son wiped a string of stray spit from the butt end of his fishing rod. "You can't just hang the bait out in front of them. Gotta put on a show for the little buggers."

Grant demonstrated this by giving his rod a series of quick twitches as he reeled.

"Yes, sir," said Nat, pretending to be hearing this advice for the first time.

Bump-bump-bump went the sound of the barker on the oil pump in the distance, produced by a hinged flapper device attached to the exhaust of the pump's engine. The noise didn't bother Nat; he was used to it. The hit-and-miss cadence of a barker system communicated the status of a pump to its engineer, who could tell just by the sound of the exhaust whether the engine was chugging along smoothly without resistance, pulling oil out of the ground and into its corresponding pipeline, or if it was laboring, which would indicate a loss of productivity. It was common for engineers to manipulate barkers to produce higher or lower pitches, or varying time signatures that were—to the engineer's ears, at least—as distinct as a songbird's melody. Even from a distance, they could tell what pump they were hearing and how it was performing. Nat was so accustomed to hearing barkers echoing through the oil-rich valleys that he hardly noticed it. Certainly not enough to let it disrupt an evening of fishing with his dad.

"Home field advantage is a heck of a thing," his father added. "Got to play by the fish's rules. We're visitors in their neighborhood, you know."

"Neighborhood." It was one of those words that Grant MacCulloch tended to say differently than the other fathers. The man had been only three years old when his family had immigrated to the United States. He usually spoke without any noticeable accent. But there were certain words that gave away his heritage in an instant. "Neighborhood," which came out with an unnaturally long first syllable, happened to be one of them. Another, coincidentally, was the word "oil," which he imbued with an oddly dull and clipped pronunciation, making it sound more like "*oll.*" And seeing as Grant MacCulloch had lived most of his life in the Oil Region, working at the Germania Oil Well Supply Company, along Rock-Oil Creek, there were plenty of opportunities for him to showcase this verbal quirk.

"You know, your ma's been wondering what's had you so excitable these past few days," said Grant MacCulloch. "She thinks it's your birthday, but your da knows better."

Nat looked up at his father, and his father looked down at him. His curly dark hair was much like Nat's, albeit receded into a horseshoe pattern around his sunburned forehead.

Grant winked at his son and said, "It's that Gideon Rust."

Nat smiled sheepishly. "Yes, sir," he said.

"Little wonder," said Grant. "Poppy Hart said he doubts there's a single piece of old Gid Rust's sheet music in his shop that hasn't had your fingers on it. If I were a rich man, maybe we could've gone to see him at the Derrick Theatre tomorrow, you and me."

"Maybe if he comes back again sometime, we can," Nat offered. "Maybe in a few years—"

"A few *years*?" said Grant. "No, no, no, I've heard you blowing that horn of yours! God—if he comes back in a few years, you're bound to be *touring* with him, the way you can play."

The suggestion made Nat smile so hard that it turned into a laugh—the kind of childish, unrestrained laugh that even he had noticed was getting rarer on his lips these days.

"Maybe . . ." said Nat, cranking his reel but paying little attention to his fishing. He forgot to "put on a show" for the little buggers, but Grant didn't call him on it. "Yeah, maybe I really could."

"Hell, if your grand-da could come to this country with nothing but the clothes on his back and faith in the good Lord, and in five years be driving locomotives from here to New York City and back, what can't *you* do? You've already got the faith. And the clothes. *And* a trumpet, to boot! Or, cornet, I mean—I know there's a difference. Any case, you're two steps ahead and not even ten years old!"

This time, Nat smiled so hard it hurt. Grant MacCulloch was a hard man and fiercely uncompromising when it came to matters of principle. But he was just as fierce in his expressions of love, understated though they tended to be. He was not a hugger. But for young Nat, encouragement from his da was never lacking.

"You think so. . . ?" said Nat. "You think I could really get good enough to—?"

Nat's question was interrupted by a noise from behind them—the sound of a dry twig snapping underfoot.

Nat and his father turned toward the sound and were met by the sight of the very thing that Grant MacCulloch always came to this particular remote fishing spot to avoid. A warden of the Fish and Boat Commission of the Commonwealth of Pennsylvania.

Grant MacCulloch scratched at his jaw and, in the same motion, used his hand to partially cover his mouth as he mumbled under his breath so that only Nat could hear, "Ah, Jiminy Damn Christmas. . . ." Then, at full volume: "You come to steal my secret honey-hole there, Sam?"

"Depends," said Sam McClintock. "Anything biting?"

"Just the black flies," said Grant.

"Boy, they are bad today, aren't they?" Sam replied amiably, swatting at the cloud of them that hovered in front of his face.

"Bad as hell," agreed Grant. "Wouldn't mind a rain shower to get rid of them, but God knows if that's bound to happen anytime soon."

"Yeah," said Sam. "Sure enough been one dry summer."

"Sure enough," said Grant.

Then Grant returned to his fishing, as if Sam were no longer there.

Young Nat watched Sam McClintock for a moment. He knew him from around town, but he had never seen him in uniform before. Until today, he and his father had managed to avoid that sight. The shirt and pants were beige, but the spotless, wide-brimmed hat, sort of beveled on the top, was a darker brown. The embroidered keystone symbol on his shoulder appeared to Nat as unassailable at that moment as a Five-Star General's stripes, never mind the silver badge pinned to his breast pocket.

Sam watched Grant cast out his line. He whistled between his teeth. "Yeah, that's right where I'd put it, too."

"That's where they are," agreed Grant.

Finally, Sam said it. "You know I have to ask, Grant. May I see your fishing license?"

Silence hung in the air.

Grant watched the lake. Sam watched Grant. And Nat watched Sam.

"You know, we're out here to celebrate my son's birthday," said Grant. "He's ten years old on Saturday. I can't get much time off work, but I thought a quiet evening of fishing might be a nice early present."

Sam nodded at Nat—or vaguely toward him, anyway. "Happy birthday, son," he said.

Nat, who had not moved, managed to say, "Thank you, sir."

Silence again.

"I remember the summer when you and I turned ten years old, Sam," said Grant. "Seem to remember your da taking us for trout at French Creek. That was a good year, don't you think?"

"Need to see your fishing license, Grant," said Sam.

"Yeah?" said Grant.

"Yeah," said Sam.

Until now, Grant's attention had been on the lake exclusively. From Nat's position, he could see that his father's face was blank.

Grant looked down at Nat. "Cast your line, son," he said. "They aren't likely to jump into your pocket."

"Yes, sir," Nat said and made a halfhearted cast.

"Grant," said Sam.

"It's in my shirt pocket," said Grant. He twitched his rod a bit—putting on a show for the little buggers, as it were. "But you won't get me to step away from this spot. Not now. Got a good feeling about this cast. You know how it is."

Grant kept watching the lake as he spoke. Only Nat saw Sam McClintock close his eyes and shake his head with an expression that looked like heartache, as if he were committing himself to a grim task ahead and regretting it already.

"I know how it is, all right," sighed Sam. And he stepped forward.

As Sam came toward them, tromping through the tall reeds and wading into the water, Nat found himself unable to look away from the revolver on the warden's hip.

"God's sake, boy," said Grant, "pay attention, or you'll hit that snag there."

Nat, in spite of everything, had the presence of mind to heed his father's instruction and pull his line so that the bait skirted the edge of the dark shape in the water—an old fallen limb along the shore that had stolen a dozen or more of Grant MacCulloch's hooks on aquatic safaris past.

Sam stepped up, directly beside Grant, within arm's reach of him. Grant, however, only had eyes for the lake.

"I've got to see it, Grant," said Sam. "It's nothing personal. It's just how it is."

Grant shrugged. "I guess if you've got to see it, you've got to see it. Left breast pocket. Go ahead."

For the second time, Sam shook his head in frustration. Then he reached for Grant's pocket.

Somehow, Grant MacCulloch's expression still did not change, even as he threw his hip to the side and removed his right hand from his fishing rod. At the same instant that Grant's hip bumped Sam in the stomach, his right hand clamped around the scruff of Sam's shirt collar. Sam, thrown off-balance by the hip-check, went down on both knees in the shallows and was still trying to reach for Grant's pocket—not yet comprehending what was happening to him—as Grant leaned sideways, and, putting his full weight into it, shoved Sam McClintock's head down under the water with one hand.

With his free hand, Grant held his fishing rod out to Nat. "Son, hold this for a minute, will you?" he said.

Bubbles were erupting from the water around Grant's submerged hand and Sam's arms flailed in the air as Nat dumbly accepted the fishing rod. Nat checked the tautness of the line, knowing that his father would never let him forget it if he got a bite and wasn't paying attention.

Grant held Sam underwater a few seconds longer. Then he pulled him up.

Sam McClintock, coughing and gasping for breath, looked up at Grant MacCulloch with eyes as wide as silver dollars. His warden's hat floated upside down in the water beside him like a boat, with a sharp fold in the previously perfect brim.

"*Judas priest*, Grant!" Sam sputtered. "You realize you just assaulted an officer of the law?"

"If you weren't fixing to be assaulted," said Grant patiently, "you wouldn't have interrupted my boy's fishing trip with his da. His birthday present, I said. Wouldn't your father be ashamed of you, Sam?"

"Birthday." Another one of those words where the barest hint of an accent could be heard creeping into Grant MacCulloch's speech. And all the more pronounced in a moment of temper; it sounded more like *barth-dee*.

Before Sam could answer Grant's question one way or the other, he was pushed back under. Again, the water boiled. Again, Sam's arms flailed, his hands now slapping the surface of the lake like a pair of smallmouth bass putting up a worthy fight. Grant didn't hold him under long. But when he let him up, it was only for a split-second, so the man could catch his breath before he promptly dunked him under again.

This third time was the longest of all—long enough that Nat began to grow concerned by the steady stream of bubbles. *Bump-bump-bump* went the sound of the pump barker in the distance.

Finally, Grant pulled Sam's head out of the water, grabbed him by both shoulders to stand him up straight, and gave him such a shove that Sam fell over backward and landed ass-first in the soupy mud along the drought-low banks of the lake.

"Now, let that be a lesson to you," Grant said.

Sam coughed and sputtered. "Dang it, Grant!" he said. But he sounded to Nat more like a little brother bested at backyard wrestling than an officer of the law.

After a few failed attempts to stand, Sam finally gained his feet. When he did, Grant was holding his hat out for him.

"Sam," said Grant calmly, "if you want to make a fuss over something as silly as a fishing license, then come and talk to me on a day I'm not with my boy. Then I'll show it to you, and we can have ourselves a civil conversation. Like men. Get me?"

Sam balled his hands into fists, then snatched his hat back. "You must be every bit as cracked as your old man was—and more!" he shouted.

"And a good day to you, Officer," said Grant.

Nat was still staring at the revolver on Sam's hip as his father took his fishing rod back.

"Nat," chided Grant, "you've got a bite."

Nat felt the tap-tap-tap of his line and managed to regain his wits and start reeling. But he was still watching Sam McClintock, who stood there, staring at Grant's back, sopping wet, fuming, trying to decide what to do.

Finally, Sam muttered, "Oh, the *hell* with you," and tromped off the way he'd come.

As soon as Sam was out of sight, Grant took Nat's rod from his hands. Nat only had the fish halfway to shore, but Grant spat out a line of tobacco juice, grabbed Nat's fishing line, and bit the line off between his eye teeth.

"I hate to let one go like that," said Grant as he quickly reeled in his own line and propped both rods over his shoulder, "but we'd best be going before Sam works up his courage to try again—discretion being the better part of valor and all."

"Discretion." Another one of those words that came out funny. *Dis-cra-shun.*

The *bump-bump-bump* of the oil pump engine continued to echo across the face of the lake as the MacCullochs beat their retreat.

Chapter Nine

Latonia City, Pennsylvania
July 2019

THE DIGITAL DISPLAY on the dash of the Ford Focus read 5:54 as Owen removed the keys from the ignition, prompting the dome lights to switch on and the windshield wipers to freeze in mid-swipe.

He sat his keys in his lap as snare-beats of rain rattled against the roof of the vehicle. And then, as he had done almost every day for the past two weeks, he sat in the car with the keys in his lap, staring out the windshield, trying to work up the courage to enter the building, thinking how easy it would be to put the keys back in and drive away. He sat long enough that the dome lights finally faded out. And, as was also his habit, he eventually slipped the keys into his pocket, opened the door, and stepped out.

The rain was tepid as bathwater against his face. He hadn't thought to bring an umbrella, so he grabbed the light Columbia jacket he kept in the back seat of the Focus and held it up over his head as he crossed the parking lot, doing his best to savor his final few moments of freedom before entering those doors.

He still didn't know why *Morning–Herald* was hyphenated. But two weeks into his new job was long enough for the bitter irony of his work schedule to have sunk in. He had enjoyed his career as an archaeological field technician, but the demands of traveling five days a week and the resulting turbulence in his relationship with Kayla had nearly destroyed their marriage. He'd quit so he could spend more time with her. And yet, today, he had seen her for a grand total of one hour. And Emma, he had seen for about two.

Working the six-to-midnight shift was turning out to be more taxing than he'd anticipated. That morning, after getting to bed at 2:00 a.m. the previous night, he had gotten up with Kayla and Emma to help with the frantic 6:00 a.m. to 7:00 a.m. rush and to see them out the door. After that, he'd gone back to bed for a while, but he never slept very well during the day. He'd woken up around 11:00 to a text from Kayla, apologetically informing him that she had to stay late at work, and would he be able to pick Emma up from Ruth Lee's at 4:00 and fix dinner? And also, if he had time, they needed stamps.

Fast-forward to 4:30, with Emma watching a TV show from the front-row seat of her high chair, and Owen neatly arranging a row of frozen chicken fingers on a plate for the microwave while the water boiled for the macaroni and cheese—the extent of his culinary prowess.

Kayla had gotten home just in time to trade places with Owen so he could throw on fresh clothes and hurry out the door. He would get home tonight at about 1:00 a.m. again. He would change out of his work clothes, get something to eat, and stand in the doorway to Emma's room for a while, watching her little stomach rise and fall as she lay in her crib. He would brush his teeth and crawl under the covers beside Kayla, trying not to wake her up. And then, he would lie awake in bed for a while, secretly hoping that Emma would wake up so he would have to rock her back to sleep. Maybe out on the front porch. He missed getting to do that every night. And tomorrow morning, around 6:00 a.m., it would start all over again.

Don't forget why you took the job to begin with, thought Owen as he reached the front door. *The benefits. The health insurance. And the steady paycheck, even as small as it is. For the family.*

He pushed through the front door and made a perfunctory attempt to wipe his damp shoes off on the thin black rug that resembled the floor mat of a minivan. His shoes squeaked against the marble mosaic of the great keystone as he crossed the lobby.

He blinked hard, trying to shake off the haze. How was he this tired before work even *started*? Not since his first week back from Iraq had he slept this poorly. But he'd actually had a relatively easy time of that, compared to some of his friends. People adjusted differently. He was lucky enough to be one of the ones who'd had trouble sleeping, instead of one of the ones who'd dug foxholes in their backyards. Or drank themselves to death, in the literal sense.

At the main desk, Felicia was packing up, getting ready to leave for the night.

"Hope you brought an umbrella," said Owen.

Felicia raised a short umbrella—it appeared to be in the pattern of a ladybug—and used it to favor him with a salute. "Too bad nobody warned you."

Owen looked down at his rain-splattered khaki pants and polo shirt and shrugged. He hadn't yet adopted the kind of shorts-and-tee-shirt vacationer's outfit that Dave Albaugh seemed so fond of wearing to work.

Felicia leaned forward over her desk and lowered her voice. "Just a warning, you might want to try to steer clear of Mae."

"Uh-oh," said Owen. "Why?"

Felicia, who was a mother of two, wore very dark lipstick and eyeliner, and had some of the longest hair Owen had ever seen, tilted her head to the side and scrunched up her almost black lips in what could only be described as a look of pity—as if addressing a boy who'd just struck out his first time at bat. "She might be over it by now," Felicia whispered, "but this morning, Mae was pretty pissed about the edits to the Chamber of Commerce write-up."

"You're kidding," said Owen. "I barely changed *a thing* in that one."

Except to correct her errors and save her from looking stupid, he thought.

But that part never got noticed.

"Maybe I misunderstood," Felicia said in a tone that said she knew she had certainly not misunderstood. "What I heard was her telling Dave.... Well, it was something like, 'He takes too many liberties, he's only supposed to be a proofer,' and, 'If *he* wants to be a writer, he can go back to his blogs.' Or, you know, something like that."

Owen rubbed his eyes again. He was usually in the building longer than ten seconds before things like this started happening.

Felicia, whose hair was not only very, very long but also happened to be colored in that trendy, indefinable shade that seemed to vary from silver to almost purple in some places, shrugged. "Sorry," she said. "But I wanted to give you a heads up."

"Thank you, I appreciate it," he said. He threw a glance at the clock that hung above reception. "Do you think maybe she'd forget about it if I hid in the bathroom until she went home?"

"You could try, but I've known Mae to yell through the door."

Owen blinked, slightly alarmed to realize that Felicia did not appear to be joking.

"I don't want to hold you up, but I have to ask," said Felicia. "They keep calling you 'Mr. Archaeologist.' Is that what you *actually* did before you came here?"

Owen nodded. "That is what I *actually* did. I was living in Ohio at the time, working for an environmental consulting firm."

"Wow," said Felicia. "So you were, like, digging up dinosaur bones and stuff?"

"That's paleontology. Archaeology is about artifacts. Stuff associated with humans."

"Oh! So, the pyramids and Egypt. Like Indiana Jones?"

"That is archaeology," agreed Owen, "although I never personally got to go digging around in any pyramids. With the company I worked for, it was mostly compliance work. Like, let's say a new natural gas pipeline was being put in somewhere. By law, a cultural resource survey had to be conducted to ensure that no potential archaeological sites would be damaged or destroyed. Unfortunately, a lot of times if we did find something cool, the company would just reroute the pipeline to avoid it, rather than have to fund an entire excavation. There was a lot of that in southern Pennsylvania and the West Virginia panhandle because of the Marcellus Shale."

Felicia was still nodding enthusiastically, but Owen could tell he was losing her. So he added, "So, yeah, like Indiana Jones. Except instead of old ruins, it's the deep woods somewhere in West Virginia. And instead of Nazis, it's ticks."

Felicia leaned forward a bit, causing her very long purplish hair to brush the surface of the desk as she whispered, "So, like, no judgment, but what are you doing *here*?"

Owen wasn't sure if Felicia meant *here* as in the newspaper or *here* as in back home in Latonia City. Either way, the answer was the same. "It just ... didn't really work out," he said. "I'd better go get clocked in. Drive safe out there, and have a good night."

Felicia smiled. "I'll try to do both."

Owen's workspace was one cubicle in a room of six cubicles below the same sort of age-stained drop ceiling as the one in the lobby. After a few polite hellos to his coworkers, he took his place at his desk. So far, he hadn't done much to personalize his workspace except for adding a couple of pictures of Kayla and Emma. But he had begun clipping out articles that interested him, mostly the ones that had anything to do with history, and pinning them to the corkboard mounted on the inner wall of his cubicle.

You're not clocked in yet, he thought. *Still time to escape. Just get up and drive home. See how long it takes someone to notice you're gone.*

But he didn't do that. He turned on his computer, and he clocked in.

He really was grateful to have this job, but the truth was, the gig wasn't turning out quite as advertised. Dave Albaugh's proposed initiative to hire Owen as the central cog in a new, dedicated copy desk had gone nowhere so far. Instead, Owen was spending only about 25 percent of his work hours copyediting, 25 percent typesetting, and 50 percent filling ad space with preset logos and images. In other aspects, however, Dave had been true to his word. The pay was every bit as poor as he'd promised.

Owen leaned back in his chair, scanning the room. No sign of Mae Baughman yet. Mae, more than any of the other staff writers, was religious—compulsive, even—about reading every word of every one of her articles, exactly as they appeared in print, every day. And this was not the first time she'd been upset about a change that Owen had made to one or more of those words. He didn't mind owning up to a mistake when he made one. But Mae's complaints (so far, at least) had had nothing to do with right or wrong. On just his third day on the job, she had called him out in front of the entire staff to explain that by removing an extraneous comma to correct a *perceived* mistake, he had created an ambiguity in the text that had altered her intended meaning to the extent that her journalistic voice had been undermined. To have heard her talk about it, you'd have thought it was a report on the Bay of Pigs Invasion instead of a two-paragraph piece on the referendum to build a new playground at the top of Polish Hill.

But what made it so much worse was how she did this without so much as even raising her voice, without getting nasty or unpleasant whatsoever, preferring instead to dole out her wrath with a patronizing, toothy grin, and no small degree of snark.

Gun to his head, Owen would have been forced to admit that there *had* been one or two times when he'd intentionally altered her meaning. Because there were times when, frankly, Mae's words overstepped the bounds of reporting and became editorializing. And at a paper that had functioned without a dedicated copy desk for years, she was used to operating unchecked and having the final say. No one called her out when her articles strayed from fact-reporting and became essays that bordered on opinion pieces. To Owen, this was an obvious problem, as her words didn't just inform the citizens of Seneca County but also influenced their perspectives. She had no qualms about recoloring the facts in light of her own politics. And that annoyed him.

No sooner had Owen let his guard down and settled into his by-now-familiar position at his computer—the root of his worsening back and shoulder problems—than Mae Baughman stood on her tiptoes and peeked her head up from the other side of the cubicle wall in front of him. Given that she stood all of five-foot-three, it was not outside the realm of possibility that she had been there the whole time. Her silhouette was closer to five-foot-five thanks to a carefully constructed pile of hair that was unrealistically dark for a woman of her age.

"Good evening, Mr. Archaeologist," said Mae cheerfully. That wide, toothy grin was on her face again.

Mr. Archaeologist. Dave had been calling him that since day one. He'd meant no harm by it. On the contrary, Dave seemed genuinely interested in Owen's past vocation and asked him about it quite often. But when Mae called him that, it felt somehow less harmless. It bore the same sort of connotation that had been thrown his way one summer, when he'd done some roofing for a local contractor between his freshman and sophomore years of college, when the older guys on the crew had referred to him as "College Boy." It was the sort of nickname you couldn't exactly protest, given that it was factually accurate. But the way they said it, with the same inflection one might reserve for a title like "Candy-Ass" or "Nancy-Boy," made it clear that they were doing more than listing his credentials. And while Owen didn't get *precisely* the same impression from Mae when she called him "Mr. Archaeologist," the intention was similarly transparent: to take him down a peg.

"Evening, Mae," Owen returned.

He figured he might as well get comfortable, so he leaned back in his chair and folded his hands over his stomach. There would be small-talk before the hammer fell. There always was.

"How's the weather out there?" she asked. Before he could answer, she pointed to his head and added, "Must be coming down pretty hard."

Owen patted his damp hair. The jacket over his head had only helped a little. "Yeah, it's picking up. Be careful on your drive home."

"Aw, you're sweet. . . . You'd better put on a fresh pot of coffee because it looks like you've got your work cut out for you tonight. A lot of copy that needs proofing. And a lot of ad space that needs filling!"

She grinned all the wider. Her teeth were tobacco-stained but large and perfectly straight. It was really quite something.

Owen shrugged. "Hard work is its own reward, or so someone once told me. I think they might have been full of it."

"Oh, stop it—you're bad," said Mae. "Well, I'd better leave you alone and let you get to your work—and oh! Before I forget, I wanted to talk to you about that Chamber write-up."

"Okay," said Owen. "Was there a problem?"

"No, not at all," she said innocently. "No problems. I wanted to tell you that you did very good work on it."

"Oh. Thank you. I didn't have to do much, honestly, it was already so well written."

"Aw, thank you as well," said Mae. "As you said, hard work is its own reward, but it's still nice to get noticed sometimes. Some of the work we do can almost feel a bit . . . thankless. But what we do informs and empowers public opinion. It's critical work, really."

And then—as abruptly as the windshield wipers of a Ford Focus freezing in place as the keys are pulled from the ignition—her grin disappeared.

"Every word is critical, Owen," she said, staring at him. "Every word."

Owen got the impression that her look was supposed to make him squirm. Instead, he just smiled and replied, "It's a good thing I'm here, then."

Mae's grin returned, but the noise she made in her throat was anything but friendly. And seriously, that hair was just too dark to fool anyone. Felicia's silver and purple hair was more convincing.

"You know, there's something about you, Mr. MacCulloch," Mae said when she'd recovered. "You're still so new to this job, but I feel as if I already know you so well. I can't quite put my finger on why that is, but it intrigues me."

She reached over his cubicle wall and tapped his corkboard with one long fingernail, where he'd tacked the history articles that interested him and a few "On This Day" pieces—old articles pulled from the archives as curiosities.

"Maybe I can manage to dig something up that'll interest you," she said. "I hope you have a wonderful, *wonderful* night."

"You too," said Owen.

And with that, Mae Baughman turned and strode off, heels clacking against the floor. A moment later, the door to Dave Albaugh's office swung open, and Dave wandered out with a half-eaten turkey sandwich in his hand and a dab of mustard clinging in his goatee. He paused a moment outside his door, surveying the cubicles from behind his wire-rimmed glasses. His eyes stopped on Owen.

"Evening, Mr. Archaeologist!" he said. "Keep up the good work."

Owen smiled, nodded, and turned his attention to his computer.

Chapter Ten

OWEN WOKE UP to the smell of chicken and gravy.

He rolled over, carrying a portion of the fitted sheet with him, and shrugged it off in annoyance. For a moment, he couldn't remember if it was morning or evening—that was what his days were like now. But the chicken and gravy aroma was a clue.

As good as dinner smelled, it still took him several minutes to summon the willpower to get out of bed. And as he lay there, listening to the sounds of spoons against pots and a cartoon playing in the background, for some reason all he could think about was the fact that he hadn't spoken to his father since that night in the hospital three weeks ago. In all that time, not a word had been exchanged between them.

It was true that there were a great many things he and his father didn't see eye to eye on. They'd had their share of arguments in the past, but there had been no disagreements this time. No real reason for Owen to have not reached out to his father, and no real reason for his father to have not tried to contact him. And no reason was perhaps the saddest reason so far.

I haven't even told him about the house yet.

He decided he would text his mom and see if they were busy this weekend. Golfing was probably all his dad had planned anyway. Owen would show up uninvited if he had to.

Finally, Owen pushed himself out of bed, groaning at a pain in his neck that radiated down through his upper back. It was amazing that hours sitting at a desk, doing practically nothing, could put you in so much pain. But Mae hadn't been joking about him having his work cut out for him last night. It had turned out to be his biggest workload yet. It'd been 2:00 a.m. by the time he'd gotten home and at least 3:30 a.m. before he'd managed to fall asleep. As usual, he had gotten up with the girls to start the day. Ideally, he then would have slept through the morning, but for some reason, he hadn't been able to sleep. Instead, he'd spent some time doing chores around the quiet, empty house, alone. And after lunch, he had managed to collapse on the bed and squeeze in a couple of hours of sleep before Kayla got home with Emma.

All in all, the schedule he was keeping didn't feel much like a schedule at all. He hoped that as time wore on, he would develop habits that would help him do more than just keep his head above water.

As Owen crossed the bedroom, the loud creaking of the floorboards announced his movements.

"You up?" Kayla called up the stairs.

"Yup," Owen called back.

"Do you know what the deal is with this bike?"

"Bike?" said Owen.

"The one on the porch."

Owen rubbed his aching neck. He paused before heading downstairs to look in the full-length mirror that hung on the back of the bedroom door. The face staring back at him looked tired. Tired and old.

Kayla was in the process of taking a baking tray of chicken out of the oven as Owen entered the kitchen of their little rented house on 322. Nearby, Emma sat in her high chair. Gripped in her hand was a small, bright pink plastic bowl half-filled with popcorn "puffs"—white things with no kernels that looked like packing peanuts and were hopefully made from different source material.

Owen went to Emma and kissed her on the head. "Hey there, sweetie," he said.

"Ya-ya-ya-ya-ya-ya-ya," said Emma before shoving a fistful of popcorn puffs into her mouth. It was her new favorite utterance.

He crossed the kitchen and wrapped his arms around Kayla, who turned to kiss him on the cheek.

"You get enough sleep?" she asked.

The answer was no.

"Yep, plenty," said Owen. "What was it you were saying about a bike?"

"On the porch," said Kayla. "You didn't notice it?"

On his way to the porch, Owen glanced at the clock on the oven's digital display. It didn't make sense. How could it possibly be time to leave for work again, already?

He pushed open the screen door and stepped out onto the covered porch that looked out on Route 322. Leaning against the railing, directly in front of the hanging swing where he rocked Emma to sleep, was a child's bike.

Owen scratched a thin layer of scruff on his chin and looked around. It must have belonged to one of the neighbor kids, but... he didn't think there *were* many neighbor kids. At least, not nearby. And what they'd been doing on his porch, he would have liked to know. Stranger still was how anyone could leave their bike behind. Didn't you need it to get home again? But Owen wouldn't have blamed anyone for ditching this thing. Judging by the faded paint and the shocking amount of rust, it must have been a garage sale purchase or a Goodwill special. Or pulled out of a dumpster. Even the tires were flat.

"The chicken needs a little more time, can you take it out and check it in about five minutes?" Kayla called from the kitchen. "Since you're up, I'd like to actually take a shower before you have to leave. And remind me, we need to talk about signing those papers for the house, they're on the table."

"Okay, no problem," said Owen. "How was work?"

But she didn't hear him. And by the time he reentered the kitchen, she was upstairs. He heard the bathroom door shut.

He pulled up a chair to sit close beside Emma's high chair. She watched him with her round, dark eyes.

"There's my girl," he said and tickled one bare foot.

Emma made a laughing face and snorted in delight, spilling a few of her popcorn puffs in the process.

On the table were the papers in question. Papers to transfer the mortgage on Ruth Lee's house from her name to Owen and Kayla's.

That had been the plan for a while now. Move out of the little rented house on 322 and into the big place in the country with Ruth Lee, who lived month to month and struggled financially at certain times of the year more than others. The house would be theirs. And, with the mortgage transferred to their names, so would the debt and the monthly payments. They got a nice big place, and Ruth Lee got the help she needed. It was a win-win for everyone involved. The only hiccup was that Owen hadn't realized quite how much she still owed on said mortgage. And at the "standard entry-level rate" at the *Herald* . . . well, it'd be a lot of Chamber of Commerce write-ups before the interest alone was paid off.

"Emma," said Owen in his baby-voice. "Can you do me a favor?"

As she turned to look at him, her sizeable noggin rocked like a bobblehead.

"Do you think you could please make lots and lots of money when you grow up and be rich and famous?"

Emma pushed her pink bowl off the high chair tray and said, "Ya-ya-ya-ya-ya-ya-ya."

"Good," said Owen. "Then it's a deal. I'm going to hold you to it, understand?"

"Ya-ya-ya-ya-ya."

Chapter Eleven

WHETHER A SYMPTOM of the drought or the simple inevitability of time's hand, the crack in the basement wall of the MacCulloch family home had widened to a degree extreme enough that it could be overlooked no longer. And so, the day after the incident that Nat MacCulloch had already come to refer to in his mind as "The Dunking of Sam McClintock," he and his father were at work.

There were, perhaps, more entertaining ways for a boy to have spent a cloudless Saturday morning in July—which just so happened to also be the morning of his tenth birthday, not to mention the day Gideon Rust was set to play the Derrick—but Saturdays and Sundays were his father's only days off from the Germania Oil Well Supply Company. Even on birthdays, there was work that needed doing. And besides, Nat didn't mind. Just being around his father made him feel good. When he was with him, it was like he became a different version of himself—a mix of the boy he was, the child he'd been, and the man his father made him believe he could be.

As for Grant, who was known to describe his workdays on the Germania factory floor as "damn hard, damn hot, and damn dangerous," a bit of manual labor in the cool, shaded basement of his own home wasn't such a bad thing. So that morning, Nat turned ten years old, and he and his da built a wall.

As Nat mixed the plaster, Grant worked the trowel. A patch-job would be enough for most of the length of the crack. But the first step had been to carefully widen the break, which had required chiseling out the entirety of the block where the problem had started. A combination of Grant's car jack and some lengths of scrap boards served as a set of temporary supports to ensure that the blocks above didn't sink. The intended replacement block—a large gray brick that Nat knew as a cinder block but that Grant referred to, more reverentially, as a universal concrete masonry unit—sat on the floor with Grant's half-finished Pepsi-Cola on top of it.

Grant took a drink of the Pepsi-Cola, swallowed, then turned and spat a stream of tobacco juice into a nearby metal pail. How he could keep the two substances straight in his mouth and know which to expectorate and which to imbibe, Nat would never understand.

Grant gestured toward the spit in the bucket. "Don't tell your ma about that," he said.

"No, sir," said Nat.

"Meant to tell you, I had a word with Poppy Hart."

Nat's mixing hand slowed.

"He told me you were bothering his boy at work the other day. Said he overheard you whispering like you was

87

about to pull off a heist. He thought it had something to do with Gid the Great. Old Gid Rust."

Now Nat's mixing hand stopped.

Grant went on: "'That adds up,' I says to Poppy. 'My boy's been doing just about nothing but playing that horn you sold him, blowing as to wake the dead and get them stepping the Charleston.'" He turned his full attention on Nat now. "Can't say I blame you. A man like Gid, right here in our city. Something like that might only happen once in a lifetime. And on your birthday!"

Then Grant grew quite serious. His body seemed suddenly rigid like a coiled spring. Nat thought at first that he was angry. Then he realized it was excitement that he was seeing in his father.

Grant reached into his trouser pocket, pulled out an envelope, and held it out toward Nat. "Happy birthday, son," said Grant. "It isn't much. But I thought you might like these."

Nat felt his mouth drop open.

He lost all sense of decorum. Forgetting every lesson of manhood he had learned, he raced forward like a toddler after a sweet, grabbed the envelope from his father's hand, and ripped open the top. His fingers were shaking as he reached inside and pulled out two folded pieces of paper. He couldn't believe it. It was all so surreal. And he'd thought his present had been their fishing trip. A fishing trip!

He couldn't unfold them fast enough. When he finally got them open, he stood frozen, staring at them.

It was a pair of playbills. Like the one displayed under glass in front of the Derrick.

GIDEON RUST — IN PERSON
THE GREAT TRUMPETER AND HIS WORLD-
FAMOUS JAZZ BAND
ONE NIGHT ONLY AT THE LUXURIOUS
DERRICK THEATRE
LATONIA CITY, PENNSYLVANIA
SATURDAY, JULY 23, 1939

"Poppy had a few extras," Grant said proudly. "The Derrick had given him some for advertising the show at his store. He didn't want to part with them. No sir, not a one of them. I had to drive a hard bargain. But in the end, I managed to convince him to part with *two*."

Nat continued staring at the playbills, silently.

He was silent for about one second too long.

By the time he came to his senses and looked up at his father, the damage had already been done. Grant's face had undergone a change. A moment before, he'd been eager. Bright-eyed. Proud. But now, something crossed his face like a curtain being pulled over a window.

"Oh," said Grant, sounding almost embarrassed.

"Thank you, they're great," Nat said hastily.

"You thought they were tickets," said Grant.

"No," lied Nat.

Grant's eyes were still on him, but his gaze seemed to go distant and unfocused. His horseshoe-shaped hairline shifted half a centimeter downward as the muscles in his jaw relaxed, and the last traces of his smile shrank into a flat, narrow line. It wasn't anger that was on his face. Not even disappointment. It was more like regret. Or failure. Or defeat.

Slowly, Grant picked up his Pepsi-Cola. He brushed off the top of the cinder block, also known as a universal concrete masonry unit, and sat down, using it as a stool, staring blankly at the floor.

Nat's insides felt cold and empty. "They're great," he tried to insist. But as Grant lifted the glass bottle to his lips to drain it, Nat thought that his father looked as close to heartbroken as he had ever seen him.

Grant swished the drink around in his mouth, swallowed, then dug the tobacco out of the inside of his cheek with a finger and tapped his hand against the rim of the bucket to dispose of it. "Didn't mean to get your hopes up," he finally said, with a throat that sounded dry despite having just taken a drink. "I see now how that must have looked. Didn't think of that. It wasn't fair of me. I just thought these might look neat in your room. Maybe tacked in the corner where you keep your horn? I don't know."

Nat looked at the playbills in his hand and realized he loved them more than any gift he had ever received. He wasn't disappointed. He'd just misunderstood and gotten a little too excited.

What had he been thinking? The MacCullochs didn't have the kind of money it took to afford tickets to a Saturday night theater show, Nat knew that. He'd just forgotten for a second. Forgotten that there was barely enough money to keep him and his sisters in clothes that fit. Not enough money to hire somebody to fix the basement wall properly. Not even enough for a fishing license.

He'd only forgotten for a second. But a second was all it had taken to wound his father. Now his old man was just sitting there, and Nat didn't know what to say. He had always been taught to never be ashamed. But, looking at his father right now, sitting on that cinder block, Nat couldn't help but think that it looked an awful lot like shame on Grant MacCulloch's face. He wanted to tell him how much he loved this gift. But he suddenly feared that if he opened his mouth to try to say anything, he might cry.

But worse than that, worse than anything that Nat had experienced in his life so far: His father looked almost as if *he* might cry.

"All right," said Grant, as if deciding on something.

He stood up from his seated position, making the kind of noise in the back of his throat that fathers make when standing up from seated positions, and turned his Pepsi-Cola bottle over. A small trickle fell out. Then he shook the bottle back and forth to sprinkle the remaining drops across the basement floor.

"Hand me those playbills, son."

Fear seized Nat. He had ruined it. The greatest gift anyone had ever given him, and he had ruined it. Now his father was going to take them away. He wanted to say how much he loved his gift, that he was sorry for being so foolish, and that he would keep them forever. But he still felt like he would cry if he tried to say anything. And anyway, one did not talk to one's father like that.

So he obeyed. He handed back the envelope and the playbills.

Grant took one, refolded it, and slipped it back into the envelope. "I'll give you a tack to put this one on your bedroom wall. If you want."

He reached into his pocket and took out the short, stubby pencil he always kept with him to mark up boards and things when he did work around the house. He looked hard at his son. And then he spoke to Nat in a way that he had never spoken to him before.

"You know, your grand-da didn't drive locomotives for himself. He did it for me and my brothers and sisters. If it hadn't paid off so well, we wouldn't have this house or be so blessed as we are to have food to put on our table every night and heat in the winter. . . . I know what people in this town say about your grand-da, but I hope you don't listen to any of it. He was a good man who just went wrong in the end. Don't you abide any of that talk about him being crazy."

Grant waited for a moment, letting those words sink in. Then his mouth stretched sideways in a half-smile.

"Someday, because of his hard work, and the work of all the MacCulloch men before him, you'll be buying theater tickets any night you please! And hell, the way you blow that horn, I'd wager my life it really will be you that people are buying tickets to see, soon enough. And after you make the big time, if you ever come back to little old Latonia City, you'll have to buy a ticket for your dear da.

So that the first Derrick show this old oil worker gets to see—" it came out "*oll* worker," the way Grant pronounced it—"will be to see Nathaniel MacCulloch, Nat the Great and His Hot Jazz Band, opening for Gid Rust, live and in person."

Nat still felt like he might cry, but for entirely different reasons. His da always knew what he needed to hear to feel better. But who was around to make *him* feel better when he needed it? Nat had never thought about that before.

"Now you take this other one," said Grant, holding out the second playbill and his stubby pencil, "and you put it to writing."

Nat accepted the playbill and the pencil but didn't quite understand.

"Your future," said Grant. "What you plan to do. Write down what you're gonna do on that playbill right there. Only you and the Lord need know what you write, but whatever it is you're gonna do, put it into words. Exactly what you'll do. Write it down. Understand?"

"Yes, sir," Nat said. And he'd been right. Speaking did make him start to cry a little. Thankfully, Grant pretended not to notice.

Nat got down on his hands and knees, using the almost-flat surface of the cold basement floor to spread out the paper playbill face-down. He thought for a moment, smiled at what he thought of, and used his most careful cursive to put it into words. Meanwhile, Grant used his trowel to even out the edges of the gap in the wall where the broken piece had been. Then he began the process of lowering the jack to make room for the new block.

When Nat was done writing, he started to stand up.

"Don't forget to sign and date it," said Grant, pulling the jack and the scrap boards free. "In great, big letters so there'll be no mistake. It may not be a ticket. But where there's a will, there's always a way."

Nat did as he was told.

When Nat stood up, Grant was holding his hand out expectantly. Nat gave him the playbill, but Grant did not read it. He gave the Pepsi-Cola bottle one last shake, rolled the playbill into a little paper tube, and slid it down into the neck of the bottle. As an afterthought, he took a glob of plaster with his thumb and stoppered the mouth of the bottle with it. Then he placed the bottle inside the hollow innards of the new cinder block.

"Give your da a hand with this, will you?"

Nat and Grant lifted the block.

"Now," said Grant, "we commit it to the Lord, and to time."

And together, father and son fit the new block into the old wall.

Chapter Twelve

THE MOMENT OF transformation from a light shower to a full-blown downpour occurred the very instant Owen was pulling into the parking lot at the *Oildom Morning–Herald*. Again, he crossed the parking lot with a jacket held over his head. It wasn't that he'd forgotten his umbrella; he just had no idea where it was.

He was a few minutes late and was disappointed to find that he had missed Felicia leaving for the day. It wasn't uncommon for her to duck out early on Fridays to get a little extra time with her kids, and Dave didn't mind. But her absence at the front desk meant there was no one to warn Owen if Mae Baughman was on the warpath again. Fortunately, he didn't see her as he navigated through the back room to his cubicle.

Now two months into the job, Owen had decorated his workspace with quite a few photos. Plus, some of his coworkers had noticed his habit of clipping articles of historical interest, and they would sometimes set old write-ups aside for him, many of which were unearthed from the *Herald*'s extensive archive during research for the "On This Day" section of the paper. He had learned a lot about the local area as a result. He'd never known, for instance, that the city's population, which today was only around 10,000, had been over 30,000 in the 1940s. Or that battle plans recovered after the unconditional surrender of the Empire of Japan at the conclusion of the Second World War had shown that Latonia City was among their list of high-priority targets for aerial bombardment, due to the fact that a strike here would have interrupted the oil and fuel supply to the entire country.

He'd never known that Rock-Oil Creek had been so named because there were places where oil seeped up from the ground as naturally and freely as spring water, at times so vigorously that it created a black skim that nearly covered the waterway's surface. And until recently, he'd never heard the story of Petroleum City, a boom town created and abandoned within the course of a single year.

To read some of the stories of oil prospectors and well-men back in the 1800s, life in Pennsylvania oil-towns had been as cutthroat and debauched as the Wild West, especially aboard the notorious riverboat casino that had once trawled the Allegheny between Latonia and Drake's Landing, drawing in gamblers, pimps, robbers, and unsavory types from across the entire Union.

Nor had he ever heard the story of the Conflagration Flood of 1892, in which Rock-Oil Creek overflowed its banks and took a path of least resistance straight through the store-yard of a petroleum processing facility, where a row of great storage tanks containing the byproducts of crude oil refining—gasoline and naphtha—ruptured. The people of Latonia City woke to the sight of an inferno moving downstream at the pace of a locomotive: a thirty-foot wall of flames riding the top of the floodwaters, racing straight into the city. The resulting fire and flood had caused millions of dollars in damage, and 161 individuals had been declared dead or missing and presumed dead.

Presently, Owen adjusted his chair and winced. When he'd started here back in July, the pain in his neck and back had been a dull ache. Now, it was a radiating, sharp pain that at times was so bad he found it difficult to concentrate. He reached into his desk drawer and pulled out a bottle of Ibuprofen, which had become as much a staple of his daily routine as his cup of coffee.

If Mae *was* still here, Owen expected he would receive an earful. Week by week, he was growing bolder about changing a sentence here or there to lend the *Herald* a more unbiased, less subjective tone. He may have only been making a paltry wage, and this little paper may not have been the great institution it had been in the days when its ornate mosaic floor was first set down. But he was going to do his best to see that *Oildom Morning-Herald* was a name that still stood for something—even if he still didn't know why it needed to be hyphenated.

He had just thrown back two painkillers and swallowed them dry when the door to Dave Albaugh's office swung open. Dave stepped out first, followed by an older gentleman. He was in his 80s at least, short, and had what was surely fewer than fifty individual white hairs on his head. These he had grown long, carefully pomading them across his scalp to create as much surface area as possible. He was round in the belly and wore his pants the way older guys tended to—*on* his gut instead of under it. Owen had always thought this was a more dignified look than allowing one's stomach to roll forward over the front of a belt, but he also wondered how one knew when the time was right to make the shift from under-gut to on. It seemed like a significant rite of passage in a man's life.

Something was said between the two men—something that apparently had to do with Dave's shirt, because he looked down and wiped at his collar with the palm of his hand. Ten to one odds it was mustard. The guy loved the stuff. Then the older man gave Dave a good-natured clap on the back, and he shuffled off. When he was gone, Dave noticed Owen. But instead of a good-natured "Mr. Archaeologist" greeting or a wave, Dave seemed to sigh. He smiled a flat smile at Owen, nodded once to him, and walked back into his office.

"Huh," said Owen.

It wasn't uncommon for an exchange with Dave Albaugh to feel awkward, but for Dave to be aware of the awkwardness—*that* was odd.

"Hey, Owen."

Owen turned, wincing yet again at his neck pain. Standing behind him was a short, middle-aged man. He wore a blue ball-cap with no logo, with two masses of unkempt hair sprouting from beneath either side of the brim. His name was Dave White, the paper's dedicated photographer, though he sometimes served other roles. And because there was already one Dave in the office,

Dave White was sometimes called "Dave" to his face but, in third person, was never referred to as anything except "Dave White," in full. Uttered quickly, as it usually was, it came out more like a two-syllable given name: Davewhite.

"Hi Dave," said Owen.

"Hey," said Davewhite. He was a quiet man with a reedy voice, whose shirts were commonly coated in a thin layer of ginger cat hair. "You doing okay?" he asked.

Owen blinked. "Yes."

"Okay, good," said Davewhite.

One awkward moment with one Dave was an event. But two awkward moments with two Daves was a pattern.

"Why wouldn't I be?" pressed Owen.

Davewhite shifted uncomfortably. His face crinkled up in a sour way that somehow made his voice even reedier. "You didn't see today's paper?"

"I haven't opened my computer yet."

"I mean today's paper. As in, the one published this morning."

"I saw the digital proof," said Owen. "I didn't see it in print...."

Owen felt the bottom drop out of his stomach. For his first few days on the job, he had reviewed his work in print every day the following morning. He'd since gotten out of the habit and had been content to trust in the digital proof. But it was written all over Davewhite's face: He had missed a mistake, and something had slipped through. Or worse, he had *created* a mistake during one of his edits. A big one. A royal blunder. And it had gone to print.

"Here," said Davewhite. "Better take a look for yourself."

Davewhite grabbed that morning's paper from the nearby desk. He flipped through the first few pages—good, not a front-page error then, at least—and then held out the paper for Owen to see.

Owen braced himself as Davewhite pointed. A typo in a headline, perhaps? An autocorrect resulting in a sexual innuendo? But instead, at the end of Davewhite's chewed-down nail was the paper's "On This Day" section. The place where articles from the archives were printed.

"Huh?" said Owen.

Most of the page was exactly as he remembered it from the digital proof the night before. But the article that had been scheduled to run in the "On This Day" section—an old fluff piece about how John D. Rockefeller had once held a private office in the Seneca Transit Center at the height of the Standard Oil monopoly—wasn't there. A different article had been printed in its place. The headline read:

> "On This Day" in 1982 — From the *Herald* archives
> Disgraced MacCulloch resigns from embattled Chamber amid scandal

Owen snatched the paper out of Davewhite's hands so quickly that it made Davewhite flinch.

"Sorry, Dave," Owen said, and began to read.

"Former director of the Latonia City Chamber of Commerce," as he will hereby be known, Nathaniel G. MacCulloch, tendered his resignation from that organization Friday morning, sending waves of relief through a populace that has been calling for his ousting for the better part of two years.

While his written announcement is flavored with the same sanctimonious moralizing that many have come to expect of a man who, in the opinions of many, ran the Chamber with unilateral disregard for its members, MacCulloch could not resist taking a farewell shot at the people of Latonia City. Wounded ego on show for all to see, MacCulloch opined, 'I have always tried to do what is right for the future of our city, but I fear that the Save Our Hospital movement has manipulated good people into believing I would best continue my efforts elsewhere.'

Observed one concerned Latonian, "One can only hope that MacCulloch, his tail now thoroughly between his legs, will 'continue' his 'efforts' far from here."

The byline read: *Mae Baughman, Staff Writer*.
Somehow, Owen managed not to indulge his first instinct and crush the paper into the smallest possible ball.

A good thing, too, for a quick look around proved that several other employees had taken notice of the interaction between Owen and Davewhite and were watching him. As soon as he looked up, the audience ducked their heads back behind their cubicle walls.

Maybe I can manage to dig something up that'll interest you, Mae had said.

There was no reason for this little write-up to have made the "On This Day" section. No reason other than to spite Owen.

When Dave Albaugh had learned that Owen was Nathaniel MacCulloch's grandson, his response had been to tell Owen a story—true or not, it didn't matter—about Nat sneaking into the Derrick Theatre. But someone like Mae was more interested in salting old wounds, determined not to let Nat's checkered past go.

And she wasn't alone, either. Even decades after the fact, there were still people in this town with strong convictions about the "hospital situation" and the role that Owen's late grandfather had played in it.

"Sorry," said Davewhite. "I didn't realize you hadn't seen it."

Owen had nearly decided to smash the paper into a ball after all. But instead, he got a better idea. He took a deep breath to calm down.

"Thanks for checking in on me," he told Dave. "I'm cool, I promise. How about you? How's Mary Ann?"

Davewhite smiled. "Doing better. They've got her on a corticosteroid, and she doesn't seem quite as uncomfortable now."

"Good."

"Well, I'll leave you alone and let you get to work."

"Have a good night, Dave."

"You too," said Davewhite.

Before leaving, Davewhite brushed some of the orange fur from his sleeve—fur from Mary Ann, the remaining survivor of a pair of ginger cats that Davewhite had owned for most of his adult life. It was probably not an exaggeration to say that Davewhite talked more about Mary Ann and the dear, departed Ginger (rest her kitty soul) than Felicia talked about her human children, which, let there be no mistake, said more about Davewhite than it did about Felicia.

With the morning's paper in hand, Owen sat down in his chair and reread the article. Then he grabbed the scissors from the desk organizer in his cubicle. He clipped out the article, found a pushpin, and carefully positioned it on his corkboard, higher and even more prominent than his collection of historical and local interest articles. If Mae Baughman was proud of her little last-minute switch, she would have the chance to gloat over it every time she passed his desk. But if there was a heart in there somewhere—and Owen strongly suspected that there had to be—and if Mae walked by and *even once* regretted what she had done, then it would be worth having to look at the story every day.

Chapter Thirteen

Latonia City, Pennsylvania
July 1939

TO BE PERMITTED to leave the house alone, and after dinner, no less, was a first for Nat MacCulloch. Art Hart had organized a backyard campout, and although Nat's mother didn't much care for that idea of him walking there by himself, certain uncommon exceptions were being made on account of today being a birthday of such monumental, double-digit proportions.

The MacCulloch house was situated at what was almost the terminus of Alcorn Avenue, in one of Latonia City's tiny outlying neighborhoods. This made a journey into town on foot no small matter, and Nat's mother usually encouraged him to take the bus. "Our city hospital has the best emergency care in the county," she was known to tell him at times when she worried for his safety, "but I still won't abide unnecessary risks."

Nat had appealed to his father at that point. The Harts' place was all the way up on Franklin Avenue, but Nat promised that he wouldn't be making the trip alone. He would meet up with Dick at the edge of Silvern Row, and the boys would walk together. After some discussion, both of Nat's parents agreed.

Everything he'd told his parents was true. It just wasn't the full story of what he planned to do that night.

As he was preparing to set out, his father favored him with a sort of smile that Nat had never seen before. And although Nat was a smart boy, he was still only ten; the world and its people were painted in colors from a finite palette. Only later, looking back, would he identify that look on his father's face for what it was: a knowing grin, with no small degree of pride.

It was seven o'clock and still sunny and hot. It was about a five-minute walk from the MacCullochs' house to the suspension railroad bridge just outside of the Silvern Row neighborhood. The bridge was unique in that it utilized a set of switches on the north side of the river, where the track diverted in a *Y*-shape. Depending on the position of the switches, a locomotive traveling across the river from the South Side could either be directed downriver—into town and on down the Allegheny toward Cornplanter—or upriver to pass within a stone's throw of the MacCulloch house on the line to Kiersburg.

Nat stopped beside the bridge and strained to listen for the echo of a distant locomotive whistle or the bells of signal stations farther up the line. There were none.

He looked back the way he'd come, half-expecting to see the silhouette of his father walking up behind him, perhaps to tell him he had forgotten something or to remind him to be back in the morning with plenty of time to spare before church. He was a novice when it came to deceiving his parents. Some of the kids at school even thought of Nat as a bit of a goody-two-shoes because he tended to avoid mischief. But he wasn't a kiss-up, and he had no choir-boy aspirations. Rather, he suffered from a combination of characteristics that tended to hamstring the proverbial devil on his shoulder before the race could ever begin: a pragmatic spirit and the inability to suspend his imagination. As a result, he generally erred on the side of caution, not because he was so devoted to upholding the rules but because usually, when one thought carefully enough about it, most trouble simply wasn't *worth* the trouble.

He looked back down the road, then at the railroad bridge. Was there anything he had forgotten? He had the rope. He had the flour sack filled with sand. And he had a change of clothes and his overnight things. Was there anything he had neglected to consider? They had scouted the location two days prior and agreed on where they would meet. And they had a contingency plan—a location to meet up in the event that it all went terribly, terribly wrong.

He stood there, trying to imagine every possible thing that *could* go wrong. And to his great dissatisfaction, he succeeded.

There were, he realized, several dozen things that could go wrong. And he knew that the longer he stood there, brainstorming disastrous scenarios, the more likely it was that he would arrive at one plausible enough to convince him to abort his mission and turn back.

He waited a few seconds longer. His father's silhouette still did not appear on the road. And there were still no train whistles or signal bells.

Dick's waiting for me, he reminded himself. Then he shouldered his pack, left Alcorn Avenue, and stepped onto the train tracks.

He'd been practicing walking on rails for seven of the ten years he'd spent on Earth, and his balance was so keenly developed that he found it no more difficult to walk tightrope-style on a right-hand steel rail than to saunter down a sidewalk. A pedestrian on the railroad bridge was a common enough sight, and although the signalman gave Nat a longer than usual circumspect glance as the boy passed, he did not call out or make any attempt to stop him. Eventually, the signalman looked away, but Nat wondered if he'd been recognized. What if the man knew his father or mother? Another theoretical scenario trying to make him turn back. He took a deep breath and banished the thought. Or tried to, anyway.

On the other side of the bridge, Nat left the railroad tracks and cut over to First Street, in front of the riverside mansions—the *right* side of the tracks, this neighborhood was. From here, he could follow First Street all the way to the intersection of First and Central: the corner where the Derrick Theatre stood.

Chapter Fourteen

Latonia City, Pennsylvania
September 2019

OWEN LINED UP his shot, adjusted his grip, and let out a deep breath to steady his shoulders.

Don't overthink, he told himself. *Just grip it and rip it.*

He hauled back, then swung hard.

The club's head striking the ball produced a satisfying *thwack*. It was a straightforward chip shot, made slightly more difficult by the dampness of the grass thanks to a morning shower that, judging by the clouds, might make a curtain call before they were through. A less than ideal day for eighteen holes. But he rarely got a chance to golf anymore, and beggars couldn't be choosers.

Irons were Owen's strong suit. He was consistent enough that, nine times out of ten, it was just a matter of choosing the right club, and this was one of the times when he'd chosen correctly. His ball sailed in a neat arc and landed on the green, leaving a brown divot in the soft, manicured earth.

On the other side of the fairway, his father, who had been watching Owen while leaning on his club like a cane, turned away with no visible reaction to Owen's shot.

Lou MacCulloch took two practice swings, stepped up to his ball, and took a real swing which bore very little resemblance to his practice swings. Even from here, Owen could see that he had pulled his head up, striking the ball with the blade of his club instead of the flat, angled surface. Instead of rising in an arc, Lou's ball shot forward like a base-hit line drive. It skipped over the fairway like a flat stone on water, skittered across the green, throwing up a mist of stale rainwater in its wake, and rolled over the fringe and down the hill to land in the rough behind the green.

Lou's reaction to his shot was precisely the same as his reaction to Owen's. None.

Owen slipped his eight iron back into his bag, slung the bag over his shoulders, and walked toward the green. On the opposite side of the fairway, his father did the same. Lou preferred to walk when he golfed. "The pros don't use carts," he always said. "If a guy can't walk the length of the course, maybe he should take up bowling."

As Owen fixed the divot left by his chip, his father took off his aviator-style sunglasses—he always wore sunglasses while golfing, even on an overcast day—and took his shot. He bladed this one, too, but the downhill lie gave him some room for error; the ball bounced up the hillside and landed on the green with a slight backspin, about the same distance from the pin as Owen.

Lou put his sunglasses back on and climbed the hill, his spikes slipping a little against the wet grass. He was dressed in long khakis and a plain blue, breathable athletic shirt—

Lou MacCulloch wore more formal attire for the golf course than Dave Albaugh did for work.

Lou didn't rush himself while he was on the course, but he did walk with purpose. He did not dally and had no patience for anyone who did. By the time he got to the top of the hill and approached his ball, he was breathing heavily. More heavily than he probably should have been, really.

"Do you know if they've got him on anything for his blood sugar now?" Kayla had asked Owen the night before. "Does he check it like he's supposed to?"

"I don't know," Owen had said. "Golfing tomorrow will be the first time I've seen him since the hospital, and we don't exactly chat."

"You should text him once in a while."

"I know."

But it just wasn't that simple.

The truth was that Owen felt he should not be here today. He had noticed a distance forming between him and Kayla thanks to his work schedule, and it was growing. There seemed to be less and less time for them to just sit down and talk, and when they did, they seemed to have less and less to say to one another. So to spend valuable weekend time golfing with his father, in the hopes of reconnecting with the old man, was a decision not made lightly. The point of the outing had been for them to catch up. But hardly a word had been spoken between them so far. Oh well. In Owen's book, anything short of a fight would be a win.

Silently, Lou MacCulloch took his putt. And silently, he missed.

Lou had always been athletic. He'd been a talented ballplayer back in the day, or so everyone always said. But baseball wasn't exactly a lifetime sport. When it came to golf, Lou was not so good. Not so good at all. For a start, his form was too much like a batter at the plate—he swung with a hard, quick turn of the hips, with elbows straight and arms extended like he was swinging for the fences. It gave him a consistently long tee shot that tended to go anywhere but straight. And his short game? It was cringeworthy. But he still golfed almost every weekend, weather permitting. Whether or not he had someone to golf *with* was irrelevant. He was just as happy to go out on his own. He'd even coached the golf team for a few years at the high school where he taught. The poor kids.

In a slight breach of etiquette, albeit a forgivable one, Lou decided to finish up and tap his ball in rather than marking his position and letting Owen take his shot from farther out. He came up short by two inches.

"Close enough," said Owen.

Lou picked his ball up wordlessly and stepped back.

Owen couldn't think of anyone who spent more time doing something they were so bad at. He didn't even seem to particularly enjoy himself. But there was a possible explanation for his devotion to the game. Lou's father, Owen's grandfather, Nathaniel MacCulloch, had died of a heart attack on a golf course, alone.

According to some, Nat had been the most recent victim of the "curse" of the MacCulloch family, a bloodline in which the men tended to die young, and not always peacefully. But Lou didn't care much for superstition. And over the years, Owen had begun to suspect that Lou's decision to spend nearly every Saturday on the links was his way of thumbing his nose at anyone who did believe in such things. Or perhaps daring fate to try to take *him* that way.

Owen frowned, thinking of Mae Baughman's vindictive stunt in the previous day's paper. An old article about his grandfather during the "hospital situation."

Wonder if Dad saw that, he thought.

He crouched on the green to pick out his line, stood, and then sank his putt for par. He was careful not to let his satisfaction show. Anybody who thought the MacCullochs were cursed had never seen his short game.

Lou's only response to Owen's shot was a brief nod before he turned to head off toward the next hole.

As Owen followed, he found himself staring at the back of his father's head and wondering what was going on in there. In doing so, it struck him how gray his father's hair was. When he pictured his dad, the image that came to mind was a man with the same dark, almost black, thick curly hair he'd had when Owen had been a kid. But an objective analysis showed that the gray hairs vastly outnumbered the black ones.

At the Hole 13 tee blocks, Lou stepped aside and waited for Owen to take his shot. But Owen decided that the silence between them had gone on long enough.

"Mom mentioned something about a problem at the house?" he said. "Water damage?"

Lou nodded. "From all the rain we've had. But that's Grandpa's house for you."

No matter how long Lou and Deb MacCulloch lived in that house on Silvern Row, it would always be "Grandpa's house." Owen hadn't grown up in it; they'd lived out in Cornplanter for most of his childhood. It was later that Lou and Deb moved into Grandpa MacCulloch's old home. Lou seemed to have a love-hate sort of relationship with the place.

"Well," said Owen, "if you need any help."

Lou only nodded.

Owen stepped up to the tee blocks and had to remind himself to relax his shoulders before he took his swing. Not his best shot of the day, but not terrible. "I was meaning to tell you," he said casually as he plucked his tee out of the ground, "Kayla and I are moving out of the house on 322."

Lou, who had his five-wood in one hand and his ball in the other, cocked his head to the side a bit but didn't take the bait. He waited for Owen to explain himself.

"We've been talking about it for a long time," said Owen. "And we've decided to move into Ruth Lee's place."

"No kidding," said Lou.

It was difficult to gauge his reaction, if any, through his sunglasses.

"Yeah," said Owen. "That place has always been too much house for her, really. It'll be perfect for all of us, though."

"So she's staying? You're moving in with her?"

"Yep. It seems like the right move. Especially for Emma as she gets older. It's very private, practically no traffic out there. She'll have a big backyard for playing and catching fireflies—er, lightning bugs. I always loved doing that when I was little. Remember?"

Lou's face warmed with a smile. "Yeah. . . . Yeah, I always liked that, too."

Lou stepped up to the tee blocks. The rain was starting again. Just a light mist. It didn't seem to bother him as he sent a scorcher dead-center down the fairway. It surpassed Owen's drive by a good fifty yards.

Owen whistled. "That'll do," he said.

Lou declined to comment on it. "Ruth Lee's been in that house a long time," he said. "I assume she owns it free and clear by now?"

Owen scratched his neck. "Not exactly. We'll be taking over the payments on her mortgage."

Lou frowned.

"She went through some rough times," Owen said. "You know, after Kayla's dad passed away. She, uh, actually had to refinance at one point, which extended the term of the loan."

This time, Lou's feelings on the matter were anything but unclear. He stared at Owen for a moment, then shook his head.

"I mean, that's part of the deal, though," Owen said. "We need a bigger place, she needs help. It's kind of a win-win—"

"Have you signed anything yet?" said Lou.

"Yes. We just need to meet with the people from the bank and finalize things."

Lou sighed, slung his bag over his shoulders, and started off down the fairway.

Owen hesitated. He knew his father. And he knew himself. He knew that if he let it go and didn't press the issue, the conversation would be over, and they could agree to an unspoken disagreement.

But he didn't let it go.

"You don't think we should do it?" Owen said, grabbing his bag and hurrying to catch up.

"Doesn't matter what I think," said Lou. "You're adults. You can do what you want."

"Right," agreed Owen. "But you don't think we should."

"No, I do not."

"Why?"

"For one thing, it's not an either-or situation."

"Meaning?"

"Putting the house in your name is a mistake. You lose your chance at the benefits that come with being a first-time home buyer if you put your name on the paper. You could easily move in as planned and pay her mortgage without putting your name on any documents. The living arrangement isn't the problem. It's that once the house is in your name, you're stuck with an obligation that you can't get rid of, saddled with a property that you're going to have a hell of a time selling if you ever decide you want something more modern. And besides that, the place is dated, it's probably got wiring from the 50s, it's a fire trap, and you're telling me my granddaughter's going to be living there. So, no, I do not think it is a good idea. There are other options out there for people like Ruth Lee. Have you looked into a life-tenant arrangement?"

Owen, now tasked with fielding a good deal more objections than he'd bargained for, only managed to say, "What's that?"

"I'll take that as a no," said Lou. "Little late for that, anyway. It'll be all right. You and Kayla both have steady jobs. I'm sure you won't have any trouble paying the mortgage off."

"Yeah, well, I'm quitting the paper," said Owen.

The words just came out. He hadn't meant to say them—hadn't even given the idea serious thought yet.

Lou stopped walking in the middle of the fairway, forcing Owen to stop as well. The rain was getting harder. Lou turned to stare at him from behind his aviators.

"What?" Lou said. It didn't sound like a question. More like a demand.

Owen shook his head, venting his frustration in a sharp breath. "The job isn't what they advertised. The hours are killing me. I never see Kayla and Emma. I make next to nothing—and did you see what they put in the paper yesterday—?"

"I saw it," Lou said. "So what?"

"That Baughman woman published it just to get under my skin," said Owen.

"I see it worked. Somebody hurt your feelings, so you're going to quit your job over it?"

"It's not just that. Stuff like that happens every day."

"And how long did it take you to find steady work the last time you quit your job because you didn't like it?"

Owen felt his nostrils flare.

"You don't announce that you're taking on a mortgage in one breath, then quit your job in the next. Sorry the work doesn't thrill you, but that doesn't mean your responsibilities go away. There are certain things you give up for yourself for the sake of your obligations. Believe it or not, being an art teacher in Latonia City, Pennsylvania, was not *my* first choice in life, either. But I did it for the sake of the people who depended on me."

Maybe Owen should have felt grateful that his father was opening up. Instead, he just felt angry. "Well, speaking as an obligation, sorry for messing up your life," he said.

Lou threw a sidelong glance at him. "That is not what I meant." And he continued walking.

"When you're right, you're right," Owen said. "Family. What an annoyance, huh?"

He could see Lou's jaw muscles tighten beneath his skin, but his voice remained low and even as he said, "Let's just drop it, all right?"

Then something occurred to Owen. "This is about *your* house, isn't it?" he said. "Talk about an obligation. Grandpa left it to you. You were hoping I would take the old water-damaged MacCulloch home off your hands someday, right?"

"Hell, no," Lou said. And this time, he did raise his voice.

"Must be frustrating," said Owen, "that I haven't followed your plan for my life."

"My plan!" Lou said.

He wheeled on Owen suddenly, and Owen blinked in surprise.

"My *plan*," Lou said so loudly that it might have echoed down the fairway if not for the intensifying rain, "was that you would get out of this place—not work at the town paper for chump change and get pushed around by the same people who pushed your grandfather into an early grave."

Owen's surprise was wearing off, replaced by anger.

"Everything I did," said Lou, "I did so that you could escape. Like I never could."

"Well, I never asked you to do that, so it's not my fault," Owen said. "Sorry I turned out to be such a disappointment."

Lou threw the bag of clubs off his back and took a step toward Owen so fast that, for a moment, Owen thought his father was about to strike him. His response was automatic: He tightened his shoulders and stuck his chin out, feeling his blood pumping in his head with that rush of adrenaline that always came from facing off against another man—whether that man was your father or not. But Lou didn't strike him. Instead, he raised his hand and jabbed a finger into Owen's sternum.

"Don't you *dare* say that," Lou hissed through gritted teeth, inches from Owen's face.

Owen glared at his own reflection in his father's aviator sunglasses.

Lou kept his finger there a moment longer, then disengaged by giving Owen a small shove. But Owen's body was like a wall, and instead of knocking him backward, the force caused Lou to recoil a step. Owen had to catch Lou to prevent him from tripping over his golf bag.

Without another word, Lou picked up his clubs and continued down the fairway in the rain. A moment later, Owen turned and walked away in the opposite direction.

Chapter Fifteen

State Route 322, Pennsylvania
November 1982

LOU MACCULLOCH—always Lou, never Louis—shifted his K5 Blazer into third gear and punched the gas. He wasn't eager to reach his destination, but he could at least make the journey fun. In the back seat were a green duffel bag and a backpack. On the floor were two six-packs of Bud. It was two days before Thanksgiving Day.

With headlights cutting through the autumn night, Lou took the downhill turn wide, accelerating through it and drumming his thumbs against the hard plastic ring of the steering wheel. The tune was in his head; the radio in this thing had never worked, not since he'd bought it at a used car lot a couple of years ago. He'd been a junior in high school at the time. Other than a few minor problems, the Blazer had been good to him. And it could go a lot faster than most people thought.

Lou held in the final inhale, then cranked the window down and released his cigarette butt to float away on the chill wind. He let the smoke trail out through his nostrils as he grabbed the pack of Marlboros from the cupholder beside him and pressed the cigarette lighter on the console into the warming position. Ahead, a bright green road sign announced the upcoming attractions:

> Latonia City 8
> Cornplanter 15

Lou tightened his grip on the narrow wheel. His biceps, sore from a tougher than usual workout with the team the day before, flexed a bit beneath a ratty old shirt that probably should have been thrown away.

Just eight more miles. Eight more miles to the old man's house. And, not for the first time since climbing into the Blazer an hour before, he thought, *I hope that letter hasn't arrived yet.*

He was almost past the green road sign with its mile indicators by the time he noticed the silhouette standing beneath the sign, with its hand raise and its thumb held out. Lou swung wide to allow plenty of space between his vehicle and the grassy berm and continued on his way.

"Sorry, pal, but I don't really do that sort of thing," he muttered as he drove on.

Nevertheless, out of curiosity, he tapped his brakes and glanced into the rear-view mirror. In the red hue cast by the brake lights, he saw the guy lower his thumb and drop his hand to his side. Then Lou noted the long red hair and realized that the guy wasn't a guy at all.

It was easy to see how he'd made the mistake. She was quite tall and wearing long, heavy blue jeans like a boy. But she wore no jacket. Only a tee shirt. And as Lou watched in the mirror, she rubbed her hands against her bare arms.

Lou slowed to a stop in the middle of the road—there was no other traffic in sight—and continued to watch her in the glow of the brake lights for a moment. He still had the pack of Marlboros in one hand. He put them down and ran his hand through his curly dark hair. He'd been trying to grow it long ever since leaving for college, but it just would not cooperate. No matter what he did with it, his hair would not grow *down*, only *out*. He kept telling himself that it would eventually have no choice but to hang down, if for no other reason than finally becoming too heavy to support itself. But so far, that had not happened. So instead of the long-haired rock star look he'd been going for, he had the beginnings of a pretty impressive afro.

"Nothing on this road for another three miles," he mumbled to himself. "Where's she think she's going? And on a cold night like tonight, dressed like that?"

The cigarette lighter popped out.

Lou drummed his fingers against the steering wheel, then shifted the stick into the reverse position and backed up along the road.

When the woman saw him coming, she stepped further into the grass, away from the vehicle, as if she were no longer sure that this was what she wanted.

Lou leaned across and pulled the handle to allow the passenger-side door to swing open, causing the dome light to come on with a yellowish glow. The woman maintained her distance but ducked so as to get a clear line of sight at him. She was tall, but she was younger than Lou had expected—several years younger than he was and closer to a girl than a woman. She was hugging her arms tightly against the cold. Her stick-straight red hair was tangled on one side but not on the other. On the left side of her face, a wide bruise blotted out her freckles. And there was dried blood on her forehead, though Lou could not tell where it had come from.

"Are you okay?" said Lou.

It was a stupid thing to say, really, to someone who looked like that.

"No," she said.

Something seemed to let loose inside her as she said it, as if the only thing holding her together until now had been *not* admitting that she was not okay. Her lower lip quivered. Tears broke from her eyes, one trail running down her freckled nose, the other trail pushed sideways across her cheek by a sudden gust of wind, which picked up her red hair and threw it across her face, making her wince and sort of fold in on herself.

"Get in," said Lou, beckoning with his hand.

She hesitated. She pushed her hair out of her face to get a better look at him.

"It's okay," said Lou. "Come on."

It took her another moment to be convinced, but once she had made the decision, she rushed to the vehicle and practically leaped in, throwing the door shut behind her. The dome light turned off as the door closed, and she sat huddled in the seat, rubbing at her arms. It took Lou a second to gain the presence of mind to crank the heat.

"Who . . . ?" Lou started to ask but at the last moment changed his question to, "Where are you headed?"

"Toward Latonia," she said. She started to wipe at her tears, flinched when her thumb brushed the swollen, blackened cheek under her eye, and added, "Twin Oaks Road, outside town."

She ducked her head to check the mirror, looking for lights on the road. Raindrops began to fall on the windshield.

"Maybe you should start driving," she said. "Now."

CR&O

PART THREE
ROCK-OIL RAG

C8&O

Chapter Sixteen

LOU SHIFTED THE Blazer into gear and hit the gas. By the time he was back into third, the rain was coming down pretty hard. He grabbed a Marlboro from the pack in the cupholder and pulled the lighter out of its socket on the console. He held the orange-hot coil to the end of the cigarette and took a drag. When he offered the pack and the lighter to the girl, she accepted them wordlessly and lit up. Then, as an afterthought, Lou asked, "How old are you?"

"Eighteen," she said.

"Okay," said Lou.

A moment of silence.

"Sixteen," she said.

"Okay," said Lou. "There's a coat in the back seat if you want it."

The girl found it and pulled it over herself like a blanket. There were a few more moments of silence as Lou navigated the wooded twists of 322, the rain sounding like a marching band against the roof of the vehicle.

"So," said Lou, "probably none of my business, but I'm going to ask anyway. Are you sure I should be taking you to Twin Oaks Road? Not a hospital?"

"I think I'm okay," she said. Taking another puff of the cigarette, she checked the vanity mirror on the underside of the Blazer's sun visor and scraped some of the dried blood off her forehead with a fingernail. "I was a little dizzy, but it's better now. And my arm's not as bad as it looks."

Lou glanced over at her and realized that she hadn't just been hugging her arms against the cold. She was currently lifting up his coat to examine her right arm, which had a large, bloody gash below the elbow.

"You want to talk about it?" Lou asked.

At this, the tears almost came on again. But at the last moment, she managed to will herself to be angry instead. "Got in an argument with my dad," she spat.

"Your *dad*?" said Lou.

Another few moments of silence.

"Again, probably none of my business," said Lou, "but no dad should hit his daughter. Ever."

She turned away from him, propping her elbow against the door and shifting her head so as to hide her face behind a curtain of red-orange, stick-straight hair.

"He didn't hit me," she said flatly. "He threw me out of his car."

She smoked two more cigarettes over the next five miles. She said nothing, and neither did Lou. He wanted to say something, but nothing he could think to say sounded quite right, no matter how many times he tried to draft and reorder and revise his thoughts. He had never been very good with words. But the closer they got to their destination, the more the silence weighed on him. Finally, he had to ask.

"This isn't your dad's place I'm taking you to, is it?"

"No," said the girl. "It's my grandma's."

"Will he come looking for you there?" asked Lou.

"Probably not for a while."

"I could take you to the police or something."

"No," was all she said.

Lou shifted in his seat. "I'm Lou, by the way."

"I know," she said.

Lou looked at her.

"I used to watch you play ball," she said. She furrowed her brow and made a face as if he ought to know this. "You played with my brother, Mike."

"Mike? You mean Mike Schultze. . . ?" Lou looked at the girl again, in a way seeing her for the first time. "Oh my God. Angie."

Her smile, the first of the drive, showed off two buck teeth and stretched out her freckles a bit, and some of the little girl he remembered shined through.

"Angie Schultze," said Lou. "Of course. I'm sorry—I didn't even recognize you." Then quickly, to clarify: "You've really grown up."

"You picked me up and didn't even know who I was?" she said, incredulous at the very idea. "I thought you recognized me and that was why you stopped."

Lou shrugged. "I just saw someone who needed a ride."

Now the full truth of the girl's destination became clear.

Twin Oaks Road.

Amity Court.

"I'm sorry," said Lou, and was not quite sure what he was apologizing for.

"It's okay," said Angie.

Mike, never a great student but an exceptional athlete, had been the black sheep in the Schultze family. Although, come to think of it, maybe it was more like he was a white sheep in a family full of black ones. With the exception of Mike, every Schultze in Latonia City that Lou could think of had been a problem student at school, and a fair share had grown into problem citizens. And they all seemed to live at Amity Court on Twin Oaks Road.

Lou did not look down on the Schultzes. Or anyone else who lived at Amity Court. His father had come from poverty, and it had always been drilled into him to never look down on anyone. Nevertheless, Schultze was one of those names you were never surprised to see pop up in the Monday-morning police blotter. Throwing one's daughter out of a car certainly fit the bill.

Was the car moving when he threw her out? Lou wondered, but he didn't want to ask. *Happy fricking Thanksgiving. . . .*

Several minutes later, he turned onto Twin Oaks Road.

"How is Mike, anyway?" asked Lou.

"He's fine," said Angie. "He's working at a garage out in Knotts Corners. Got a big twelve-point, first day of archery."

"Nice," said Lou. "He'd kill me for saying this, but ask him if he ever finally learned how to slide into third base. He'll know what it means."

"What? No, gross!"

Lou blinked. "Huh? No—no. Oh God, *no*. It's about baseball. *Actual* baseball."

"Oh," said Angie. "Oh."

"Yeah, jeez. . . ." Lou shook his head. "See, we were playing Seneca Regional this one time—you might have even been there that day—and they had this real big guy who played third. He used to crowd the baseline whenever he covered the bag, and we all said if he tried that on us, we'd run him over. Just stupid talk, right? Guys being guys. Anyway, it's the first inning, and their pitcher's throwing garbage, and Mikey's on second. And I can see it in the way he's hopping around, he's gonna try to steal third. And he's got his eyes on that big third baseman.

"So, then he gets his chance: a called ball four in the dirt. And Mikey takes off. As usual, the big guy's standing right in the baseline—not even ready, not covering the bag, just standing in the baseline, right in Mikey's way. Well, I don't know if it was all our tough talk before the game or if Mikey just didn't like the look of the guy, but he doesn't even slow down. He lowers his shoulder and just *plows* right into this third-baseman. Knocks the guy *flat*! But Mikey's going too fast. He trips and falls forward, lands right on his face, and goes rolling through the dirt. And when Mikey finally stops rolling, he stretches his arm out and smacks his hand down on the third-base bag—as if he *meant* to do that, like the whole thing was a slide.

"So now there's this cloud of dust like somebody got in a fight in an old cartoon. Mikey's on the ground, the big guy from Seneca Regional's on the ground, and the whole field is silent. Our head coach is standing there in the box on third-base line, and Mikey just looks up at him with this big grin on his face, thinking Coach is about to tell him what a great job he did stealing third. And Coach says, 'Schultze, you dumb-ass, there's a guy on first.'"

Lou could see from Angie's polite smile that she wasn't quite getting the joke.

"See, it was a called ball *four*, and Mikey was on second," said Lou, "but he forgot that we had a guy right behind him on *first*, too. So the walk advanced both runners. He could have just walked to third. So he'd basically run down this poor third baseman for no reason."

"Oh," said Angie. "Oh!"

"Yeah!" said Lou. "We gave him all sorts of hell for that one. Every game from then on, if Mikey got on second, you could bet your life that somebody was gonna yell, 'Slide into third, Mikey! Slide!' Seneca Regional's third baseman hated him for the next two years. . . . But he didn't stand in the baseline anymore."

"Next time I see him, I'm totally gonna say that," said Angie.

"Do it," laughed Lou. "And tell him MacCulloch says hi."

"I will," she said. "He still talks about you sometimes. He said you still play ball?"

"Yeah. At Pitt. How about Mikey?"

Angie said nothing for a second. The way she turned away and shook her head told Lou that that had been the wrong question to ask. "No," was all she said.

Finally, Lou turned off of Twin Oaks and onto the dirt road that marked the entry to Amity Court. The rain had stopped, and before him, laid out in rows, was a grid system of mobile homes, each with its own driveway and little front yard. In the double-lights of the Blazer's headlamps, children's toys and pipe-framed swing sets cast shifting shadows on faux siding, cinder blocks, and empty brown bottles. Not every trailer court was rough. But in Seneca County, Amity Court was about as rough as it got.

"The third one on the right over there," said Angie, pointing.

"That pink one?" said Lou.

"Yeah."

Angie's buck teeth were no longer showing, and Lou noticed that she was rubbing her arms again beneath his coat.

"You sure about this?" Lou asked.

"I'm sure," said Angie.

Lou kept driving, but much slower than necessary. Because *he* was not so sure. But he couldn't rightly refuse, either.

He swung wide to avoid an overturned charcoal grill whose briquettes had been scattered across the lane. He almost kept driving past the pink trailer. Almost. But in the end, he slowed and put the vehicle in park. If she wasn't going to go to a hospital or a police station willingly, what else could he do?

He turned and looked very seriously at the straight-haired girl with the freckles, the girl he knew better as a tiny child in pigtails who was always in the stands for their home games. On her father's lap.

"Angie, I will only let you out of this vehicle," said Lou, "if you promise me that this is a safe place for you to be tonight."

Angie nodded. "It's safe."

"I could take you to stay with your brother," said Lou. "Or to my mom and dad's place. Or the YWCA or—"

"It's safe," she said again. "I promise. My grandma's the only one home, and maybe her boyfriend, but he's nice to me."

Lou hesitated. Then he reached into the back seat. He pushed aside the green duffel bag to get at his backpack, dug out a notebook and a pen, and jotted down two phone numbers.

"This first number is my parents' house," he said. "I'll be there until Sunday night. The second number can reach me at school if you ever need to call me there for any reason."

It was the number for the payphone in the hallway of his dorm at Pitt, which meant that at least *in theory* she could reach him there. But that would depend on whether

(a) someone bothered to pick up the ringing phone, (b) the person who answered had any clue who Lou was, and (c) they cared enough to go looking for him to tell him he had a call.

Lou tore the sheet of college-ruled paper loose and handed it to Angie.

"Even if all you need is a ride somewhere," said Lou, "or somewhere safe to be, call me."

Angie stared at the piece of paper.

"And Angie," said Lou, "if your old man ever lays a hand on you again. . . ."

Just thinking about it made Lou's fingers close tightly on the wheel of the Blazer, causing his forearms to bulge.

"You find me and tell me," he said. "And whatever he does to you, I will do to him twice over."

Angie's good eye went wide.

"Oh, and tell Mikey to get ahold of me sometime," he added. "He can come down to Pitt for a weekend, and we'll catch up. Or maybe he could come and see me play ball sometime. I'm in his old position. Second base."

Angie hesitated. She looked down at the paper again. "What if I call the house and your dad answers?"

Lou sighed. "Don't believe everything you hear about my dad. He's a good guy. Really."

"Okay," said Angie, removing his coat from her lap. "Thanks, Lou."

Lou nodded. And with that, Angie climbed out of the passenger side. Lou waited until she'd made it indoors, hoping he hadn't made a terrible mistake by bringing her here.

A few seconds later, as he pulled out onto the dirt drive, the Blazer's headlamps shifted, shining their full glow on a small sign on wire posts in the front yard of the pink trailer. It read, SAVE OUR HOSPITALS. Lou frowned at it. Then he hit the gas.

Chapter Seventeen

THERE HAD ALWAYS been something strange about that *X* on the wall.

Lou wasn't sure what it was that bothered him about it, exactly. Maybe just the fact that it was so off-center; his father, ever a practical and meticulous man, had drawn it on the wall when Lou was a small boy, as a target for him to practice throwing his baseball and catching it when it bounced back, in the winter months when it was too cold to go outside.

But for some reason, Nat had drawn it in an odd spot on the wall. It was pretty high, really, to serve as a good throwing target. And placing it in an off-center spot was nothing like Nathaniel G. MacCulloch, who contended that there was a "right way" to do everything, and tended to strive for it on every occasion. Even in something as inconsequential as drawing an *X* on a wall, Lou would have expected Nat to have placed it dead-center and at the optimal height.

Lou hauled back and gave the ball a throw. Not a baseball. Heck, a baseball would have knocked this crummy old house down. Instead, he used a blue rubber racquetball, which had been his standard weapon of choice for basement-bound fielding practice since the age of twelve. It was better practice than one might have thought. Racquetballs were a bit small, but they had a hell of a bounce and took funny hops that kept you on your toes. When it came off the wall along the seam of one of the bricks, it could produce an unexpected backspin. Good training for hand-eye coordination and reaction time.

As the ball took a hop and came back into Lou's open glove, he paused to look around the nasty dirt-floor basement. He would never understand why his father had stayed in this old house all these years. He'd had major renovations done, but Lord knew Nathaniel MacCulloch had enough money to afford a better place than *this*. Sure, the man had grown up here. But at some point, a guy had to cut his own cord and move on.

Lou was about to toss the ball again when a high-pitched wail came reverberating through the floorboards above his head.

"God help me," Lou muttered under his breath. "Miles fricking Davis, at it again."

He'd rolled into the driveway in his Blazer late the previous night, and he had thus far managed to avoid the sound of Nat blowing his horn. But his luck only lasted so long.

Hope Angie's all right, thought Lou. *I should have insisted on taking her to the hospital to get checked out. Who knows if she was telling the whole story?*

He made a mental note to keep an eye on the police blotter anytime he was in town in the future. And to pray that he never saw the name Angie Schultze in it.

He tossed the ball a few more times before the sound of his father's trumpet became too much for him. Finally, he shoved the racquetball into his glove, pulled the glove off his hand, and tossed it into the corner of the basement. The trumpet—no, no, no, *cornet*, his father always insisted on calling it—only got louder as Lou climbed the stairs. He emerged on the first floor of the house, ignored his father in the adjoining room with his horn raised to his lips, and walked down the hall to his bedroom.

Lou shut the door behind him and within seconds had his record player rotating. He cranked the knob until Eddie Van Halen's guitar was drowning out Nat MacCulloch's cornet. If there was one thing Lou had not missed since leaving for college last year, it was listening to his father play the same old songs, *every* night, badly. At least this time he would only have to put up with it for a couple of days, until Thanksgiving break was over.

I've got to find some other place to stay after next semester, thought Lou, throwing himself down onto his bed. *I cannot take another whole summer of this. I just can't. Got to get out of here.*

Lou's grandfather had built this house, and his father had lived in it for almost his entire life. He could have bought something bigger, in a nicer neighborhood, but he'd instead chosen to have the old place restored, renovated, and added onto. So the little house that had been practically a shack during Nat's boyhood was transformed into a beautiful middle-class home with respectable square footage and an enviable view of the river across the railroad tracks, though no trains ran on them anymore. Nat often spoke of one day handing the family home down to Lou.

Me? Live in this house? thought Lou. *Over my dead body.*

Lou wasn't surprised when he heard the quiet knock from his door, barely audible over the wail of Eddie's guitar.

"Come in," Lou called without turning down the volume or moving from his bed.

The door opened a few inches, and his mother ducked her head in. Her blonde hair was done up high and tightly curled. An unlit cigarette was pinched between fingers with long, bright red nails.

Rose Stewart MacCulloch said something that Lou didn't hear, then waited for a response. She did not raise her voice or strain herself in order to be heard over the sound of the record. On principle, she never raised her voice, which forced Lou to get up off his bed and turn the music down.

"What?" he said.

"I said, is everything okay in here?" she said, same volume as before.

"Yeah, why?" said Lou.

"Well," said Rose, "just because you've been gone for a while doesn't mean I've forgotten what you're like when you're upset." Her lipstick matched the red of her fingernails, as did her heels. Lou had barely ever seen her without makeup on, and he did not think he had ever seen her wear anything other than a dress outside of the house. She leaned against the doorframe and crossed her arms, nodding toward Lou's Panasonic turntable. "When you turn the volume on that thing so high that even *you* don't enjoy the sound of it anymore, it means something's up."

Lou blinked. This behavior was news to him. But, thinking about it, she was right.

"I like the hairdo, by the way," she added, grinning.

"I bet dad doesn't," said Lou.

"No, he does not," said Rose. "So. What's wrong?"

"I don't know," said Lou.

Rose gave him a moment to think. He needed that sometimes. To collect his thoughts.

"Yeah," he concluded. "I don't know."

"Is it maybe a little strange to come home again?" she asked. "After being independent and on your own for a while?"

A particularly high note from Nat MacCulloch's cornet came through loud and clear from down the hall, and Lou felt his jaw clench involuntarily. How could a person practice all his life at something and still be so bad at it? "It is a little strange," he agreed.

"Well, I understand that, but you also have to remember," said Rose in the sing-song sort of cadence she always used when making a very good point, "neither of *us* got the opportunity to go to college."

Rose waited. From experience, Lou knew that she would not continue until he acknowledged what she had said. It was a sort of conversational tick she had. She was a sixth-grade teacher by trade, and there were times when her techniques for dealing with rowdy students permeated into her parenting style, never mind that her son was almost twenty years old.

"I know," said Lou.

"And this arrangement is just as new to us as it is to you," she continued.

She waited again.

"I understand," Lou said, nodding.

"So if we're not acting the way you think we're supposed to be acting, just know that we can't read your mind, but we are *trying*. It's a . . . a challenge to reconcile the fact that you are an independent person now but also still our child and still living under our roof, and subject to our rules. We will do our best to respect your independence. If you will also do your best to respect us."

The rules in question were the ones that had to do with the two six-packs Lou had brought home in the back seat of his Blazer. He'd stashed them in his baseball bag before bringing his things into the house, but he had expected to make it longer than a day before getting caught with them. Leave it to his teetotaling father to bring the hammer down over a couple of beers.

There were times when Lou thought the apple could not have fallen farther from the tree. The kind of words people used to describe Nat MacCulloch were "gentle," "kind," and "upright." But Lou MacCulloch was competitive. And not very gentle. Nat was kind to everyone he met. But Lou could be mean, and he knew it, especially if someone didn't deserve kindness—woe to them. And upright? Well, as a kid, Lou had been known to sneak cigarettes and curse rather creatively when adults weren't listening. He was upright in the ways that mattered to him. But outside of that, there was fun to be had.

From what Lou could tell, he was more like his grandfather, Grant, than his dad. Lou had been told that Grant MacCulloch had once fist-fought a union boss on the factory floor of the Germania Oil Well Supply Company over a labor dispute. Meanwhile, the only thing even remotely scandalous that Lou had ever heard of his father doing came from a story told by one of Nat's childhood friends, Art Hart, owner of the local music store, in which Art claimed that he and Nat had once snuck into the Derrick Theatre without tickets. But Art Hart was well-known as a peddler of tall tales. And it sure didn't sound like something Lou's father would do.

"I do respect your rules," Lou told Rose. "I wasn't going to drink in the house. There's supposed to be a party in town tomorrow night, so I was going to take them there."

"We don't want you drinking there either," said Rose. "Imagine how it would look if you were picked up."

Imagine how it would look, thought Lou. *Not, imagine what would happen. Not, imagine how it would affect you. No—imagine* how it would look. . . .

"Dad has always said, no drinking in this house," said Lou. "I wasn't going to drink in this house. I was going to take it somewhere else. I was following his rules."

Rose slipped the unlit cigarette behind her ear. Lou had left his own smokes in the Blazer—he wasn't even going to try to anticipate his father's rules regarding cigarettes in the house. For as long as he could remember, his father had smoked a pipe in the den every evening after dinner. But his mother, who smoked cigarettes, only ever smoked them outside. Lou wasn't sure if this was an unspoken rule, an official policy, or something in between. But he had a feeling that if he broached the subject, it would only lead to further disagreements, so he'd decided to let it be for now. It wasn't worth the effort.

Only now did Rose step all the way into Lou's bedroom. She glanced back over her shoulder, then shut the door behind her. "It's not so much the drinking itself," she said, lowering her voice a bit. "It's more. . . . Well, honestly, it's really just about listening to your father right now."

Rose MacCulloch sat down on the bed beside Lou, which was something she hadn't done in a long time.

"You haven't been home in a while," she said, "so you wouldn't know. But things have gotten much worse."

"What has?" said Lou. "You mean the hospital thing?"

"Yes, that." Rose pulled the cigarette back out from behind her ear and rolled it nervously between her fingers. "It's not just the talk radio call-ins or the town hall meetings anymore. There have been letters. And phone calls."

Lou leaned over to switch off the record player. It was Van Halen's newest album, released just a few months prior, and this was one of Lou's least favorite tracks on it, anyway—a strange cover of an old-timey song from the 1920s.

"What do you mean?" said Lou. "Like, threats?"

Rose sucked her teeth. "Mostly just minor, harassing sorts of comments. But, yes. There have also been some threats."

"Mom," said Lou, sitting up very straight. "If anyone has threatened you, I will—"

"No, you most certainly will not. Bite your tongue right now, and don't you say another word. Lord, that's all we need—*you* getting into a fight or mixed up in some sort of trouble. This whole hospital ... *situation* has gotten out of control. The doctors in this town have the people so riled up. . . ."

Lou's mother trailed off, and Lou realized why. His father's trumpet playing from the opposite side of the house had stopped.

"I'm not asking you to be enthused about being home," Rose whispered. "I'm not even asking you to be nice. All I ask is that you don't put your father under any more stress than he already is. Please. His doctor said—"

"Honey?" came Nat's voice from the hall outside.

"I'm in here talking to Louis, Dear," Rose called. "I'll be right out."

Lou's mother gave his knee a little squeeze. "Can you do that, Louis?" she whispered. "Just for a few days?"

Louis. No one had called him that in months. But Lou nodded.

Rose winked at him. Then she left the room.

Lou remained seated on the bed. Don't put his father under any stress. Well, he would try. But his success would all depend on whether he managed to intercept a certain letter from the university in time.

If it hasn't gotten here already, that is.

In the hallway outside, Lou's father spoke softly. No doubt, he thought he was speaking quietly enough so as not to be heard through the door. But his hearing wasn't so good these days, and he spoke louder than he knew.

"Is he going to straighten up?" asked Nat.

Lou bristled.

"We talked it over, and everything is fine," Rose replied.

"Good," said Nat. "So, what do you think? A little rusty, but do I still got it?"

"Still *got* it," said Rose. "You sound just like Gid the Great."

Chapter Eighteen

Latonia City, Pennsylvania
July 1939

"MAYBE HE COULDN'T get away," said Dick. "Maybe Poppy wouldn't let him."

A few quiet seconds passed.

"We did say right here, didn't we?" said Dick.

Another few seconds.

"We said *right here*. Right? Didn't we?"

"Yes, okay? Yes," said Nat. "We said right here. And yes, he is late. What do you want me to do about it?"

"I don't know!" Dick snapped back. "Sorry! Okay?"

Nat chewed on his lip thoughtfully, looking up East First Street and then down. For what felt like the hundredth time, a passerby lugging shopping bags forced him and Dick to retreat a bit further back on the sidewalk. They now had their backs flat against the stone of the Saint Stephen's Cathedral, which stood like an impenetrable medieval bastion amid the city's shoulder-to-shoulder shop buildings and tenements.

Nat had only been in downtown Latonia City at night a few times before, and those times had been with his parents. It was almost 8:00 now, and the sun had just dipped below the buildings across the road on Central Avenue. Before long, it would be night—well and truly *night*. And Nat was out on his own. Such a thing had never happened before.

As he and Dick stood on the corner of East First Street and Warren Street, one block from the Derrick, he found himself surprised by how lit-up the streets already were. Not a single storefront was dark. There were people everywhere, with sidewalks so choked that on his way here, he'd had difficulty navigating through the throng at the center of town. The streets were lined with parked vehicles, and the traffic came in steady, alternating streams. Cars. Trucks. Buses. He'd never seen the city quite like this before. And up until about fifteen minutes ago, the pulsing epicenter of the commotion had been the Derrick Theatre, whose facade was illuminated by a bank of searchlights shining up on it from below.

A mob of people had been waiting outside the theater. Men in suits and hats. Women in furs. There had been ticket-takers at the doors and young men parking cars and a few shabby-looking kids hanging around. And there had been police officers watching the crowd. Nat had even seen one of the aforementioned shabby-looking kids get caught while trying to reach into a theater-goer's pocket, only to be grabbed by a cop and pulled away by his ear. To where? The paddy-wagon? Nat didn't know.

But now, the doors of the Derrick were shut, and the only people in front of the theater were the usual pedestrians. Plus, a pair of city cops, chatting with one another as they paced in front of the doors, looking for all the world like a couple of troops outside an army fort.

He's in there right now, thought Nat. *Gid the Great. Gideon Rust. The show's probably already started. And I'm missing it.*

"Even if Art does show up, I don't see how we're gonna get in," said Dick, whose voice was taking on an increasingly whiny quality with each passing minute. He had to talk around a white-and-red swirled peppermint in his mouth; he'd been carrying around a bag of them for the past few days but was down to his last few. "I mean, it wasn't like *this* when we took a look the other day—"

"Course it wasn't," said Nat. "We knew it wouldn't be. It doesn't change the plan."

A middle-aged woman carrying a paper shopping bag slowed down in front of Nat and Dick. Nat did his best to look uninteresting and stepped in front of his pack on the ground—the one he'd carried here all the way from Silvern Row but had set on the sidewalk because it was so heavy—and subtly pushed it behind him a few inches.

The woman did a double-take. She watched the two of them: two young boys just standing there, alone, on the busy sidewalk. For a moment, it looked as if she might say something. Then she sniffed, seemed to decide the whole thing was none of her business, and kept walking.

With his hands behind his back, Nat drummed his fingers against the stone of the cathedral and shifted his weight nervously from one foot to the other. "What time you got now?" he asked.

"One minute after the last time you asked," Dick said.

"Don't get lippy with me," said Nat, "just because you're scared."

"It's ten minutes after eight," said Dick, "and I am not scared, I'm just tired of being asked what time it is."

"Then give me your watch."

"Get your own."

Nat grumbled a word under his breath that he'd learned from an older kid at school. "I say we give him a couple more minutes, then go, with or without him."

"Okay," said Dick, looking at his watch again. "What do you mean by 'a couple,' though?"

"Two. That's what 'a couple' is."

"Not always."

"Yes, it is. Look it up in the dictionary."

"People say 'a couple' all the time when they mean more than two."

"Well, when I say it, it always means two. At 8:12, *a couple of minutes* from now, we'll. . . ."

Nat trailed off, his attention drawn toward the sudden *pat-pat-pat* that anyone who is a child or has ever been a child can identify as the sound of another child's worn-down shoes smacking heavy-footed against the ground as they run. He turned toward the sound and saw a pair of shoppers parting just in time to make way for a rail-thin youth with wispy hair to come sprinting up the sidewalk. Panting, Art Hart came to a skidding halt in front of Nat and Dick.

"Where on earth have you been?" demanded Dick. "We said quarter till eight." And although it could not have been a single minute since the last time he'd checked his wristwatch, he consulted it again. "It's going on quarter *past*!"

"Sorry," said Art. "You could've gone in without me. I'd have caught up."

"Now he tells us," said Dick. He bit down, cracking the peppermint sweet between his teeth.

"The shop was busy," Art said. "Poppy wouldn't let me go till it'd slowed down a bit. And it still hasn't slowed—I snuck out." He giggled and shook his head. "Boy, am I gonna catch hell for this."

"Good man," said Nat. "All right. We're all here now, so let's go."

Without waiting for a response from the others, without even waiting to see if they would follow, Nat hurried down the street toward the crosswalk.

Chapter Nineteen

Latonia City, Pennsylvania
November 1982

THIS PLACE, thought Lou. *This fricking place. . . .*

"Who needs one?"

"Right here," said Lou.

The can of Budweiser sailed through the dugout, and Lou caught it with an outstretched hand. The source of the lob, the ample-framed Eddie Tarr, followed it up by tossing him the opener. Lou caught that, too, then neatly punched the top of the can. Then it was bottom's up as Eddie, Bill Mahle, and Deb McClintock watched. Out of the four of them, Lou was the only one who had left town for college. He was a sophomore now, and they were all quite impressed with how his drinking had progressed.

Lou lowered the empty can and wiped his mouth. All the colleges in the area had let out for Thanksgiving break, which meant that everyone was in town for a few days. Naturally, there would be a big party tomorrow. Everyone would be there. As for tonight, one of Lou's old buddies had gotten ahold of him to tell him to come over to the football field, where a bunch of the guys were getting together. Lou had been a three-sport athlete all through high school, and seeing the old football crew might have been nice. But had any of those guys tried to keep in touch with him since he'd left? Had any of them called him? Or returned his calls?

Eddie, Bill, and Deb, on the other hand. They returned his calls. And called him once in a while, too, to see how he was holding up in the city. He would have rather spent a Friday night with any one of them over the whole football team. Especially Deb. She'd always shot him down in high school. But, well, it could have been his imagination, but she seemed to be looking at him differently now.

The old baseball dugout wasn't glamorous—just a free-standing brick structure with a caged-in front that made one feel like a chicken in a coop. But, coopish as it might have been, it was just as good a place to sit and throw back a few as it was to take shelter in during a rain delay.

Lou stared through the wire fence, out onto the diamond. The dirt infield was even crummier than he remembered. At the university, they had a grass infield that got mowed before every game. And so far, his dad hadn't seen him play on it once.

"I don't get it," said Lou. "Why are people so bent out of shape about this hospital thing?"

"I guess I don't really know either," admitted Bill. "Never really heard the full story."

"You seen the signs yet?" asked Eddie.

Lou nodded. "I saw a few as I rolled into town yesterday."

The one in the front yard in Amity Court had been the first, but there were plenty of others. Not just posted in front yards, but hung in shop windows, taped to telephone poles, tacked to fences, and stuck to the bumpers of cars. Signs and stickers that read, SAVE OUR HOSPITALS.

"Do *you* not know the full story, Lou?" asked Deb.

"Yeah, like, doesn't your old man talk about it?" said Eddie.

"He and I haven't really talked much since I left for school," said Lou. "I mean, I know what's going on. It's people's reactions I don't understand. He doesn't like to talk about it."

"I'm not surprised," said Eddie. "People hate him."

Bill nudged Eddie with his elbow.

"What? *I* don't," Eddie clarified.

"A lot of people also agree with your dad," said Deb. "Maybe even *most* people. But the ones who don't are being stirred up, and your dad's the scapegoat."

Lou reclined on the bench and let the back of his head rest against the cool brick of the dugout wall. He was used to having his family's reputation precede him, but usually, it was in a good way. Until recently, Lou had never heard a bad word spoken about Nat MacCulloch. It was always, "You Nat's boy? Old Nat is one of the good ones." Or, "Oh, you're Rose Stewart's kid—didn't she marry little Nat MacCulloch? A good guy, Nat."

All the stories he'd ever heard about his father were the good kind. Stories like how when Nat was a boy, he would give his sack lunch to a child from one of the poor families who sometimes showed up to school with nothing to eat. Never mind that the MacCullochs were just as poor; the difference was, when there wasn't enough food in the MacCulloch house, it was the parents who went hungry while the kids ate.

Stories like how, after Nat's father—Lou's grandpa—had died young, Nat had gone to work to help support the family, tending the register at Poppy Hart's music emporium and doing tune-ups and pumping gas at the local service station. And he never complained about it, even when it stretched him thin during the schoolyear and amounted to practically a full-time work schedule in the summer. There had been no sports or clubs for Nat MacCulloch. His after-school activities had been providing for the family, which consisted of him, his mother, and his five sisters. That sort of workload wasn't technically legal for a minor to take on, but it had all been done under the table, and the family would have been bad off, otherwise.

Stories of how Nat had worked hard in school with the hopes of someday putting himself through college. How he'd gone to work at the Germania Oil Well Supply Company like his father before him when college had proven too expensive. And how, by saving up money on the side for years, he'd eventually scraped together enough to go to business school. After business school, Germania had rehired Nat, this time to keep their books. Somewhere in there, he'd enlisted in the Navy—Lou was a little fuzzy on the timeline, but he knew that after the Navy, Nat had been hired at the Latonia National Bank. Lou also knew that it was through a connection at the Bank that he'd eventually taken his position as Director of the Latonia City Chamber of Commerce.

The Chamber was one of many local organizations in which Nat MacCulloch played a role—he was on so many boards and a member of so many committees that Lou had never been able to keep track of them all.

But it was there, at the Chamber, that the trouble had started.

"Pass me another one," said Lou.

Eddie did, and Lou punched it open and threw it back. When it was gone, he placed the empty on the dugout bench beside him and stared down at his feet. "Not a drop of alcohol has ever touched these lips," Nat MacCulloch was known to boast. "Not once in my life."

Yeah, the apple certainly had fallen a long way from the tree, that was for damn sure.

Lou hadn't been a straight-A student. He suspected that he was capable of such a thing. Maybe. But he'd always felt that the sort of hard work that studying required was best reserved for wind sprints, lay-up drills, and batting practice. He had also developed an interest in landscape paintings. But his father was about as interested in art as he was in sports.

Growing up with a *good* family reputation, Lou thought, was in some ways even more oppressive than living under a bad one. He sometimes envied a person like Mikey Schultze. Because an anomaly from a ne'er-do-well brood was praised when he rose above the standard. But coming from "good stock" ensured that even minor childish infractions didn't go unnoticed. Boys like Lou were told things like, "I know you were brought up better than *that*," and, "what would your father say?"

Still, Lou was just being impudent, and he knew it. When he thought of Angie over at Amity Court, he knew which option he would have preferred. The trouble was that he just felt so penned in. Nat and Rose had always had a plan for him. He was their only son, and he was going to college. He would get a degree, and then he would get the kind of good job that opened up the sorts of doors that had always been locked tight to kids like Nat and Rose. And he had been content to go along with this plan, so long as he could play sports while he did it. That was how he'd come to begin a four-year Bachelor's program in Business Administration at the University of Pittsburgh, where he'd managed to secure a walk-on spot on the baseball team his freshman year. By the third week into the season, he'd been starting at second base and batting clean-up. And maintaining a low B average. This semester, he was set to pass all his classes again without any issues.

To Nat and Rose's knowledge, this academic arrangement would continue as planned. And they would keep believing that. As long as Lou managed to intercept a certain letter. He'd checked the mailbox that morning and again that afternoon. But it hadn't been there.

"It all started civil enough," said Deb, pausing to open a can of her own. "Just some opinion pieces in the paper. Then some town hall meetings. But then. . . . I don't know. It got ugly."

Lou sighed, thinking back to his mother's talk of harassing phone calls and threats at home.

"The whole thing will blow over eventually," Bill said cheerfully.

"I don't know," said Eddie. "My dad said every time he goes in for an appointment, the doctors are talking their patients' ears off about it. Telling them how if the city hospital closes, the doctors will all lose their jobs, and the people will lose access to their health care and have to travel out of the county."

"That is *not* true," said Deb. "Rumors like that are the problem. The doctors think they're going to lose their jobs, so they've turned it into a smear campaign to try to discredit Mr. MacCulloch. And that Baughman woman is the worst of the lot. The things she writes, trying to rile people up. It's shameful."

"I heard a rumor that Nat's taking bribes from some corporation in Pittsburgh slated to build the new place, once the old hospitals close," said Eddie.

Lou turned on him. "That's a damn lie."

"I know, I know!" Eddie said, hands raised defensively. "But that's what they're saying."

"Eddie, that's probably enough," said Bill.

"All I meant is that I heard it—"

"My dad isn't perfect," said Lou, "but making this town better is all he's ever cared about. I sometimes think he cares more about that than he cares about *me*. He isn't taking any bribes, and anybody who says he is will answer to me."

"You're gonna have to be careful this summer, then," said Eddie.

"You think I'm afraid?" demanded Lou.

"Nah, man, that's not it," said Eddie. "I just mean. . . . Well, you're gonna have to fight a lot of people, if that's how you feel about it, and it probably wouldn't help your dad's case anyway. Did he say if he's gonna resign?"

"Resign?" said Lou. "From the Chamber?"

"That's their latest thing," said Bill. "People are calling for him to resign as director."

"Yep," Eddie chimed in. "Because of the scandal."

"Eddie, cool it," said Bill.

"Scandal?" said Lou. "Since when is it a scandal? He's done nothing wrong."

"I don't know," said Eddie. "But a bunch of business owners signed a petition. And the ones that didn't sign, well, people are boycotting their stores now—"

"Eddie, for the last time, would you cram it already?" said Bill.

"What?" Eddie protested. "He didn't know."

"I know," said Bill. "But that's enough, okay?"

Lou hauled back and pitched his empty. It rattled against the fence.

This fricking place, he thought again.

"You know, I was always told to stay away from the MacCullochs," Deb said playfully, breaking the silence.

"Me too," Eddie cut in. "Because of the curse. Because of what happened to old Grant and—"

"Eddie, *seriously*," Bill said.

"What, I can't say *anything*?" said Eddie.

"No, not because of a stupid superstition," said Deb. "I was told to stay away from the MacCulloch family because they were 'bad news.'"

Lou grinned. "Really?"

"Really," said Deb McClintock. "Something about a dispute over a fishing license. But even *my* dad knows that a bad word said against Nat MacCulloch's character is a lie."

Deb was sitting with her shoes together and her elbows in her lap, holding her Budweiser on top of her knees. Lou smiled at her. She smiled back at him.

Chapter Twenty

"OH, SON OF A BITCH," Lou said, plenty loud for it to be heard all the way on the parallel fairway.

He had just watched his ball go slicing through the air, like the off-kilter flight of a cheap boomerang, ending with a resounding *crack* as it struck an unseen tree trunk along the wood-line. Lou stared for a moment, hopeful. But the ball did not bounce out.

"Damn it," he swore again.

He looked across the fairway. The November sky was cloudless, and it was unseasonably warm. So warm that any golf enthusiast with the day off or otherwise had flocked to the nearest course to capitalize on it. And beneath that cloudless sky stood his father, a good deal closer to the green, with an iron propped over his shoulder as he waited for Lou.

Nat MacCulloch was a man of average height. He wore a fedora when he golfed to shield his eyes from the sun, in addition to the shaded horn-rimmed glasses that he always wore—these dark lenses had become quite fashionable. His shoulders had been strong and squared once but now were rounded and a bit slouched. He wore a blue button-up shirt and shorts, and his legs were skinny and pale. His face was cleanly shaven, and his hands were free of callouses. And at his midsection was a belly that one might have easily mistaken for a pillow stuffed under his shirt. It was, in not so many words, the quintessential white-collar body.

He watched Lou for a moment, then slowly shook his head. Lou could practically hear the disapproving sigh from here, which was about as close as his father got to obscenities. In fact, as far as Lou could remember, he had ever heard the man swear in his entire life.

Nat lined up his shot, then took a slow, graceful swing. The path of his ball was like a rainbow. It landed in the center of the green, bounced, and stopped.

Lou grumbled under his breath, slung his bag over his shoulder, and started walking toward the wood-line. He knew he shouldn't have sworn so loudly like that, but it was a bad shot—what was he supposed to do? Be happy about it?

It had been Rose's suggestion that the two MacCulloch men take advantage of the day to share a round of golf. Doubtless, she had intended the outing to be an icebreaker, and to help reduce the stress constantly weighing on Nat as the result of "the hospital situation," which was less a "situation" than it was a snowball that had careened downhill and grown in strength until it destroyed or knocked loose everything it touched. Until the snowball itself was indistinguishable from the avalanche it had caused.

Lou didn't know all the details, but he knew that trouble had been brewing since at least the 1960s. The gist of things was that the two major medical centers in the area, a pair of hospitals in Latonia City and Cornplanter, were both going broke. Some blamed the declining populations in the two cities—a direct result, Nat's father was always quick to point out, of the "devastating loss of industry" across the once highly productive Oil Region. He always, *always* used the word "devastating" when he referred to the "loss of industry."

It wasn't that the wells had gone dry. There was still oil in the ground. The problem was that it was less financially feasible to reach the reserves here than it was to reach them elsewhere. It was a numbers game, pure and simple. It had been cheaper for the locally grown oil giants to move their operations to places where one needn't drill so deep. So, they had left. And the pumping of Pennsylvania crude out of the "Valley that Changed the World" had all but ceased. The once-busy refineries and foundries and factories associated with that industry now sat empty. And the resulting loss of employment had spurred a mass population exodus from little towns like Latonia City. By some estimates, within twenty years, half of all Latonians had left for greener pastures.

There was no enterprise that did not suffer as a result of the drop in population, including the health care industry. It hadn't taken long for the Latonia City Medical Center and the Pennswood Hospital in Cornplanter, each of which had been built to support much larger communities, to feel the impact.

Lou stopped beside the wood-line, dropped a fresh ball at the approximate location where his first one had left the fairway, and pulled out his seven iron. Golf was the only sport Nat had ever shown any interest in, but Lou was of the mind that any sport that could be played by old men was hardly worth playing at all. Or maybe he was just too impatient to care to get any good at it.

He lined up his shot, hauled back, and swung with all his might. He always swung with all his might. How else should a man swing?

The ball did not sail nicely upward the way it was supposed to. Instead, it traveled like a bottle rocket fired horizontally. After about seventy-five yards, it hit the fairway, skipped hard, bounced, and rolled up to sit beside the green. One of his best shots all day.

On the opposite side of the green, Nat sat on a small bench beside a wire wastepaper basket and a ball-washing machine, waiting patiently. Lou slid his club back into his bag and headed toward his ball.

Many potential solutions had been brainstormed in an attempt to solve the Seneca County health care crisis: two large hospitals, both hemorrhaging cash. In the 1970s, a division-of-labor deal had been struck between the two facilities. Instead of a full range of services offered at each hospital, certain services took place exclusively at one of the two. It was a less than ideal solution, but it was what the people got. The Pennswood Hospital in Cornplanter lost its maternity department and cancer center. And Latonia City Medical Center lost, among other things, a dedicated emergency ward.

To many, the loss of the emergency ward had seemed outrageous. But a full impact study had determined that Pennswood Hospital was within sufficient proximity of the main population of Latonia City, meaning that its location was suitable to service both communities. Nevertheless, the whole arrangement didn't sit right with a lot of people, including Nat G. MacCulloch, whose father, Grant, had died in the back of an ambulance. He, perhaps more than anyone, knew the importance of having access to high-quality and prompt medical care.

As the newly appointed Director of the Chamber of Commerce at the time, Nat MacCulloch was a pillar of the community. (Lou thought "pillar of the community" was a stupid term, but there it was.) And it was no surprise when he accepted a chair on a newly formed board whose purpose was to facilitate the collaboration between Latonia City Medical Center and Pennswood Hospital. What *was* a surprise was when Nat and a few of his contemporaries spearheaded an altogether new initiative: a proposal to replace the two outdated hospitals with a new, state-of-the-art facility built in a more central location. This would provide easier, fairer access to health care—not just for residents of Latonia City and Cornplanter, but for some of the smaller surrounding towns throughout the county as well.

And that was where it had all gone wrong.

The new initiative was quickly met with fierce and vocal opposition from a group that was as influential in the community as it was well-funded: the medical professionals who worked at the two hospitals. Keenly aware of the loss of jobs that would follow if such a merger took place—an inevitability in a county where jobs were disappearing for *everybody*, not just health care workers—this group felt threatened, and they started a movement of their own.

The Save Our Hospitals Coalition was an initiative aimed at preserving the old medical centers. At first, they attempted to refute the numbers, claiming that a new medical center would prove more expensive for the county and detrimental to its citizens. But the data did not support their position. So when that didn't work, they targeted the individuals at the heart of the matter, first simply attempting to discredit them, then implying that the persons in question had something to gain personally from the arrangement—that they were lining their own pockets instead of doing what was in the residents' best interests. A daringly ironic premise. And there was perhaps no individual more at the heart of this matter than the Director of the Chamber of Commerce and the chair of the merger committee, Nat MacCulloch, who soon became the object of their ire.

In a way, they could not have picked a more difficult target. Nat was well-liked, and his background was squeaky clean—"Not a drop of alcohol has ever touched these lips," lest we forget. But things got nasty as time wore on, and the opposition found ways to make their claims stick.

As it now stood, it looked like the initiative for the hospital merger and the construction of a new medical facility would indeed pass. But the Save Our Hospitals

Coalition hadn't given up yet. They were still fighting. And they were fighting dirty. Misinformation. Rumors about bribes from big Pittsburgh corporations. Boycotts of area businesses. Harassing phone calls. And words like "scandal" printed in the newspaper by staff writers like Mae Baughman, who discriminating readers might have done well to note was married to one Dr. Baughman of Cornplanter. Things had gotten so bad that the chief of the Latonia City Police Department had urged Nat to stay far away from any more town hall meetings, as authorities had reason to believe that his life might be in danger.

The petition calling for Nat to resign from the Chamber had been news to Lou. He'd wanted to ask him about that today. But so far, it just hadn't seemed like the right time. His father seemed upset with him. He *always* seemed upset with him.

It was like there was a veil between them. Nat had the gift of gab. He was a social butterfly, right at home in the middle of a conversation. But Lou had not inherited that gift. This, in addition to their personal differences, made Lou one of the few people with whom Nat did not easily converse. Lou had always found this idea difficult to accept.

Lou stepped up to his ball and pulled his nine iron from his bag. All the while, Nat watched him from the bench, arms crossed, waiting for his son to catch up with him.

I hate golf, thought Lou, and swung hard.

Chapter Twenty-One

Latonia City, Pennsylvania
December 2019

DESPITE THE STRONG assertion he had made during his argument with his father, Owen MacCulloch did not quit his job. In fact, he continued to work faithfully at the paper for weeks. Weeks that turned into months.

Before he knew it, it was December of 2019, and he had been working at the *Oildom Morning–Herald* for almost five months. He still did not know why the name was hyphenated, and he very much doubted that he ever would. But he had witnessed his daughter taking her wobbly first steps and saying her first words. And he and Kayla had signed the papers to take over Ruth Lee's mortgage, and they had moved out of the little rented house with its neighbors within arm's reach, and into Ruth Lee's country home. And, hoping to smooth over some of the rough patches that had been brought on by his daily six-to-midnight schedule, Owen had bought his wife a puppy. A Welsch Corgi named Bandit. He knew it was shameless, but in marriage, sometimes one had to score points however one could.

It was a Thursday afternoon, and Owen had just woken up to prepare for work. Kayla was still at work, and Ruth Lee was watching Emma while Owen slept. This was their standard daily schedule. But as he emerged from the bedroom that he and Kayla shared at the back of his mother-in-law's house, the place was quiet.

A lot had happened in the past few months. But there was one thing that had not happened. Owen hadn't once spoken with his father. Not a word had been exchanged between them since their argument on the golf course, not even on the day that he and Kayla had moved out of their tiny rented house and into Ruth Lee's place. Owen's mother had come over, bringing a housewarming gift of freshly baked cookies, apologizing and explaining that Owen's father had been "busy" that day. Such a long-lasting fight was unprecedented in the MacCulloch family.

Owen went to the kitchen, poured himself a cup of coffee from Ruth Lee's ancient-looking coffee maker, then went into the dining room to look out the bay window where two cactus plants and a flowering peace plant grew in pots on the sill. There, the reason for the house's silence became clear.

It was a sunny, warmer-than-usual day for early December, and Ruth Lee was taking advantage of it. Emma, as usual, was strapped into the small pink plastic swing in the tree, with her head tilted to the side, asleep. Under the swing, Bandit the Corgi puppy and a mostly-beagle named Wilma lay in the grass. Ruth Lee was on her knees nearby, holding a can of WD-40 in one hand and an old rag in the other, tending to a rusty, child-size bike.

"What is. . . ?" said Owen.

He squinted and realized that Ruth Lee was tending to the same bike that Kayla had discovered on the front porch of the little rented house on 322, months ago, before the move. The one that one of the neighbor kids had left there.

Owen took another sip of coffee, tossed on a light jacket, and stepped outside. Immediately, Ruth Lee looked up. Even in her late seventies, her ears were still good enough to hear a screen door turning on well-greased hinges. Bandit and Wilma were slower on the uptake; Owen had taken a few steps before the dogs rushed over to greet him. He got down on his knees, petting them both, playfully rolling Bandit over and ruffling the fur behind his long, perked-up ears. He still had those sharp puppy teeth, but he never bit hard.

"You get enough sleep?" asked Ruth Lee. The volume of her voice, high-pitched and sweet at most times but capable of sharpness when necessary, indicated that she was not concerned with Emma waking up.

"You bet," said Owen. Still engaged in a one-handed wrestling match with Bandit, he gestured with his coffee cup. "Where did you find that bike?"

"Have you been looking for it?" asked Ruth Lee.

She started to push herself up off the ground and didn't manage it the first time. Owen moved forward to help her, but by the time he got there, she'd done it on her own steam.

"No," answered Owen. "It's not even ours."

She made a face. "Not yours?"

"No," said Owen. "How did it get here?"

"Uh-oh," said Ruth Lee. Then she slapped a hand to her head, blew a raspberry, and erupted in a peal of laughter that excited Bandit enough to make him jump and yip. "Oh my. I've had this in the garage since youns moved in here! It was on your porch when you were moving. I thought it was yours, so I tossed it in the trailer and brought it over here. Put it in the back of the garage and forgot about it!" A flash of something crossed Ruth Lee's face—the look she made when she remembered something that made her shift topics in mid-thought, which she tended to do a lot. "Oh! Did you want me to make you something for dinner since Kayla's working late tonight?"

"She's working late?" said Owen.

"Busy day, apparently. She didn't text you?"

Owen shook his head. It had been several days since he'd received one of the midday texts that Kayla always used to send him during her lunch hour, just to let him know how her day was going. Sometimes it felt like they barely saw each other anymore. And when they did, it was either after a long, hard shift, or as one of them was rushing to prepare for the next one. Weekends were usually spent recovering from the week and arguing over little things.

Kayla's job was stressful and took its toll on her every day. And Owen knew that his schedule at the paper only added to her overall stress. He wanted to fix it. To save her from it. But he didn't know how. The distance between them was growing. He wouldn't have said they were *fighting*, necessarily, but they seemed to be consistently getting the worst of one another.

"I wonder if she's left work yet," said Ruth Lee. "Let's find out." And she pulled the cell phone from her pocket.

Owen resisted the urge to roll his eyes. It had taken Ruth Lee several years to fully embrace the idea of carrying a cell phone, but boy, had she embraced it. Owen thought that the ability to track someone's location using their phone was a bit much. Even a little creepy. But Ruth Lee loved it.

"Nope," said Ruth Lee after a few harder-than-necessary taps on her phone's screen. "Still at work." She pinched her fingers on the screen to zoom in. "And in the North Wing of the facility, looks like."

"Good to know," said Owen.

Ruth Lee put her phone away and slapped the handlebars of the bike, laughing at herself all over again. "Well, guess I'd better take this old thing back over and ask your old neighbors if anybody's been looking for it! I was wondering why you bought Emma a bike in such rough shape, but I thought maybe it was a hand-me-down."

The possibility gave Owen pause.

He looked hard at the bike. Its surfaces were coated in rust, with faded yellow paint on the body. The rubber grips on the handlebars were suffering from dry rot. The spokes were brown with jagged surfaces. And the tires were as flat as tires can be. Leaning forward, he saw that there was a piece of foam between the handlebars. A thin strip of fabric clung to the foam that read, in a flaming, extreme-looking font that was badly faded, *2 Cool 4 Words*. And beneath it, hanging from a dirty old plastic zip-tie, was a keychain that read *Seneca County Fish Hatchery, Kiersburg, PA*.

And just like that, the penny dropped. Suddenly, Owen could see the extreme-looking font not so faded, the tires not so flat. The yellow paint, he realized, only looked yellow because it had been bleached by long days or years beneath the sun; it had been green, once. A bright, electric shade of green. He could feel himself riding— remembered how, when you first started out, the gearless little rig's tires would spin in place and throw up gravel behind you before the treads could find enough purchase to propel you forward. And that zip-tie. He remembered taking it from a tiny storage container of plastic drawers on his father's workbench and using it to attach that keychain he'd gotten as a souvenir from his Cub Scout troop's visit to the Fish Hatchery. Why he had wanted it so prominently displayed, he could only imagine. But he had done it. He had.

"This is my bike," Owen said. Then repeated, "This is *my* bike."

"I won't tell if you won't," said Ruth Lee. "I doubt anybody will come looking for it after all this time. A bit of a lemon anyway, if you ask me."

"No, I mean, it's mine," said Owen. "Jeez, this was my bike when I was a kid."

He stepped forward and touched the dry-rotted rubber of the handlebars. One memory gave way to another. He could see the wrapping paper coming off of it on Christmas morning. It hadn't really been *wrapped*, per se, so much as draped in paper with a bow stuck on top. He couldn't have been older than five or six years old at the time.

The obvious question was how, twenty-some years later, it had found its way onto his back porch. The just-as-obvious answer was that his father or mother had brought it over and left it there. And the fact that not a word had been said about it pointed to his father.

He brought my old bike over, thought Owen, *and left it without saying a word.*

The sheer absurdity of it struck Owen, and he shook his head in frustration. "Ruth Lee," he said. "I do not understand my father."

"I imagine," said Ruth Lee, "that you aren't the first young man to feel that way. But it might help if you spoke with him."

Owen grimaced. Ruth Lee Hart Woodford was not a woman known to pull her punches, and he had walked right into that one.

"How long has it been?" she asked.

"I haven't heard from him in four or five months. He's acting like a child. He didn't even call or text when we moved out of the old house."

"So that means *you* can't call or text?" said Ruth Lee. "Or go over and visit?"

"Well, if he doesn't want me to . . ." Owen began, but he didn't finish.

"He doesn't have the only say in the matter," said Ruth Lee. "You only get one father, and if he was gone tomorrow, it wouldn't be *his* fault you hadn't talked."

Owen said nothing.

"Someone once said," Ruth Lee went on, "that a man ought to forgive his brother seventy times seven times. I imagine the same applies to a father. Your dad lost the right to be a boy—to act like a child, to use your words—the day his father died. So if he's acting like a child now, maybe there's something else going on you don't know about. Maybe, just this once, he needs you to be the man in the relationship for him."

Ruth Lee brushed her hands off on her pants. "Well, I'm heading in to get a drink," she said. "Can I get you anything?"

Owen felt that he could barely speak. "No, thank you," he managed after a few seconds.

His mother-in-law headed toward the screen door. As she pulled it open, she turned toward the dogs. "You coming?" she asked.

Wilma the beagle lumbered after her. Her comma-shaped tail wagged back and forth, slapping hard against the doorframe as she entered the house. But Bandit remained sitting at Owen's feet, looking expectantly up at him. Owen got down on his heels and scratched the top of Bandit's head.

A thought occurred to him, and he rolled up the sleeve of his jacket to look at his left elbow. There was a small semicircle of white in the skin on his funny bone—a scar he'd gotten from riding the bike in front of him too fast down a gravel driveway as a boy. He'd forgotten all about it. But now, he could remember everything, right down to what the weather had been like that day. He remembered how the front tire had twisted between two larger-than-usual chunks of gravel, causing him to pitch forward. How he'd landed and looked down to see a piece of skin missing, which had frightened him more than it had hurt. He remembered the smell of the freshly cut grass. And the shirt his dad had been wearing when he'd come to lift him up and carry him to the house for a Band-Aid and an orange push-pop.

Chapter Twenty-Two

AN HOUR LATER, light snow was falling, and Owen was just stepping out of the front door when he saw Kayla pulling into the driveway. She parked in the driveway and, for a moment, just sat there in the car. He waited. But she didn't get out.

He walked toward the car. When she saw him coming, she opened the door, but even before he said hello, he noticed her body language. Rapid blinking. Clenched jaw. Red nose. She'd been crying.

"Are you okay?" said Owen.

"Fine," Kayla said.

She wore baby blue scrubs, and her long dark hair was done up in a tight bun. She wouldn't look at him but tried to step past him toward the house.

"Kayla," said Owen. "What's wrong?"

"Nothing," she said. "Just a bad day at work."

"Did something happen?" said Owen.

"Nothing, really," Kayla said, glancing at the time on her phone. "Don't you need to get going?"

Owen looked at his phone, too. He did need to get going. When he looked back up, she was biting her lip, clearly trying not to start crying again.

"Kayla," said Owen, touching her on the shoulder. "Are you okay?"

She made an exasperated noise in her throat. "What do you want me to say? Yes?"

Owen felt his forehead pinch as he tried to restrain his annoyance. "I just want to know what's wrong."

"Well, I'd be happy to tell you, but thirty seconds in the driveway isn't going to cut it."

"Fine. Sorry for trying."

If his goal had been to get her attention, that one had done it. *Now* she was looking at him.

"So I'm not trying?" said Kayla. "Just because I don't want to talk when *you're* ready to talk, it means I'm not trying?"

"I didn't realize I needed to make an appointment," said Owen. The annoyance he'd managed to hold back up until now broke through, loud and clear. "Next time, I won't bother."

Kayla stared at him for a moment, then turned away. She rubbed her hands against her shoulders, shivering against the cold. Owen shut his eyes, already regretting his words, and hating himself for not keeping his cool. When Kayla turned back to him, she was wiping away fresh tears.

"I just had a bad day, that's all," she said.

"I'm sorry," Owen said, and he meant it. "I didn't mean to. . . . I'm just sorry, that's all."

"I know," said Kayla.

"We will get through this," said Owen.

She nodded. But not in a way that said she believed him.

"I'm cold," she said, and she started toward the house. "Have a good day at work."

"We will get through this," Owen said again, this time to her back, and thought, *We will, won't we?* Standing alone in the snow, he watched the door of the house swing shut behind her.

Chapter Twenty-Three

WHEN SOMETHING BOTHERED Owen MacCulloch, his response was usually to do everything in his power to avoid thinking about it at all costs. So, as he sat in his red Ford Focus, waiting at the same red light he got stuck at almost every day on his way to work, he was trying not to think about Kayla.

But the more he tried not to think about her, the more he thought about her, and the tears in her eyes, and the way her jaw always clenched when she'd been crying. And the more he thought about all that, the more he hated himself for taking a bad day and making it even worse for her. And the more he worried about their future.

He looked up through the driving snow at the marvelous facade of the Derrick Theatre. At this time of year, it was nearly dark by five o'clock in the evening, and the snow made the visibility far worse. But he had practically memorized the features on the front of that grand old building, given that he had so many chances to stop and look at it every day. And now that it looked like the theater would indeed be torn down this summer, he paid even closer attention.

Owen detested the idea. Demolishing a defunct parking garage was one thing. But this was the Derrick. He hoped someone would at least have the courtesy to chisel off and preserve the carved theatrical masks on the building's heights before they destroyed the place. It would be strange to look up and not see those empty stone eye sockets gazing back down at him—or that lone, gnarled tree that grew inconceivably from the corner of the roof.

When the light turned green, Owen proceeded through town, his wipers swiping slowly at the snow accumulating on the windshield.

As much as he hated the change, it wasn't surprising, given Latonia City's depressed, blighted status. Back in the late 1800s, Pennsylvania crude had been some of the highest-quality oil to be found anywhere on Earth, and nowhere was it more prevalent than it had been here. Hence the region's nickname: the Valley that Changed the World. But the real story was what this had done to the region's people.

In a strange bit of serendipity, drilling rights had made many a lucky landholder into a millionaire, and even after the industry had dried up and left town, trust funds managed at the Latonia National Bank had kept the local economy afloat for a time. But with no fresh influx of commercial enterprise, the city had slid into a decline, and it was still falling.

Davewhite, the ginger-cat-loving photographer at the paper, had turned out to be a man of strong convictions and many, many theories—not all of which would have been wise to share in polite company. And for some reason, he seemed to enjoy sharing them with Owen any chance he got. Davewhite had, on multiple occasions, condemned the "local rich boys" who were "the sons and daughters of farmers lucky enough to have owned oil-soaked ground" and content to "live off their family money and enjoy the ride while it lasted." Owen didn't know about all that. But he couldn't deny that Latonia City seemed cursed to never escape the shadow of its own former glory. And Owen knew a thing or two about curses.

Though the snow slowed him down a bit, he still arrived at the *Oildom News–Herald* with a few minutes to spare before his shift started. Not long enough to dally, but long enough to quickly say hello to Felicia at the front desk as she was packing up to leave, and ask if her kids were excited for Christmas.

"Excited?" was her response. "You have no idea. Just wait until yours is old enough."

Owen smiled at the thought. "Have they been to the mall to see Santa yet?"

"Yes, and now they want to go back a second time," she said as she slipped a hat over her head, careful not to muss her long, silver-purple hair. "I swear, we do all this work, and then we give the guy in red all the credit. I have no idea why we do this to ourselves. By next year, Emma will be old enough that you'll get to join in the fun."

"I can't wait," said Owen, and he meant it.

"Well, good luck tonight," said Felicia. "This place has been nuts today. I still don't get why you came back to work at our rinky-dink newspaper!"

She had meant it to be funny, and normally, Owen would have favored her with a polite, lighthearted response. But today, all he could muster was a sigh and a "Yeah, me neither."

Felicia winced. "That came out wrong. I didn't mean that to be, like, negative or anything."

"It's okay," said Owen.

He hesitated. There was a part of him that did want to explain the decision to her. To tell her about how the demands of his old job, constantly traveling and spending five nights a week in hotel rooms, had nearly destroyed his marriage. How, as much as he'd enjoyed the work, he had left that position to save his relationship with Kayla and spend more time with her. How, as hesitant as he'd been to move back to his hometown, he'd done it to provide Emma with a good place to grow up, and so he could be closer and have a better relationship with his parents.

Those were the reasons why he had come back. But he didn't have the heart to articulate this, considering the irony that he was presently failing on almost all of these fronts.

The conflict must have shown on his face, because Felicia stepped around her desk and placed a hand on his shoulder, rubbing it softly.

"Hang in there," she said.

"I'm trying," Owen said.

As Felicia exited through the front doors, Owen proceeded into the back, where he turned the corner and nearly ran straight into Mae Baughman.

"Sorry," he muttered.

"No, no, my fault," she said sweetly, smiling up at him. "Is Felicia still out there?"

"She was just leaving as I came in."

Mae pursed her lips. "Shoot. I was going to have her fax something."

Owen might have offered to do it for her if it'd been anyone but Mae, a woman who had not so long ago run an article that had incensed him to the point that he'd considered quitting.

"Sorry," he said. "You just missed her." After all, she knew perfectly well how to fax something.

"Oh, well. It can wait until tomorrow," said Mae. "She's a sweet girl, really. It's always nice to see someone like that doing well. Even overlooking her . . . *lifestyle* choices . . . in a town like this, it's not easy to come from a family with a reputation." She paused and looked up at Owen as if realizing she'd just said something rude. She put a hand to her sternum and said, "Oh dear, no offense, of course."

Owen, who had not taken any until now, gave Mae his thinnest smile. "Don't mention it."

"Have a nice *niiight*," she said in a sing-song voice as she brushed past him.

By the time Owen got to his desk, the few extra minutes he'd had going for him were gone, and he was officially late signing in at his work station. He had barely finished hitting the Enter key, confirming his clock-in time, when the door to Dave Albaugh's office opened.

Dave stepped out. As ever, there was a moment when he looked legitimately lost. Then he scanned the room through his wire-framed glasses, spotted Owen, and seemed to be found again.

"Owen," he said. "Come over here a minute." And he stepped back into his office.

Owen gave his clock-in time a second look. Two minutes late. He had never been late before. Not once. But late was late.

One might have expected Dave Albaugh's office to have matched the man—a nucleus of chaos and disorganization threatening to spill out and contaminate everyone and everything around it. Instead, the room was neat and tidy. Owen put it down to the fact that it was almost empty. Dave seemed to keep no mementos. No photos. No extraneous supplies that could have cluttered his desk. In short, his office was clean because there was so little in it to mess it up. It wasn't a bad strategy.

Dave sat at his desk, looking down at his computer screen with that look that anybody over a certain age looks at a computer screen: his eyes squinting suspiciously, his nose pointing slightly up in the air, a look on his face as if he'd just smelled a fart.

Owen knocked on the doorframe.

"Owen," Dave said, looking up. "We were just talking about you—Mae and I, I mean."

"You were?" Owen said, expecting the worst.

"She was telling me," said Dave, "that she thinks you have a tendency to *rewrite* as opposed to edit. And that got me thinking. . . . Mae is talking about retiring soon."

"No kidding," said Owen, making a mental note to celebrate privately later. "Good for her."

"Yeah, well, I don't know what 'soon' means to her. Could be a month, could be a year. But she's been here forever, and if she's thinking about leaving, I've got to be thinking about hiring a replacement. In my head, that meant a replacement for her. But maybe instead of rewriting, you'd like to try your hand at doing the writing yourself."

For a moment, Owen had nothing to say. "Well, that would. . . . I've never really thought about it before."

"Is that something you'd be interested in?"

"I'd be willing to give it a shot."

"As far as I'm concerned, you've proven you know your stuff," said Dave. "I know my plan for a dedicated copy desk didn't work out quite as I'd planned, but you rolled with the punches and were patient about the whole thing." He lowered his voice and leaned forward over his desk. "And, frankly, Mae's not the only staff writer who's getting up there in years. Their time is passing, and I just think we're wasting your talent on ad space and proofreading. . . . Depending on how it goes, I may just move you into writing full-time. The pay's better. It's a salaried position. Plus, the hours are friendlier for a family man. Ten to six instead of six to midnight."

Owen was usually good at hiding his feelings, but this time, he couldn't hold back a smile. A normal schedule.

Time with his family. And what if he started making enough for Kayla to quit her job and find some less stressful work? Something that paid a little less, perhaps, but didn't give her so many bad days or make her cry alone in the car on the way home.

"How do we make this happen?" asked Owen. "What do you need from me?"

"Well, it's not a sure thing just yet," said Dave. "But now that I know you're interested, I'll see what I can do. Until then, do me a favor and keep this between you and me. Deal?"

Owen extended a hand across the desk. "Thank you, Dave," he said. "This means a lot."

Dave grabbed Owen's hand and pumped it, then stood and gave him a friendly slap on the shoulder. "You deserve it. For now, better get to work, Mr. Archaeologist. Got a long night ahead of us."

"Yes, sir," said Owen.

Chapter Twenty-Four

Latonia City, Pennsylvania
July 1939

SCOUTING THE AREA the day before had proven to be a prudent venture, as the sun was down by now, and the alley behind the Derrick Theatre looked a lot different in the dark.

Nat went first, leaving the sidewalk to move quietly into the alleyway. There, he crouched in the shadows at the corner of the building. No sign of anyone guarding the back of the building, no one between him and his destination: a freight entrance at the back of the theater.

HartSounds, in addition to doing the standard business of a music emporium and record shop, also rented out gear—instruments and microphones and such—to some of the music acts that toured the Northeast and the Great Lakes. Over the years, Poppy Hart's brother (Art's uncle) had delivered last-minute items to the Derrick as minor as an emergency set of banjo strings and as substantial as a full drum kit. And on a few of those deliveries, young Art had accompanied him to do a bit of the lifting. That was how he had known about the freight entrance.

"All clear," said Nat, adjusting the weight of the pack slung over his shoulder.

Art left the light of the streetlamp, trying to look casual at first. Then he ducked low and hurried to join Nat in the shadows. Dick came next, looking a bit more conspicuous while hiking up his ill-fitting short pants to hustle over.

"Nobody watching the door!" Dick whispered as he arrived beside them, grinning like Harpo Marx.

Art held a finger to his lips and shot Dick a serious look. "There could be somebody on the inside, though. Cops or security. We should only talk if it's urgent."

Dick nodded to acknowledge the warning, although he apparently found it "urgent" enough to turn to Nat and ask, "You got it, right?"

Nat lowered the pack from his shoulder and opened it. Inside, hidden beneath tomorrow's set of clothes and a *Dick Tracy* comic added for good measure, just in case his mother happened to look inside, was a length of rope arranged in meticulously wrapped coils. He had found it in his father's storage shed. It was quite sturdy and had, more than likely, "walked off the job" at the Germania Oil Well Supply Company by hitching a ride home in Grant MacCulloch's lunchbox. Nat estimated that it would be plenty long enough to get the job done tonight. Tied to the end of the rope was an old cotton flour sack. His mother always kept them for reuse purposes, not just as containers but sometimes to patch clothing.

Nat felt guilty about borrowing the flour sack. More guilty than he suspected his father had *ever* felt about the various items that occasionally found their way home from Germania in his lunch box. He would do his best to give the flour sack back, but he would have to clean and wash it first, because it was currently about half-filled with sand. Sand he had scavenged from the laid-bare shallows of the drought-low Allegheny River across the tracks from his house.

While Art watched the door and Dick kept an eye on the street behind them, Nat uncoiled the rope. One end was loose. The opposite end was tied the best he knew how to the flour sack of sand.

During their pre-heist scouting mission, when it had become clear that getting in through the door of the freight entrance would be impossible, it had been proposed they might somehow climb up to the second or third floor. Ultimately, the boys had decided—Art, in particular, had been the herald of reason in this regard—that scaling a vertical building-side was a feat best left to Dick Tracy and his contemporaries.

And then, Nat had noticed the fire escape.

It was a clever little contraption; most of the fire escapes in town were of the kind that looked like exterior metal walkways with little ladders at the bottom, inaccessible from the street below, able to slide down from above in the event of an emergency. But this one was different. Instead of a ladder, the bottom of this fire escape was like an additional set of steps, held aloft by what appeared to be a counterweight—like a great teeter-totter balanced on a fulcrum in the middle. When someone from above descended, the stairs would extend downward automatically by way of the escapee's body weight. How *much* weight was required to make the rig move, Nat didn't know. And whether or not some sort of lever or safety mechanism had to be engaged from above before the stairs could be lowered, he also did not know. These two variables would ultimately determine whether or not his plan would work.

Nat could feel his heartbeat in his fingertips. He drew a long breath in through his nostrils and tried to ignore how even his insides seemed to be shaking.

This was it. They weren't searching for treasure on the riverbanks anymore.

"All right," he whispered to his coconspirators. "Watch my back and snap your fingers if anybody's coming."

Art and Dick nodded.

Nat approached the back entrance to the Derrick building with his rope-and-sandbag invention in hand. He stood, looking up at the bottom of the fire escape.

Here goes nothing, he thought.

Doing his best impression of the Lone Ranger, he held the loose end of the length of rope in his off-hand and grabbed it near the flour sack with the other, gripping it like a lasso. He had practiced in the backyard a few times, but in the heat of the moment, he was having trouble remembering how he'd done it. He tested the weight, trying to relocate the optimal hand position.

He moved his arm in a loop to swing the flour sack, first back and forth, then in a full circle. He did three full circles, building up momentum with each swing until finally, he heaved with all his might and let the flour sack fly upward. It sailed in an arc toward the fire escape.

But the thing was too heavy, and his throw didn't have enough height. The length of rope unspooled through his loosely gripped hand as the flour sack went up, up, up, fell short of its mark, and came down, down, down. It hit the ground in the alley with a muffled *thump*.

Nat shot Dick a look, thinking about how much noise he'd have just made if they'd gone with *his* first suggestion: a wrench. Easier to throw, maybe, but that wouldn't matter if they alerted the whole block.

He retrieved the flour sack from the ground, undid his knot, and opened up the top of the bag. He tipped it to the side to allow some of the sand to fall out onto the ground. Then he tested the weight of the bag, tied it shut again—

A snap of fingers in the dark.

Nat turned and saw that Art had one hand raised, pointing back toward the street where they'd come from—the direction Dick was supposed to be watching. There, parked alongside the curb, was a police cruiser.

In the light of the streetlamp, the vehicle's weight shifted on its shocks, and a potbellied officer of the law exited the driver's side. The man stepped up onto the sidewalk, took out his flashlight, and started walking toward the darkened alley.

PART FOUR
SOUTH SIDE STRUT

Chapter Twenty-Five

CROUCHED LOW, with his weight balanced on the tiptoes of his one-size-too-small shoes, Nat hurried back to join Dick and Art behind the trash can situated along the side of the alleyway, where he managed to wriggle in between them, his homemade grappling hook in hand. If they'd been much older than they were, and if Art hadn't been so rail-thin, they never would have been able to all fit behind a single trash can. But, as it was, they sat crammed together like kippered herring in a barrel and did their best to stay still. Nat could smell the scent of HartSounds on Art—he didn't know what that odor was, maybe a combination of paper record sleeves and the polish they used on the brass instruments—and could tell that Dick had his last peppermint sweet in his mouth.

The full focus of an electric flashlight's beam landed on the door of the freight entrance, and lingered. Then, like a prison searchlight, it swung across the alley, moving slowly from one exterior building wall toward the other. It was coming straight for the boys' trash can when it suddenly halted and redirected itself, trained on something in the middle of the alley.

In the center of the cop's flashlight beam was the small pile of sand Nat had spilled from his flour sack.

Nat grew lightheaded, like the first time his father had let him share his cup of coffee with him before work. He was smashed arm-to-arm with Dick so tightly that he could feel his friend's pulse pounding through his skin. He heard sharp footsteps getting closer to investigate, and the flashlight's beam changed. It grew no larger but, as its source drew nearer, became more focused on the damning evidence on the ground. Until finally, the toe of a polished black shoe stepped into view just a few feet away from the trash can.

There, the officer stopped.

For several excruciating moments, the officer's shoe did not move, and the flashlight's beam did not deviate from the sand—fine, nutmeg-brown sand that had no business being in an otherwise empty alleyway several blocks from the river.

In the silence, Nat exchanged looks with his accomplices. Art was pale yet stone-faced. Dick, meanwhile, had both hands clamped over his own mouth and his eyes squeezed shut. Which was good, because Nat was certain that if Dick could have seen how close the officer was, he would have ralphed liquefied peppermints all over the bricks.

The beam of the flashlight shifted and came to rest on the freight entrance again. Then it swung back to reexamine the sand. The officer made a thoughtful noise in his throat, stepped back, and walked away. Neither Nat nor Art nor Dick dared move a muscle until what felt like several minutes later, when they finally heard the police cruiser's door shut with a thud and the engine roar to life. Then the brake was disengaged with an audible grind, and the car revved and drove off.

No sooner had the sound of the cruiser faded away down the street than Nat was back out in the center of the alley. As the middle portion of their trio, mashed between a pair of human bookends, he was immediately missed; Dick and Art toppled inward and into each other in a heap. But Nat didn't look back. He returned to his position below the fire escape ladder, resumed his rodeo posture, and swung the flour sack of sand—now half its previous weight—into the air. Behind him, Dick uttered an incoherent syllable, the beginning of a protest. But he seemed to forget what he was going to say when the flour sack sailed over the bottom step of the fire escape stairway, and hung there. Nat felt a grin tug at his cheek.

Slowly, carefully, he began to feed the line out through his hands. The rope slid over the metal step. And like the slow descent of an elevator lift, the flour sack was lowered in a straight line toward the ground. He checked and confirmed that he did, indeed, have enough slack. His estimate had been nearly perfect.

The sack came to rest on the ground directly below the fire escape, and Nat stepped forward and tied the loose end of the rope to it. What he now had was the equivalent of a set of reins. But instead of a bit in a steed's mouth, he'd roped the bottom step of the stairwell.

He looked back at the others, who were still too shocked by what had *almost* just happened to fully comprehend what *had* just happened, what he had accomplished.

"Well?" said Nat. "Get over here!"

The command snapped Dick and Art out of their shared stupor, and they ran to join him.

Together, the three boys grabbed the improvised reins and tested their weight against the rope. Above them, the counterweight of the fire escape responded, and the set of stairs pivoted on its fulcrum, so well-greased that it gave only the tiniest, tinny squeak as the stairs came gently down.

"Jiminy Damn Christmas, it actually worked," said Nat. It was something his dad would have said. And saying it himself made him feel quite grown-up.

When the staircase was low enough, the boys grabbed hold of the bottom and pulled it the rest of the way down. Nat positioned the flour sack between the metal step and the brick surface of the alley. When he stepped up, the sand-filled bag served as a cushion, perhaps preventing a loud clang. He nodded in satisfaction and was about to take a second step up when a hand suddenly grabbed him from behind and held him tightly by the wrist. It was Art who had snared him, preventing him from going any further. He spoke no words, but his face said it all: *Are we really doing this?*

Nat said nothing either. He set his jaw, and he nodded.

Art exhaled, nodded back, and let go of Nat's wrist. And the boys started climbing.

Chapter Twenty-Six

Latonia City, Pennsylvania
November 1982

NAT DIDN'T ASK for Rose to pass the corn. He stood up, an indignant look on his face, and grabbed it off the table for himself. Then he sat back down, spooned a pile onto his plate, and placed the bowl to the side, loudly, without looking at anyone. It took a special sort of person, thought Lou, to be able to sit in a nice warm house, in front of a home-cooked meal, on the night before Thanksgiving—knowing there were people only a few miles away who would have given anything just to have something, *anything* to eat tomorrow—and still manage to be so fricking miserable.

When the phone rang, Nat gave no indication that he had heard it. Just took a bite of his corn and kept looking down at his plate through those shaded horn-rimmed glasses.

Maybe the stress really is getting to him, thought Lou.

By the third ring, it became clear to Lou that his mother, who had *just* sat down after preparing the meal and had barely taken a bite for herself, was the one expected to answer it. She removed her napkin from her lap, but Lou got to his feet before she could put down her fork. "I'll get it, Mom," he said.

Rose nodded gratefully.

The olive-green rotary phone sat on its own dedicated stand in the kitchen, around the corner from the adjoining dining room. Lou stepped in and picked up the handset.

"Hello?"

"Nat MacCulloch," said a voice. A woman's voice. Grating with age and heavy from a lifetime of tobacco smoke. "You will go to hell."

Lou blinked.

"Do you hear me, you son of a bitch?"

Lou's grip on the phone tightened. "Who is this?"

"You *will* go to hell for what you've done, and good riddance. Latonia will be better without you. You'll die, and you'll go to hell, and you'll rot there. And keep your bastard of a son away from my family."

Lou had just managed to pry open his teeth to reply when there was a click from the other end. He was squeezing the handset so hard that it hurt, but he made himself replace it on its mount as gently as possible. When he got angry, he sometimes had to force himself to be gentle. Otherwise, things around him tended to break. He took a moment to compose himself, then returned to the dining room.

"Who was that, Dear?" asked Rose.

"Wrong number," said Lou.

Nat made a noise in his throat. "Another concerned citizen, I take it."

Lou sat down without saying anything.

Nat continued to focus on his food. Those glasses of his were supposed to look stylish, but Lou thought the darkened lenses made the man behind them seem less a part of the world he looked out on. Less human, somehow.

Suddenly, Nat dropped his fork. It hit the china with a *ping*.

"You know," he said, looking up at the ceiling as if musing on a funny anecdote. "Those calls started as legitimate, well-thought-out concerns expressed by reasonable people. There were times when I would take half an hour or forty-five minutes out of my evening, my own personal time, for a conversation with an unsolicited caller. Sometimes, I changed my plans for an entire night just to take a few calls, often from people I didn't even know." He frowned. "I miss the reasonable folks."

Nat threw a glance at Rose. It was the first eye contact he'd made with anyone in several minutes.

"HartSounds is closing," Nat said. "Did you hear that?"

"No," said Rose.

"Oh, yes," said Nat. "That place has been in business since 1912. It never made the Harts much money, but it was their livelihood—in the same spot on Venango Street for *seventy* years. Then Art speaks out in my defense, in support of the hospital deal, and they call for a boycott on his store. They picket outside his door. Nobody wants to be seen going in anymore. Well, they won. Come the first of the year, HartSounds will be gone. Another empty storefront. . . . 'What are you doing at the Chamber to fix our town, Nat?' they all want to know. 'Why aren't you bringing in new business, Nat?' The oil industry's gone, Main Street's going dark, and it's, 'What are you going to do about it, Nat?' What am *I* doing about it? 'What are *you* doing about it,' is what I want to ask them. 'Where's all the money your daddy and granddaddy made off the mineral rights? Where's all the wealth pulled out of the earth from beneath *your* family farm?' I'll tell you where it is. It's gone. 'And did you reinvest it, put it back into our local economy? No, you lived comfortably off the dividends until it ran out. The money didn't dry up like an old well—you bastards pissed it away. And now you drive honest, hard-working people out of business because a few doctors who are scared to lose their jobs told you to.' *That's* what I want to say to them."

It was the first time in Lou's entire life that he could remember hearing his father swear. But even as angry as he was, Nat still did not raise his voice; even his tirades were gentle. All he did was mop his brow with the edge of his cloth napkin and take a deep breath before continuing.

"You give your whole life to this place, and what do they do to you?" he said in a near whisper. "They turn you into the villain. Well, no more. After I resign from the Chamber, they can find themselves a new whipping boy."

"What?" said Lou.

Nat looked up at him. It was as if he had only just remembered that he was not alone in the room. He hesitated, then nodded. "The press release is all written up. It'll go out Friday, day after Thanksgiving. And that'll be the end of it."

Judging by the look on Rose's face, this announcement was news to her, too.

"But then, they win!" said Lou.

Nat shrugged. "Win, lose. Either way, if I stay on, nothing gets done. I've lost track of the number of members the Chamber has lost because of its association with me. It'll be better for the city, better for everyone, if a new director is appointed. Someone who can move the wheels."

There was a moment of silence. Maybe the thing to do was to quietly finish eating. But Lou felt he had to say something.

He looked at his mother. There was no expression on her face, but somehow, it was clear; she could tell Lou was about to say something, and she was silently begging him not to. But Lou didn't listen.

"Dad," he said. "You're better than this place."

Nat looked up at his son through his shaded lenses.

"You're a great man, Dad," said Lou. "A lot of people know that. But this town. . . . It's just *one* little town, you know? There are thousands like it. You're giving your life for it, but what does it give you in return? This place is destroying you. And for what?"

Nat chewed on his tongue. "For *what*, eh?"

Lou hesitated. "I just mean, all this stress you're going through. . . . You're better than all this. It isn't worth it."

"Hmm," said Nat. "I see. Not worth trying to save this dying little town. That what you mean?"

"No—" Lou began, but Nat cut him off.

"Oh, believe me, I've heard *that* one before. 'This crummy little town,' they say. 'This dying city.' May as well give up on her, right? Gather 'round, everybody, it's an open-casket affair! Let's lay the old girl to rest so we can move on and go our separate ways."

"I didn't mean it like that," said Lou.

"Sure you didn't," Nat growled.

"I didn't," said Lou. "All I meant is that these problems seem big when you're up close. But maybe if you got away from this place, you'd see that those problems are pretty small."

Nat's cheek twitched. "Small. Yes, small problems. Of course they are. Why didn't I see it before? Just a hill of beans, really!"

Lou wasn't sure what to say. It wasn't just his father's cynical attitude. He had never seen him so openly combative before. Over the years, no matter what sort of issues Nat had been forced to deal with at work—or what stupid thing Lou had done to get into trouble—Nat always managed to keep his cool when they bumped heads. But now, he wore a sour face as he reached inside his vest, into the inner pocket. And pulled out an envelope.

Lou's spirits sank. Even from the other end of the table, he could see the seal of the University of Pittsburgh, and could see that the envelope had been opened.

He'd done his best, but his postal dragnet had failed.

"It's not just about this *town*, you know," said Nat. "It's about our family."

Slowly, deliberately, Nat removed a letter from the envelope and unfolded it.

"This place, *dying* though some people claim it is, is still where we come from," he said. "Your grandfather took great pride in that. I was ten years old when he passed away. I didn't have the option to leave. I had to stay here and care for my family. And when I finally did have the means to leave, I chose not to because I thought this was the best place to give *my* son a good life. So I stayed. And I worked. And I saved so that my boy could be the first in his family to go to college. Get a four-year business degree and make something of himself."

Nat passed the letter to Rose.

"We owe our son a toast of congratulations, Rose," said Nat. "Our son, the art student."

Rose took the sheet of paper and traced the typing with a red-painted nail. When she was done, she looked up at Lou.

"You changed your major?" she said.

Lou said nothing.

"Honey," she said gently. "That was not the deal, you know that. You *know* that."

The "deal" was that Nat and Rose would pay for Lou's schooling until he got his business degree. He was welcome to pursue other interests on his own time, and his own dime.

"Were you planning on telling us about this?" asked Rose.

Lou looked down at his plate.

"Son," said Nat, "I want you to know that your mother and I would be happy to assist you in whatever ambitions you have—after you get the business degree we talked about. It would be one thing if we'd forced this on you. But we didn't. We had a deal. You agreed to it. Remember?"

"Yes," was all Lou said.

"I am going to try to be reasonable here," said Nat. "But I can't abide outright deceit like this. I just can't. There are going to be consequences for your actions. Understand?"

Lou could feel his hands balling into fists in his lap.

"Louis, are you listening to me?" demanded Nat.

"Yes," said Lou through clenched teeth.

"Watch your tone," said Nat.

Lou's fists were as tight as they would go. He felt his biceps bulging, shaking. His mother's words rang in his ears: *I'm not even asking you to be nice. All I ask is that you don't put your father under any more stress than he already is. Please. His doctor said. . . .*

"Now, I want you to hear this, in plain English, so there's no mistake about it in the future," said Nat. He stabbed his finger against the tabletop in a steady rhythm as he spoke. "I did not work and save my entire life so that my boy could learn to paint. But *far* more important than that, I did not raise my son to be a *liar* who takes advantage of—"

Finally, Lou could take no more. His fists flew out from beneath the table and came down hard on either side of his plate. There was a thump, a crack, and every glass and dish in the room rattled. Nat flinched. Rose jumped.

"You didn't come to any of my games," said Lou.

Nat appeared more surprised than taken aback. Rose, on the other hand, was horrified. But all Lou could see was red.

"I am playing college baseball," said Lou. "I walked on to the team. My *freshman* year. *At Pitt*. Do you know how proud most dads would be of their sons for that?"

Nat looked as if he was going to answer this question, but Lou didn't give him a chance. The ball was rolling, and now, he couldn't stop it.

"Not a single game," said Lou. "Not even when we played at Slippery Rock. What is that, a thirty-minute drive? You can't leave this town behind for a *couple of hours*? Not even to watch your son play ball? Did you know I stole three bases that game? Season batting average of .410—there are people who say I could play in the pros. And I kept my grades up, too, even though I hated my classes. Did I change my major for next semester? Hell yes, I did, because that's what I want to do. And no, I *wasn't* going to tell you because you don't care what I want to do, you only want me to do what *you* want. Get a business degree. Why? So I can move back here and take over right where you left off? Shit, maybe if I'm lucky, everybody will hate me, too."

"Louis!" Rose gasped.

Lou stood from the table so fast his chair fell over behind him. He went to the front door, but he paused with his hand on the knob and looked back toward the dining room table. Rose's hands were shaking. Nat was staring at him, stunned.

"You know," said Lou, "you act like the hospital situation is what caused all these problems. As if everything was fine and this family was perfectly well-thought-of before, but even then, everybody said the MacCullochs were cursed. Because of what happened to Grandpa. And his dad. But I know what the curse really is. It isn't us. It's *this place*. It takes good people, and it catches them in a web, and it sucks the life out of them. Well, I'm breaking that curse. Maybe you want to die here, Dad, but not me. And just because you gave up on your dreams doesn't mean I have to give up on mine."

Lou heard his mother trying to call for him as he opened the front door, threw it shut behind him, and marched out into the night.

Chapter Twenty-Seven

Latonia City, Pennsylvania
December 2019

Despite Owen's best efforts to remain quiet each night when he came home, Wilma the almost-beagle and Bandit the Corgi puppy always heard him coming and were waiting for him at the front door. Fortunately, Wilma never howled, which would have been enough to have woken the neighbors half a mile away. But Bandit had developed a habit of making tiny, sneeze-like woofs anytime he heard a car in the driveway, so Owen always tried to hurry to the door to get him to quiet down before he disturbed Kayla, Emma, and Ruth Lee. Tonight, in his rush, he slipped and nearly fell on the icy stoop, and for some reason felt that the appropriate response was to creatively defame the mother of the front step. It was something his dad would have done, but he tried not to think about that.

It was 1:46 a.m. when he opened the front door to Ruth Lee's house—no, *his* house, he had to keep reminding himself—and found Kayla sitting at the dining room table in a nightshirt.

For a moment, Owen assumed that Emma had woken up. Emma was a good sleeper, in general, but on at least a once-a-week basis, she would wake up in the middle of the night for no particular reason and be wide awake and ready to play.

But Emma was nowhere to be seen. Kayla was alone. She sat, leaned forward, with her arms folded on the tabletop. She smiled flatly at him.

"Good dogs," Owen told Wilma and Bandit, distractedly.

Wilma's comma-shaped tail thudded repeatedly against the doorframe, and Bandit, who had no tail except for a furry nub about the size of a chicken nugget, settled for jumping back and forth enthusiastically as if Owen were a wayward sheep that needed to be directed back to the pen.

Ten years had not been enough to learn everything about the woman in front of Owen. Not nearly. But he knew enough by now to pick up on that sticky, heavy feeling that hung in the air before a TALK.

Owen was not too proud to stall for time. He removed his coat one arm at a time, and it took him several tries to get it on the coat rack just the way he wanted it. He checked his pockets, wondering if he had left his phone or his wallet in the car. No dice. When he could think of nothing else to do and finally crossed the room to the table, he was holding his breath.

"Couldn't sleep?" he asked.

"I miss you," said Kayla.

Owen nodded. "I miss you, too."

The dragging sound of the chair's legs against the floor sounded very loud as he pulled it back from the table and sat down.

"I didn't mean to be a jerk today," he said. "I really did just want to know about your day, but my timing was not great."

"My day sucked," Kayla said. "And I don't really want to talk about it. And I need you to just be okay with that sometimes."

Owen thought for a moment. This was the sort of time when it was wise not to be hasty with one's words. "I can be okay with that," he said. "When you do want to talk about your day, I will listen. Anytime."

Kayla let out a long breath. "It feels like we never *have* any time."

"Then I will make the time," said Owen. "I'll be late to work. Big deal. I'll skip work if I have to. I'll let every article go to press full of typos and inconsistencies and faulty parallelisms, and we'll see how miss-smarty-pants Mae Baughman looks with her dangling modifiers hanging out for God and the whole county to see."

Kayla snorted a laugh. It was like pressure being vented from an overworked system; her face did not seem quite so tight, and her shoulders no longer looked as if she were lugging a heavy suitcase in each hand. "My day wasn't really *that* bad, honestly," she said. "No worse than usual, anyway. Just the same old story. You don't want to hear about it, believe me."

"Your job is really, really hard," said Owen. "Even on a normal day, I don't know how you do it."

"I didn't mean this to be a pity party, you know. I'm not looking for sympathy."

"I know."

For one brief, misguided moment, Owen considered bringing up his potential promotion at the *Herald*. Dave had said the pay was *better*, and terms did not get more relative than that. But it was salaried. And his benefits were already good. Again, he entertained the idea that he might make enough for Kayla to quit her job and find a line of work that was less stressful on her. But something told him that now was not the time to bring it.

A few seconds passed. The only sound was the ticking of a very old clock on Ruth Lee's kitchen wall.

Finally, Owen said, "If there's anything I can do to help—"

"There is not, Owen," Kayla said patiently. "None of this has anything to do with you."

It didn't take a genius to catch the implied unspoken follow-up to that thought: *And don't try to make it about you, either.*

He nodded. "I'm pretty tired. I think I'm going to go to bed."

He was on his way to do just that when the dam burst:

"There's a bad flu making its way through the dementia unit," said Kayla, "so we've had to isolate some of the residents to their rooms, and the nurses all have to wear masks and protective gear. But...." She sighed. "You just can't understand the scope of dementia until you see it for yourself. Everyone thinks it's just your memory that goes, but it's not. It's a steady decay of the mind. The entire mind. A decline back to the brain of a child. And what would a child think—what would Emma think—if suddenly they weren't allowed to leave their room, or go home, or see their families? And on top of it all, everyone around them is suddenly wearing masks. They think they've been kidnapped. They literally think they are prisoners. These people are scared *all day*. Some of them, their bodies are still strong enough that they could overpower a nurse if they really wanted to, but their mental faculties are barely above a one-year-old. Meanwhile, building enrollment is down, so the facility is losing money. And you'd think that would give the staff more time to take care of our patients, but instead, the administrators see it as a way to justify cutting our hours. And because our hours are being cut, there's extra pressure on us not to 'waste' any time, meaning we can't give the residents the attention they need.

"Yesterday, one of my favorite ladies got so agitated and worked up that they wanted to sedate her. And I said, 'I know this woman. She doesn't need *sedated*! All she needs is someone to sit and hold her hand and smile and tell her everything is all right.' My supervisor said, 'Well, we don't have time for that.' So I said, 'I'll make the time, then.' So I skipped lunch, and I sat with her instead. And I held her hand. And I took my mask off because she needed to *see a smile*. Yes, I took off my mask—sue me, why don't you? And after a few minutes, she calmed down and fell asleep. And this morning, I got to work, and guess what? She died last night. Alone in her room, in the dark, with no one there, she died. And you'd think it would make me feel good that I chose to take that time to sit and hold her hand. Nope. I can't even feel happy about that, because her daughter has wanted to do that for the past two weeks. To just sit with her mother and hold her hand and smile at her, but she wasn't allowed to because they had the floor locked down. Part of me wants to tell her that I got to sit with her mom and hold her hand for that short time, but I'm not sure I should because it's so, so unfair that I was allowed to and she was not. I might almost resent that person, if it was me.

"There is not a single resident who hasn't declined *sharply* in isolation. It's only been a couple of weeks, but they're miserable because they can't leave their rooms and can't see their families. The old ladies can't get their hair cut, either, and as unimportant as that sounds, for some of them, that is one of the only things in their lives they can still control. They're depressed, they're losing weight, they're getting sick. And I'm not saying that what the facility is doing is wrong—it has to be done, because the flu could kill a lot of these people. So what else can we do? We *have* to do it this way. But it just . . . just. . . ."

"Sucks," said Owen.

Kayla took a deep breath, then let it out, long and slow. "Yes," she said. "And when you see it every day, it wears you down more and more, little by little. And I'm trying to be strong. But it's so hard. It is so, so hard. And I don't know what to do anymore. I mean, I *know* what to do: Do my job. Take care of these people the best I can and follow the new rules as best I can. I do what I do because I want to help take care of these people. And that includes when it's hard."

The kitchen went silent again, and Owen found himself feeling two things very strongly. The first was an overwhelming surge of love for this woman. And the second was an almost equally overwhelming sense of relief that he had kept his mouth shut about his potential promotion and his idea that she might be able to quit her job.

What did you think was going to happen? he wondered. *That you'd ride in like some knight in shining armor and save her from all her problems?*

Owen had just stood up to leave when Kayla started speaking, and it hadn't occurred to him to do anything but remain standing as the words flowed out of his wife. Now, he sat back down and looked at her, and it was like he was seeing her clearly for the first time in months. No promotion, he suddenly realized, was going to save his wife. Nothing he could do was going to save her. Because she didn't need saving. What she needed was backup. This woman wasn't some damsel in distress. She was his comrade in arms. And maybe it was time he started treating her that way.

"I was worried there was some sort of trouble between us," said Owen. "I thought you were unhappy with me. Or depressed. But you're not. You're stressed. Stressed up to your eyeballs."

Kayla made a noise in the back of her mouth. "Uh, *you think*?"

Owen laughed a little. "Okay. I see that now. And I'm sorry I didn't before. I didn't mean to—"

"Stop, stop, stop." Kayla shook her head. "I haven't exactly made it easy for you to understand that." She reached across the table and grabbed his hand, squeezing it tightly. "Thank you for asking me about my day."

"You're welcome."

"I can see why you might have thought I was depressed," said Kayla. "I've been pretty freaking depressing to be around."

"No!" objected Owen. "I'm the one who's depressing to be around. You and Emma definitely have not gotten the best of me with this crazy schedule. Sometimes I feel like I don't know how to be a husband."

"I didn't marry a *husband*," Kayla said. "I married my best friend." She let go of his hand and punched him in the forearm. "Just be that. You're good at it."

"That I can do," said Owen.

Damsel in distress, he thought. *Yeah, right.*

Who had taught him to see women that way? Society? His upbringing? It didn't matter. Enough was enough.

"Oh, man—I almost forgot!" said Kayla. "Mom told me about the bike! That rusty old thing is actually yours?"

Owen rolled his eyes. "Oh, yeah. That."

"How's it feel to be so old your childhood bike has turned into tetanus on two wheels?"

"Hey! It's not that bad. Fresh coat of paint, a little WD-40, slap some training wheels on there for Emma—"

"Emma is *not* riding that thing. How did it get on our porch anyway?"

"I'm assuming Dad must have brought it over."

"That was . . . nice of him," said Kayla. "He didn't tell you?"

Owen sighed. "Kayla, honest to God, I don't think I will ever understand that man as long as I live. I've tried. All I can do is make sure Emma doesn't end up feeling the same way about her dad."

Kayla thought for a second, then said, "Maybe you should call him."

"You're probably right."

She smiled. "You're tired, aren't you?"

He smiled. "Eh. Not that tired."

Chapter Twenty-Eight

THE NEXT DAY, when Kayla got home from work, Owen made the time. He went into the house with her, they each grabbed a cup of coffee, and he talked with his wife for almost half an hour, just the two of them (plus Bandit and Wilma at their feet). When she asked if he was going to be in trouble for being late, his response was, "Who cares."

He was, admittedly, feeling notably less cavalier by the time he pulled into the parking lot at the *Herald*—twenty-five minutes late for his shift. Felicia was long gone for the day, but he was surprised to encounter Mae Baughman on his way through the front doors. Here, she drew up short and, in a manner so over the top that it would have made the weekend thespians at the community theater blush, took an exaggerated look at her watch.

"We were starting to worry about you," she said.

Owen, who had by now concluded that the only weapon this woman had was the ability to get under his skin, smiled at her. "It happens," was all he said. Then, "Have a nice *niiight*."

And he went inside.

Today, as Owen walked into the offices of the *Herald*, what he noticed was not the walls that needed painted or the old NO SMOKING sign, but the framed photo on the wall above reception. The one with the caption that read, *Oildom Morning–Herald Celebrates 150 Years*, with a staff picture. Owen was in the front row, between Mae and Davewhite. Dave Albaugh was back and to the right of him, with Felicia beside him—who had taken the opportunity to pop a two-fingered pair of bunny ears over Davewhite's baseball cap. Along with the rest of the small staff, they had been photographed standing proudly in the center of the marble floor, with the mosaic keystone prominently displayed. It was so clean you could've eaten off it.

Owen all but snuck to his cubicle. But he hadn't even hit the Enter key to clock in when the door to Dave Albaugh's office swung open. Out stepped Dave. And with him was the same older guy—the octogenarian-looking gentleman with the oversized nose and white hair—whom Owen had witnessed visiting Dave's office several times before. He had since learned that the man was Dave's father and occasionally stopped by the *Herald* to have a late dinner with his son in his office.

Dave turned, scanned the cubicles, and looked straight at Owen. Owen braced himself, preparing to be reprimanded for being late. Instead, Dave raised his hand and smiled, beckoning Owen to come over and join them.

"Me?" said Owen, pointing to himself.

Dave opened his mouth, but it was the older man who answered: "Yes, you! I'd recognize a *MacCulloch* anywhere—just look at that damn hair. Get over here!"

When Owen was close enough, Dave gave a wary look both ways, leaned in, and said in a whisper, "I was just telling Dad about how my young copy editor has been ruffling Mae Baughman's feathers, and he got a big kick out of it."

"Couldn't happen to a nicer lady," the older man said, making zero effort to remain quiet.

Dave smiled as he shushed his father. "When Dad asked who this young copy editor was and I mentioned your name, he just about couldn't believe it." Dave placed one hand on Owen's shoulder and the other hand on his father's shoulder. "Owen MacCulloch, meet Richard Albaugh."

The older gentleman gave a wide smile and held out his hand to Owen. "Call me Dick," he said.

"Nice to meet you, Dick," said Owen, surprised at the iron grip of the old man's hand.

"No doubt about it," Dick said, looking Owen over. "You got your grandfather's looks, you poor thing!"

Owen drew back as if offended, prompting a hearty laugh from Dick.

"I was friends with your grandfather when we were kids," Dick said.

"Small world," said Owen, careful to keep his response intentionally noncommittal. Thanks to the hospital situation back in the 80s, the backlash, and the fallout, almost everybody in this town had a strong opinion about his late grandfather. It was just a matter of whether they leaned to one side or the other. There were people who thought rather highly of him. And then there were people like Mae Baughman, who still, thirty-some years later, thought it prudent to take the long-dead native son down a peg any chance they got.

"Yeah, old Nat!" Dick chuckled. "We did a lot of running around town back then. Playing in the river. Getting into a little trouble here and there. Never too much, though." He leveled a thick finger at Owen and added seriously, "He was a good man, and don't let anybody in this town ever tell you otherwise. That new hospital is the only thing anyone remembers about old Nat, but he did more for this town than that. More than anyone could have asked of one man. Devoted his life to this place. And, besides the point, that hospital has been a godsend to this region. I don't think there is *anywhere* in this country where you would find such a large, state-of-the-art medical facility in a mostly rural area like this. And it's all thanks to your grandfather. He is *the one* who made that deal happen. I hope you know that."

"Honestly," said Owen, "my family's never talked about it very much."

And that was true. The "hospital situation" was a topic that Lou MacCulloch didn't like to discuss. The whole thing had a skeleton-in-the-family-closet sort of vibe. It had never occurred to him that it could be a matter of pride. Owen had always gotten the impression that Lou believed all that work and devotion had done nothing but drive Nathaniel MacCulloch to an early grave. And there was a feeling of bitter contempt for the people who had demonized him.

"I wish Nat was around *now* to see how it's impacted our two communities," continued Dick. "Those old hospitals were outdated, falling apart, and so damn broke they couldn't even make payroll toward the end. As far as I'm concerned, it ought to be Nat MacCulloch's name on that new hospital. You and your whole family should be proud."

"I appreciate you saying that," said Owen. "I'll. . . . I'll have to tell my dad you said so."

"That's right—your dad! He was the ball player in the family!" said Dick. "I used to watch him play at the high school. And I hear Art Hart's kid sister is your mother-in-law? How's she doing?"

Owen actually laughed out loud at the thought of Ruth Lee being anybody's kid sister. "Oh, Ruth Lee is doing great," he said. "No sign of slowing down. Ever."

"Ha-*ha*! Good," said Dick. "That reminds me: Anybody ever tell you about the time me, Art, and your grandfather snuck into the Derrick?"

"Actually," said Owen, "the first I ever heard of it was when Dave brought it up on the day I interviewed for this job. I thought he was pulling my leg."

"No, no—it happened!" said Dick. "Swear to God. Snuck in to see ol' Gid the Great."

Owen cocked an eyebrow. "Gid the Great? As in Gideon Rust? The trumpet player?"

"Gid Rust himself. The one and only."

"Hold on," said Owen. "You're telling me that *Gideon Rust—the* Gideon Rust—played at the Derrick Theatre? Here? In Latonia City, Pennsylvania?"

"Sure did!" said Dick. "Hell, back in the 20s and 30s, Latonia and Kiersburg were on the circuit for all the old traveling vaudeville shows. Houdini came through here, my dad saw Charlie Chaplin. And Old Gid Rust played a show at the Derrick in, let's see, guess it must've been round-about '39 or '40. Your grandpa and I...." Dick caught himself, seemed to remember where he was, and shook his head. "Oh, I'm rambling on. Next time I'm here, I'll have to tell you the whole story. But your grandfather, he was a good man, I mean it. A *good* man. He'd just love the idea of his grandson replacing that Baughman woman.... And your grandmother—what a peach she was."

"Well, thank you," said Owen, banking on the assumption that to be a peach was a good thing. "It was nice to meet you, Dick."

"Good to meet you too, young man," said Dick, pumping Owen's hand hard a few times and giving him a wink. Then he said goodbye to Dave and headed toward the exit of the *Herald*, wobbling a bit to carry his size.

"So, what do you think?" Dave asked after Dick was gone.

Owen, whose thoughts had moved on to the world-famous trumpet player and singer Gid Rust, and was currently wondering if the city library might have kept any records of the musicians who had performed at the Derrick Theatre, had no idea what Dave was referring to.

"About doing a bit of writing for the paper," said Dave. "Still interested?"

"I am," said Owen.

"Good," said Dave. "Mae turned in her official notice tonight. Two weeks can't go by fast enough, far as I'm concerned."

Funny how time could play tricks on you. Because that night, Owen's work shift seemed to positively race by. And even though he had to stay late (again), and by the end of the night, his neck and back hurt in all the usual places (again), he somehow didn't feel quite so weary— nor quite so relieved when it was finally time to make the walk back through the cubicles toward the lobby. In fact, he took his time tonight, pausing to note some of the decorations in the other work stations. There were pictures of his coworkers' children or nieces and nephews. Like him, many of them had cut-outs from the *Herald* pinned on their corkboards, some because they were interested in the subject matter and others because they'd had a hand in creating them and were, presumably, quite proud of that.

Owen said his goodbyes to the employees who ran the printers, then headed out for the night. But not before pausing to take a look at the peeling paint on the wall in the back corner of the lobby. And instead of thinking, *Somebody should do something about that*, what he thought was, *I should do something about that.*

Chapter Twenty-Nine

Latonia City, Pennsylvania
July 1939

ON THAT SWELTERING summer night, every window of the Derrick Theatre was wide open. And with the fire escape leading to several windows, getting in was just a matter of choosing the right one.

As the fire escape stairs swung quietly upward into their prone position behind the three intruders, Nat cautiously raised his head to peek into the first window he came to. The second-floor room inside was dark but for a sliver of light at the bottom of a single closed door.

Nat had only been inside the Derrick a couple of times. The theater showed films as well as live shows, and he'd seen a few war pictures here with money earned from metal and rubber drives. He called upon his mental map of the building's interior, trying to visualize the entryway and its location relative to his current whereabouts. He remembered that there was a half-spiral staircase in the lobby with a wrought-iron railing. It extended upward to a balcony that looked down from a second floor. There were large double doors on the ground level of the lobby leading to floor seats; an identical set of doors on the second level led to balcony seating.

So where was he now, relative to the lobby and the entrance to the theater proper? Which direction would he have to go, once inside? The fact that he had less than a single clue forced him to reconcile the fact that *this* was precisely as far as his plan had extended. From here on out, they were winging it.

He hesitated long enough that one of Dick Albaugh's pudgy fingers began tapping him furiously on the shoulder from behind.

"We're not really doing this, are we?" Dick whispered. "I mean, not *really*?"

"Nat," said Art Hart's voice from behind him. "I'm game if you are."

Nat took a deep breath. Not since his moment of indecision back at the railroad bridge had he been so close to turning back. His hands were on the window frame— what was he doing? This was illegal. This was breaking and entering. This was insane. . . !

And then, a gentle vibration. A sort of pulsing sensation, reverberating from the window frame, trembling up from the painted wood, through Nat's fingers, all the way up his arms, in a rhythm that he thought he nearly recognized.

And then, from somewhere inside the building, a distant squeal of notes. A trumpet playing a series of high C's.

No one could hit notes like that. Not all in a row, not so quickly. No one but the Rust Man. No one but Gid the

Great. And Nat was hearing him play. Not on a record, not from a radio receiver. He, Nat MacCulloch, was hearing *him* play.

Live and in person, just like the playbill said.

Nat barely remembered climbing in, but his feet had only just hit the floor when an even more frantic series of pudgy-fingered taps jabbed his shoulder. He turned to find Dick, wide-eyed, pointing back down toward the street. A police cruiser was parked beneath the light of the streetlamp again. Was it the same cop coming back to check the alley again? Or a different one? It didn't matter. They couldn't go back down now. So Nat grabbed Dick by the arm and pulled him into the room, and Art vaulted in behind them.

"The rope!" Dick whispered in the dark. "He's gonna see it!"

Nat chewed on the inside of his cheek. The rope and the flour sack were still hanging from the bottom rung of the fire escape. It would have been smart to haul it up behind them, but none of them had thought of that.

"Listen," said Nat.

When Nat said nothing else, Dick demanded, "What?!"

"Shh!" said Nat. "*Listen. . . .*"

The three boys went silent. There was only the sound of their breathing and the sounds of the band somewhere down in the theater.

Art broke out in a smile. There was a distant look in his eye as he recognized the tune. "Golden aces!" Art said. "It's 'Limehouse Blues'!"

"We're gonna get caught, do you understand that?" demanded Dick.

"That's him playing," said Art. "We're hearing Gid Rust right now!"

"And we're gonna see him, too," said Nat. "Come on."

He crossed the room, which appeared to be a small office of sorts, and paused at the door. There was no keyhole and not enough of a gap under it to get a look at what lay beyond. For all Nat knew, someone was standing right on the other side.

Where there's a will, there's always a way, echoed the words of Grant MacCulloch in Nat's head.

Nat opened the door.

The hallway on the other side was abandoned but smelled of expensive cigars. Electric bulbs burned in copper wall fixtures. The walls were papered not in the green and gold color palette of the building's exterior but with a blood-red and cream paisley pattern. The floor was thickly carpeted in long, bushy gray fibers that looked like grass, and Nat found himself wondering what it would feel like between his toes.

Despite its fine decor and well-lit interior, the hallway did not appear to be a heavily trafficked area of the building. There were a few doors similar to the one Nat had just emerged from, and that was all. The music was louder here. It sounded like it was coming from the left, so that was the direction Nat started walking—after making a mental note of which door he'd come from.

With Dick and Art close behind, Nat passed beneath a series of portraits on the wall. They were presumably figures of some importance, but he neither looked at the paintings nor cared who it was they honored. He stopped at the first door he came to and reached for the knob, then thought he heard voices coming from the other side and changed his mind. He looked back at Art and Dick. Art wore a serious expression flavored with a devilish little grin, while Dick looked as if a stiff breeze would have knocked him flat. Nat gestured with his chin, indicating that they should keep moving, and they continued down the hallway.

Finally, they reached a door with a squat pane of beveled glass set in its upper half. The room beyond appeared to be dark. Painted on the glass, in silver, were the letters PROJ.

"Limehouse Blues" had come to an end, and Nat could hear the audience applauding as he pushed the door open and stepped into the Derrick Theatre's projector room.

Chapter Thirty

Pittsburgh, Pennsylvania
November 1982

"WOO-WOO! WOO-WOO!"

If any police had been sitting along the side of I-79 that night, Lou MacCulloch would have gone straight to jail—do not pass GO, do not collect two hundred dollars. But life was not fair. And young men often did not get what they deserved, lucky for them.

His plan had been to party that night. The only thing that had changed was where he was doing the partying.

The combination of the dried blood on Angie Schultze's head, his conversation with his friends about the hospital, his father's bitter complaints over dinner, and his own outburst had left a sour taste in his mouth for everything to do with his hometown. He'd sucked down two beers in the Blazer before he'd even left the Latonia City limits. It was the night before Thanksgiving, and he had no intention of going back. An hour and a half later, he found a party in the city, and a half-hour after that, the room was a blur.

He was in the bathroom with a bottle of beer in his hand. Then he wasn't.

Then he was talking to somebody in a kitchen.

Somebody put a shot glass in his hand. Whatever was in it, he downed it without tasting it.

His head swam. His stomach was a ball of fire.

And overtop of it all, the music kept playing. A rock song with a repetitive chorus that had the whole party chanting along.

"Woo-woo!" they all called out. *"Woo-woo!"*

Some good Samaritan put a fresh beer in Lou's hand. He punched the top of the can with the key to his Blazer. "He didn't come to a single game," he was telling someone as he punched a second hole in the side of the can. "Business degree. What a joke."

He lifted the can high and drained it from the bottom. Most of the beer went down his throat. The rest spilled down his chest.

"Woo-woo!" chanted the whole party. *"Woo-woo!"*

A moment of clarity: *I'm not even asking you to be nice. All I ask is that you don't put your father under any more stress than he already is. Please. His doctor said. . . .*

The party faded to black for a few minutes, and Lou regained focus when a fist hit him in the mouth. It sobered him up long enough to realize that he was in a fight for some reason.

"Woo-woo!" he said, and he swung his fist.

There was an impact. The guy on the other end went down. Someone patted Lou on the back, called him Balboa, and handed him a cigarette.

Fade to black again.

This time, when things came back into focus, he was looking up at a ceiling. A ceiling that would not stop spinning. All was dark. And quiet.

Lou rolled over and touched a wall. He was tangled in thin sheets, lying in a bed. Not a bed that he was familiar with. His mouth ached from a split lip.

Nat MacCulloch, you will go to hell, rang an old lady's voice in his head.

Don't believe everything you hear about my dad, he heard himself telling Angie Schultze. *He's a good guy. Really.*

Now, Deb McClintock's voice: *I was told to stay away from the MacCulloch family because they were bad news.*

You'll die, and you'll go to hell, and you'll rot there, snarled the old lady. *And keep your bastard of a son away from my family.*

"Not a single game," Lou mumbled into the darkness, unsure if there was anyone there to hear him. He rolled over. "Woo-woo."

Fade to black.

Chapter Thirty-One

Latonia City, Pennsylvania
December 2019

OWEN'S GREETING AT his parents' home was a reminder that when fathers and sons fight, it's the mothers who suffer.

The door opened to the generation home on Silvern Row in Latonia City—the house Owen's grandfather had grown up in, fixed up and remodeled, and left to his son. Deb MacCulloch, who had hardly seen her son for the totality of the disagreement between Owen and Lou, stepped out of the house, threw her arms around his shoulders, and squeezed him hard.

"Oh, I have missed you, kiddo," she said into his ear.

"Me too, Mom," said Owen.

"Please tell me you have come to see your dad," she said.

"Yeah," said Owen. "I have."

Deb finally released the hug but kept a grip on his shoulders. "Good. He's out golfing again."

Owen made a face. "It's like 35 degrees."

"Yes, but it's sunny, which is good enough for your father. The course isn't technically open, but the owners let him walk on when he wants to because he always slips a twenty under the clubhouse door. I'm glad to see you making the effort to reach out. He needs it."

He needs it? thought Owen.

Owen gestured toward the big white van parked in the driveway. "Who's here?"

"Oh, those are the contractors fixing the water damage in the basement," said Deb. She sighed. "I finally convinced your dad that he ought to call in some experts to get it taken care of. And good thing, too. It was worse than we thought." She pulled her cell phone from her pocket. "If you wait a minute, I can check your dad's location to see if he'll be done golfing soon. . . ."

"Oh, Mom, not you too," said Owen. "Don't you think that's creepy?"

"Oh, I like it," said Deb. "Easy to tell if he's sneaking around on me."

Owen shook his head. Sometimes he couldn't believe these were the same people who had told him he "didn't *need*" a cell phone the first time he'd asked for one in high school. "But what if the car breaks down or something, and I don't have a phone?" he had asked, to which his mother had replied, "Then you do what people have always done: You flag someone down and hitch a ride." This same woman was presently zooming in on a digital map in her hand to pinpoint her husband's location—not just the golf course where he was playing, but the exact hole he was on.

"Looks like he's on the 6th green right now."

Owen made a face, wondering if Kayla ever tracked him.

"I've been worried about you," said Deb as she put her phone away. "Ruth Lee told me. . . . Well, she sent me a message and said that you and Kayla were having some troubles staying connected with your schedules."

"Wow," said Owen. "No secrets when Ruth Lee is involved, are there?"

"Not really," said Deb.

"We're figuring it out," said Owen. Normally, he would have left it at that. But, to his surprise, he said, "I want to take care of Kayla. And Emma. And I want to do what I'm supposed to do, but sometimes, it feels like nothing I do is right. Or enough. Or at the right time."

There was a long silence, during which Owen stared at the ground and could feel his mother watching him.

"Louis Owen MacCulloch," she said.

The stern, clear enunciation of his full name—his given name, not the name everyone called him by—had its intended effect. Owen looked up, giving his mother his full attention. She was smiling. But her eyes were intense.

"What you need to do," said Deb, "is not think so much."

Owen squinted. "Huh?"

"Those girls don't need anything," said Deb, "except you, just as the man you are. But for them to get it, you have to give it."

"Hey, Mrs. MacCulloch!" a voice called from inside the house.

A young man wearing a mask, the kind used to block particulates, emerged from the house carrying a small object in his hand.

"We was replacing the problem area of the wall," said the contractor in a thick western Pennsylvania accent, "and when we pulled out that busted brick in the middle of the crack—you know, the one with the *X* painted on it—we found something inside."

"Inside the brick?" said Deb.

"Yeah," said the contractor, and he held it up.

It was a brown glass bottle. On the side were the words *Pepsi-Cola*.

The contractor gave the bottle a shake. "Pretty sure there's something inside. Figured the homeowner oughta do the honors."

Deb accepted the bottle. She gave it a look, but instead of opening it, she handed it to Owen.

"Me?" said Owen.

"You're the archaeologist," she said.

Owen shrugged and took a look. The mouth of the bottle appeared to have been plugged up with something. Plaster, maybe. So he pulled out the Focus keys and dug through the obstruction. Proper archaeological technique this was not, but oh well.

He broke through the plaster easily and emptied the pieces into his hand. Then he shook the bottle upside down until a rolled-up sheet of paper fell out. He did his best to open the paper carefully, but it still cracked along the edges as it uncurled, emitting little puffs of dust. When the sheet was fully unrolled, Owen held an antique theater playbill, featuring a black-and-white printed image of a man's face. Anyone with a passing knowledge of twentieth-century music or popular culture would have recognized the face of vocalist and trumpet player Gideon Rust. Beneath the picture, the printed text read:

GIDEON RUST — IN PERSON
THE GREAT TRUMPETER AND HIS WORLD-
FAMOUS JAZZ BAND
ONE NIGHT ONLY AT THE LUXURIOUS
DERRICK THEATRE
LATONIA CITY, PENNSYLVANIA
SATURDAY, JULY 23, 1939

But it was what had been written at the bottom of the playbill that had Owen's full attention. In pencil, in the large-looping, careful cursive of a young writer, were the words:

Nat was here, on the day Gideon Rust came to play at the Derrick.
Nat is going to sneak into the Derrick Theatre to see him tonight.
Nat will someday play trumpet with Rust and will be the most famous trumpet player in the world.
—Nat MacCulloch, July 23, 1939

Chapter Thirty-Two

Latonia City, Pennsylvania
July 1939

NOT FOR THE FIRST time since this escapade had begun, Nat neither knew nor cared if Dick or Art were following behind him. He practically floated into the projector room, thunderstruck by the volume of the crowd in the theater auditorium somewhere below. What had before been no louder than a distant murmur now sounded like it was right in the room with them. Because, in a way, it was.

The projector room was jam-packed with stacked film reels and tools and objects of which Nat had no knowledge. The far side of the room ended in what appeared to be a small set of stairs that extended upward high enough that it almost would have reached the next story of the building. There sat a great big movie projector looking like a cannon pointed out through an open square cut into the far wall.

Only now did Nat hazard a glance back. Dick and Art wore dazed, disbelieving smiles—almost certainly mirror images of the expression currently painted on his face. Art closed the door quietly behind them, and together, they climbed the stairs to the smaller upper portion of the room, with its cut-out square section in the wall. There was enough clearance between the wall and the projector's cannon-like snout that all three of them were able to stick their heads up at once to peer out.

Stretched out before and below them was the theater's massive interior hall. On the ceiling high above was an oddly shaped light fixture that Nat had remembered being fascinated by during his few visits to this place. Rather than the sort of elegant chandeliers he saw in book illustrations and associated with great wealth, this fixture was like an upside-down crystal pyramid with modern-looking, clean geometric lines. The same drama faces that lived outside on the heights of the Derrick building— masks depicting comedy and tragedy—were present as golden effigies hanging above the stage. On either side of the stage, massive, heavy-looking curtains hung suspended by elegant, tasseled gold ropes as thick as tree branches. It was Latonia City's own little slice of bohemia, and not a seat was empty.

The audience was still applauding far below—and *not* so far below, as well. The upper rows of seating, Nat was slightly alarmed to see, were startlingly close. Were one of the boys to have whispered "who was the first vice president," one of the nearby theatergoers could have answered "John Adams" as quick as you like. And if any one of said theatergoers had happened to turn and look their way for whatever reason, the young intruders would have been spotted. But why would anyone look away from what was happening down there?

There were six of them on stage, as Nat knew there always were. The Black woman at the baby grand piano wore a black dress, while the men were all dressed in all-white suits with black ties. A round-waisted, light-skinned Black man stood supporting an upright bass. Behind him, an Italian-looking guy with a pencil-thin mustache sat at a five-piece drum kit. There was a freckle-faced almost certainly Irish fellow on clarinet, a Black man with pomaded hair on trombone, and a bald-headed, reed-thin Black man with a small guitar.

And, standing at the center of them all, was a dark-skinned Black man, overweight but not fat, tall but not towering. His hair was thin, but he was not entirely bald. He held a trumpet in one hand and a white handkerchief in the other. His name was Gideon Rust.

As the applause rolled on for a moment longer, Gid looked out at the seats with a layer of sweat shining on his face. He raised his handkerchief toward the crowd and fluttered it back and forth as if waving a white flag in surrender, then laughed and beamed at them. By all appearances, he was having the most fun of anyone in the room.

When Gid finally convinced the audience to cease their applause, Gid's Hot Six began to play. The pianist's hands began to move, and her feet bounced up and down the pedals. Then the trombone, the bass, and the guitar came in together, followed closely by the drum kit and the clarinet. Even before Rust had played a single note, Nat recognized the tune from the hundred or more times he had sampled it in the listening booth up at Pastel's. The rest of the crowd picked up on the melody at the same time he did, and a cheer went up. Onstage, Gid laughed at the reaction and favored the room with a smile, then wiped his upper lip with the handkerchief and raised his trumpet to play.

He started with a run of notes, clear and piercing and crisp as an October apple. He played the melody for a bar. Then he lowered his instrument, wiped at his upper lip again, stepped up to the microphone, and sang in that booming, raspy, inimitable voice:

"Now when the saints—!"

"When the saints!" the rest of his band called out.

"Go marching in—"

"Go marchin' in!"

"Now when the saints go marching in—"

"Go marchin' in!"

"Oh, yes, I want to be in that number. . . . Yeah, when the saints go marching in."

"Marchin' in!"

By now, the audience was clapping along with the snare-hits, and Nat was certain that he could not possibly be where he was at this moment, seeing what he was seeing, hearing what he was hearing.

After another time through the verse, Gid stepped back from the can to allow the clarinet to take a solo. By the time the next verse came in, the audience had joined in the call-and-response.

"Now, when that band—" sang Rust.

"When the band!" the audience shouted.

"They begin to play—"

"Begin to play!"

"Now when that band, begins to play-yay-*yaaay*—"

"Begins to play!"

"Oh, how I want to be in that number . . . when that band—" Here, the whole band cut out as Gid snapped, "Ba-deep-a-dip-a-ree *zop*. Did, zizz-un-*razz*!"

The band came back in all at once, louder than ever, with growling encouragements from Gid, barely able to be heard over the commotion: "Come on now, cats, get that band a playin'—I believe this Derrick's struck oil!"

Gid the Great raised his horn to his lips again, and what followed was a run of notes that defied everything Nat had, up until that point, understood to be possible from a small brass horn. In the next minute, he counted twenty high-C's in a row.

It was beautiful. He was beautiful. And everything—everything was beautiful.

And it would remain so until three songs later, when Nat, Dick, and Art were spotted.

Chapter Thirty-Three

IN THE FIFTEEN minutes or so after "When the Saints Go Marching In" ended—during which Gid and his Hot Six played swinging, lightning-fast renditions of the songs that had been spinning on record players across Latonia City all week—what struck Nat most about this larger-than-life figure was that his music was only part of the show. The man was an all-around entertainer. Teasing the crowd. Goofing around with the other musicians. One moment playing into expectations by staying almost mathematically true to the melody of a well-known tune. The next moment defying every presupposition and stomping his foot against the stage like a madman as he launched into a blistering, rising-and-falling, avant-garde solo.

At times, he would stand with his fingertips poised over the trumpet valves, looking out at the crowd as if to say, "Should I do it?" and prompting shouts and hoots of encouragement. When the other members of the Hot Six soloed, Gid danced and clapped, sometimes pulling astounded faces as if he couldn't believe what he was hearing, and at one point chasing the clarinetist in a circle while he was trying to solo, as if demanding that he stop showing him up.

But when *he* soloed, there was no playing around about it. His spine went straight as a board, and he seemed to grow several inches taller than his normal height. His shoulders shifted back and went rigid and square, and everything in him seemed to freeze in place except his flying fingers and the rapidly inflating and deflating air sacs that seemed to extend from his cheeks all the way down to the collar of his shirt.

Nat, Dick, and Art didn't dare make a sound, so close were they to the spectators in the upper rows. In fact, none of them had uttered a single word since entering the projectionist's room and had only been snapped from their spellbound reverie between songs long enough to exchange silent, disbelieving looks with one another.

Presently, the audience applauded the conclusion of "Beale Street Blues," and Gid laughed wildly at himself and at them. Then he stepped up to the microphone, and the crowd quieted.

"Now, this next number is one of the good-old good ones," he said in his gravelly, New Orleans accented voice. "It's one of my favorite tunes. And tonight, we're really gonna swing it. I bet you all've heard this one before, but you've sure *never* heard it like you're going to hear it tonight."

As he spoke, he removed his suit jacket, revealing a shirt soaked in sweat from his collar to his beltline.

"This is one hot summer evening, folks, and it's about to get a whole lot hotter in this joint, because we're taking a trip south to Carolina. It's 'Dinah.' 'Dinah!' I like it! Let's swing, cats, swing. *Look out there*!"

It was during the resulting round of applause raised in approval of Gid's song choice—while Gid was in the process of sending his suit jacket spinning through the air toward the back of the stage—that the yellow beam of an electric flashlight from the theater floor below fell full upon the faces of the three boys in the projectionist's room.

"Hey, you!" called a voice.

"Up there!" said someone else.

All those heads that had gone so long without turning toward the boys now all turned at once to look straight at them.

"Busted!" hissed Art.

"Hit the bricks!" said Nat.

"We're dead!" yelled Dick.

Gid and the Hot Six paid no mind.

As the three boys abandoned their illicit balcony seating, the drummer slammed the snare to start a quick-stepping, eight-to-the-bar beat. The rest of the band came in like a rocket, launching into the fastest-moving rendition of "Dinah" that Nat had ever heard.

The piano pounded. The clarinet bawled. The trumpet soared. And the boys bolted.

Gone was the caution which Nat, Dick, and Art had previously observed. Nat took a running leap for the door. Dick, in a less successful imitation of this move, collided with a pile of film reels that toppled with a series of cymbal-like crashes.

Nat was first to the door. He threw it open and took off down the hall. At the far end, two young men in red vests and matching trousers were engaged in a frantic conversation. But at Nat's sudden appearance, their bodies tensed like a couple of cats catching sight of a rabbit.

"There!" one of them said.

"Hurry up, Dick!" Nat heard Art yelling from behind.

In the wake of Art's desperate appeal came a second round of crashes from the projection room, followed by Art and Dick tumbling out of the door just as Gid's voice called out over the mic:

"*Oooooh*, Dinah! Anyone *finer*—in the state of Caro-*lina*! If there is and you know her, show her to me!"

It was a race for the exit—the second door on the right, Nat reminded himself—between the three boys and the two young men in vests. And Nat was faster. He flung the door open, waited long enough for Dick and Art to pass through, and then jumped into the room just before his pursuers were within arm's reach of the knob. He threw the deadbolt with not a snare-beat to spare.

The knob giggled back and forth, and the door jumped on its hinges.

"Open up in there!" a voice demanded.

Nat, laughing wildly, replied, "Dinah! Got them Dixie eyes blazing! How I love to sit and gaze in—to the eyes of Dinah Lee!"

"Come on, come on, let's *go*!" Art shouted, already at the top of the fire escape.

"My shoe! Lost my mother-loving shoe!" Dick protested, hopping toward the window.

Nat, meanwhile, had broken into full scat. "Oh baby, every night, why do I, shake with fright—oh, cause my Dinah might change her mind—baba-did-um-zid-um-vee—*ooooo*-eee!"

With Art's help, Dick made it out the window and tumbled ass-over-teacups onto the fire escape on the other side.

"Doo-doo-waa, wander to China, babe!" Nat sang as he practically leaped out of the window. "I would hop an ocean liner, babe—doo-dee-zee, doo-dum-zaa! *Yes*, yes!"

The police cruiser that had been parked in the light of the streetlamp was no longer there, and the alleyway below was empty. But Nat's rope-and-flour-sack grappling hook was also gone—a dead giveaway that someone had indeed discovered their instruments of intrusion. Throwing all caution to the wind, Nat grabbed the railings of the fire escape and threw his full weight forward in a jump to the far end of the suspended stair. The stairway pivoted and dropped like an elevator with a cut cord, and the three boys screamed as they rode it all the way down.

No sooner had the bottom step bounced against the bricks with a teeth-jarring *clang* than Nat leaped free and took off running down the alley toward Warren Street, steering far clear of the main entrance of the theater. With any luck, they would be across the bridge before any ushers, police officers, or deputized marshals conscripted in stalwart defense of justice against concert-crashers even made it around to the alley.

"Oh, Dinah!" Nat intoned to all of Latonia City beneath a sky of July stars. "Anyone finer!"

"MacCulloch, you're *nuts*!" Dick vowed as he ran off-kilter, with a shoe on one foot and only a sock on the other.

"Did you see their faces?" laughed Art. "Aces! Golden aces!"

"State of Car-o-lina!" Nat sang out. "Yeah—if-there-is-'n-ya-know'er-I'd-like-to-have-ya-show'er-to-me—*Dinah*! *Yes, yes*! Dinah! Oh, babe! Dinah Lee. . . !"

Chapter Thirty-Four

Latonia City, Pennsylvania
December 2019

AT SOME POINT in Owen's adult life, he had come to the conclusion that a great deal of his expectations about dramatic moments had come from movies and television. But when dramatic things happened to real people, in real life, it rarely went the way it did in the movies. War had taught him this lesson better than anything else. Often there was no pivotal moment of shocking realization but, rather, an unfolding of many smaller moments in incremental degrees of comprehension and severity, in which one gradually gained an understanding of the situation, all the while convinced that whatever was happening couldn't *really* be happening. That was why so many people, Owen concluded, described the bad things that happened to them as being like "a bad dream" they couldn't wake up from.

Looking back on it later, Owen would marvel at the fact that he didn't remember the exact moment when he received the news that his house was on fire; he would only remember the feeling of dread, like sopping wet clothes and a sickness in his stomach, that had accompanied those many smaller, incremental moments in which he tried to hang on to the misplaced belief that it was just a bad dream and couldn't really be happening.

But he drove. And the moments unfolded. And he didn't wake up.

PART FIVE
RUST BELT BLUES

Chapter Thirty-Five

Latonia City, Pennsylvania
July 1939

THE MONDAY AFTER Gideon Rust played the Derrick, clouds hung dark above Latonia City, bloated with the promise of rain. Rain that Seneca County badly needed. Perhaps, thought Nat as he stared up at the smiling stone face on the side of the Derrick Theatre, today would finally mark the end of the long drought of the summer of '39 and help to refill the wells.

Nat returned the stone face's smile, thinking back to Saturday night.

Where there's a will, there's always a way, he reminded himself. He would never forget it.

Dick wasn't with him today. Instead, his only company was the cornet in his hand and the three nickels in his pocket. Part of him worried about the thought of being caught out in the rain with his prized instrument, but it was Monday afternoon, and everything was open—plenty of doorways to duck into, and plenty of stores and service stations and what-have-you for a boy to waste a bit of time in while he waited for the rain to pass. But maybe, if he hurried, he could still make it across the bridge and over to HartSounds before the skies let loose.

He heard a distant rumble of thunder and, for some reason, found his eyes drawn away from the smiling face, toward the one on the other side of the building. The frowning, disproportionately stretched, almost horrified-looking face that represented tragedy.

Nat's smile faltered a bit. No matter how old he got, he'd never get over the look of that one. It was like something out of a nightmare.

He reached into his pocket and closed his hand around the three nickels, counting them with his thumb to make sure they were all still there. Then he turned and ran down the sidewalk toward the bridge.

Most ten-year-olds lucky enough to have found themselves with a bit of spending money on a summer's day would have been intent on taking in a picture at one of the town's theaters or blowing it all on sweets at the drug store. But Nat MacCulloch had more important things to attend to. After all, he'd put to writing what he intended to do. He had placed it inside the basement wall and committed it to the Lord and to time, just as his father had told him to. And now, he'd witnessed his future firsthand. Had seen it onstage before his very eyes—live and in person. If he wanted it, it was up to him now. From here on out, he vowed, every free moment would be spent pursuing it, until *he* was the one up on that theater stage, performing while his da watched him from the front row.

Nat hadn't quite made it across the bridge that spanned Rock-Oil Creek when the rain began—heavy, fat drops that bespoke the prelude to a downpour. A train whistle sounded, and he was grateful that there was no chance of getting stuck at the crossing behind the street traffic.

The rain was picking up as he passed the Latonia National Bank Building, where employees were hurrying to pull the doors shut on the ground floor and close windows up on the second story, where the prices were wired from New York City—that rumored, faraway place to which his grandfather had driven locomotives, back before whatever had "gone wrong" in the old man.

Thunder growled more loudly overhead, and Nat considered taking refuge inside the Seneca Transit Center or the department store across the street. But HartSounds wasn't much further. So he tucked his cornet up under his shirt and kept going.

A block past the Transit Center, he crossed the street, feeling rainwater soaking through his shoes and into his socks. A moment after he crossed, an ambulance car with its lights flashing drove past behind him, and as he grabbed the handle to the door of HartSounds, he caught a glimpse of it coming to a stop in front of the lowered gate of the railroad crossing. The driver of the ambulance leaned out to argue with the signalman, but it was too late. The locomotive was coming through.

Nat threw open the door and rushed in, greeted by the sound of a record. He didn't recognize the tune, but he'd have bet two of his three nickels that it was Glenn Miller. Gid Rust had come and gone, it seemed, and so had the citywide mania for his music. Latonia City was moving on to other things.

There were only a few patrons in the store this afternoon, and all of them stopped and stared at this sopping-wet youth just a few days past ten years old, standing in the doorway with a distinctly trumpet-shaped bulge under his dripping shirt, looking the part of a comically inept shoplifter. At the front of the store, young Art Hart manned the register.

"Hey, Art!" Nat called as he always did, hurrying to the front of the store.

Art, in a betrayal of his usual serious nature, was smiling from ear to ear at the sight of Nat. And Nat smiled right back at him. So far, Nat hadn't bothered trying to tell anybody about what they'd done on Saturday night. For one thing, he didn't think anyone would believe him. And for another, he knew that were he to try to put his story to words, something was bound to be lost in translation and ruin its near-perfection. It would have been like trying to relate to someone a half-remembered dream, and he'd have hated to see that glazed-over look come into someone's eyes—the look adults got when they switched from listening to you to waiting for you to finish. The best things in life were always better left unexplained anyway and allowed to just *be* good, without trying to convince anyone of their goodness.

Something about the look on Art's face told Nat that he hadn't told anybody about their caper, either. For now, their secret mission was still a secret.

"Poppy says you can't hang around unless you help out," Art reminded him by way of greeting.

Nat pulled his cornet out from under his damp shirt and placed it on the counter. Then, much less delicately, he pulled the three nickels from his pocket and slapped them down.

"Who's hanging around?" demanded Nat. "I'm here to do business, my good man."

"Oh yeah?" said Art.

Somewhere in the back of the store, a phone rang, and Nat heard Poppy Hart answer—proof that Art wasn't minding the store on his own. Nevertheless, Art leaned forward and propped one elbow on the counter in his best imitation of a big-shot salesman. The effect might have been more compelling had he been tall enough to comfortably reach the counter.

"What'll it be, *Mack*?" Art asked.

"Ran out of valve oil," said Nat. "I can't solo like Gid with my valves sticking."

"Maybe if you didn't carry it around inside a wet shirt," offered Art.

Nat tapped a finger meaningfully against one of the three nickels on the countertop. "If I want advice, I'll ask for it, young feller. *Oil*, toot-sweet."

"You're the boss," Art said. He adjusted his apron before heading to the wall behind the counter where such things were stored.

It was during the interim between one Glenn Miller track and the next that the door to HartSounds swung violently open, and Dick came skidding in like a bird dog on a frozen pond. Behind him, the rain was coming down in sheets on the street. The sidewalks were deserted. Even those with umbrellas had decided to wait this one out. All except Dick.

"I just cleaned those floors, you know," Art said from behind the counter.

Nat had begun to laugh at the state of Dick and was trying to think of a comparison that would be poetic—what he really looked like was Sam McClintock after three dunks in the lake, but the present company wasn't likely to understand or appreciate this parallel. Nat stopped laughing, however, when he saw the look on Dick's face. His cheeks were sickly white, and his eyes were bulging and red.

When Dick saw Nat, his face went even whiter, if that was possible.

"Oh, Lord," said Dick. "Nat. Oh God, Nat."

Nat and Art exchanged worried looks. It was all over Dick's face: Someone must have found out what they'd done.

Had one of the ushers recognized them? Or had the police somehow figured out where that flour-sack-and-pilfered-rope grappling hook had come from? What sort of trouble could you get in for breaking in to see a show? What would his parents say? All these thoughts, and others, had time to pass through Nat's head before Dick finally managed to open his mouth. But whatever Dick was about to say was cut off by Poppy Hart emerging from the back room.

Poppy's piercing blue eyes noticed Dick first. Then Nat. And his face fell. "You're here," he said to Nat.

Nat wasn't sure if it was supposed to be a question or not, but something about the way Poppy said it made Nat sick to his stomach.

Poppy stepped out from behind the counter. He had the same wispy yellow hair as his son and might have been just as thin once but now carried a spare tire around his middle. Nat barely knew the man, which made it all the more bizarre when Poppy placed one soft, thin-fingered hand on his shoulder. Even his father didn't show this sort of affection. The MacCullochs were, after all, not huggers.

"Son," said Poppy. "I just got off the phone with. . . . There has been an accident. At Germania."

Nat found himself thinking of the ambulance car that had driven by just as he'd crossed the street. The one that had gotten stopped at the railroad crossing.

"Okay," was all Nat could think to say. It came out as raspy and gravelly as Gid Rust's vocals.

Poppy Hart's soft, thin fingers squeezed Nat's shoulder. "Nat, they're saying your father . . . fell."

Chapter Thirty-Six

Pittsburgh, Pennsylvania
November 1982

AS FAR AS LOU MACCULLOCH was concerned, drinking like a fish and laying a guy out in a drunken brawl didn't make you tough. What made you tough was how you carried yourself the day after. And the day after that night in 1982 just happened to be Thanksgiving Day.

He woke up in someone else's bed, alone, in a dorm room in a part of campus he'd never been to before. He didn't know how he'd gotten there. Perhaps some kind soul had lent him a bed to prevent him from having to travel all the way back to the Towers. He left in the early-morning hours and walked home to his dorm. By the time most people were having breakfast, Lou was showered, shaved, and ready for the day.

But the day would bring nothing. Because he planned to go nowhere and see no one. As far as Lou could tell, he was the only one on the entire floor.

The payphone in the dorm hall rang every hour, practically on the hour, all day Thursday. He suspected that it was his mother trying to reach him. But Lou never found out, because he didn't bother to pick up the ringing phone; his aversion to seeing or speaking with his father had grown temporarily stronger than his instinct not to upset his mother, and that was saying something. It wasn't until Friday night, after the phone calls stopped, that Lou considered the possibility that it hadn't been his mom trying to call him at all. He had made Angie Schultze a promise. Now, he desperately wished he'd picked up the phone when he'd had the chance. If her name showed up in the *Oildom News–Herald* police blotter on Monday morning, he knew he would never forgive himself.

Lou didn't go home on Thanksgiving, or the next day, or the day after that, or the day after that, either. He managed to find a party every night that weekend except for Sunday. Thursday night, Friday night, and Saturday night, he got just as blind-drunk as he'd gotten the night he'd driven back to campus. By Sunday, students were trickling back in, their Thanksgiving break over. Having failed to locate a party that night, Lou had to settle for a small get-together in a shady basement, but that didn't slow him down. If anything, that night was the most debauched of all. Nevertheless, he still made it to his first class the following morning, showered, shaved, and with his hair looking perfect. And fifteen minutes early.

If you weren't fifteen minutes early, you were late.

He went to each of his classes with nothing to visibly set him apart from any other typical day other than his lip, which was still a bit swollen from somebody busting his chops a few nights prior.

There was no business degree in his future. Next semester, he would have a fresh start, taking art classes on the side of the campus where classrooms looked like studios or warehouses. The credits he was earning this semester—on the side of campus where classrooms looked like classrooms—would mean nothing in the long run. But Lou MacCulloch didn't start anything without finishing it, so he would damn well finish his semester of business courses. After all, he had to keep his grades up to stay on the ball team. Might as well ace his finals while he was at it. Just to prove he could.

It wasn't until his final class on that Monday afternoon—for some reason, in the middle of jotting a note about amortization—that Lou started to feel bad about what he'd said to his father. Initially, the feeling attempted to disguise itself as self-interest. He needed to stay in school to keep playing baseball. He didn't agree with his parents about a lot of things, but yelling at them had been a stupid thing to do. He knew now that he probably shouldn't have tried to hide his change of major, either; if his father refused to pay for him to continue going to school, maybe he could borrow enough money to keep himself afloat for another year. Besides, he'd heard about an upcoming open tryout for one of Baltimore's farm teams. If he kept playing the way he had last year, he wouldn't need school to play ball.

But as class wore on, the veneer of self-interest wore thin.

I was told to stay away from the MacCulloch family because they were bad news, echoed the words of Deb McClintock—whose uncle, it was said, had been on the receiving end of a whooping, courtesy of Grant

MacCulloch just a few days before Grant's death. *Even my dad knows that a bad word said against Nat MacCulloch's character is a lie.*

All I ask, echoed the words of his mother, *is that you don't put your father under any more stress than he already is. Please.*

"Louis MacCulloch?" said a deep voice.

The entire class looked up from their notes. The only one who seemed more surprised by the interruption than Lou was Dr. Brunner, at the front of the room, who had paused midway through writing something on the blackboard and was now looking curiously at the doorway. A tall man with a full, dark black beard had ducked his head into the classroom. He had one hand resting on the doorframe. The other, he raised and used to gesture apologetically toward the professor. Lou recognized him as Dr. Emmitt Steinberg, Dean of the College of Business Administration.

"Sorry, Dr. Brunner," said Dr. Steinberg. "Is there a Louis MacCulloch in here?"

Every pair of eyes in the auditorium-style classroom turned toward Lou.

Lou raised his hand. "Here," he said loudly.

Dr. Steinberg frowned, then sighed. "Mr. MacCulloch, would you come with me, please?"

Lou looked around. "I'm in class right now," he said.

Lou wouldn't have imagined that Dr. Steinberg's frown could have moved any lower on his face than it already was. But it did.

"Come with me," Dr. Steinberg said. "Now, please."

Lou exhaled sharply—a sound halfway between a scoff and an incredulous laugh. Now, it was a new voice that was echoing in his head: *I did not work and save my entire life so that my boy could learn to paint.*

The old man certainly hadn't wasted any time.

The hundred or so eyes continued to watch Lou as he slammed his notebook shut and gathered up his things. "Can't believe this," he said without caring who heard.

Dr. Brunner, who had paused dramatically with his chalk still touching the board in mid-stroke, waited silently. At the doorway, Dr. Steinberg stepped back to allow Lou to walk past him. Then Dr. Steinberg said, "Follow me," and began to walk down the hallway. A moment later, Lou heard Dr. Brunner clear his throat just as dramatically and continue his lecture. It was the sound of Lou's education moving on without him, as if he'd never been there at all.

A few steps later, still following the tall, quiet Dr. Steinberg, Lou began to second-guess his first assumption. Blame it on the brain fog leftover from an eventful weekend.

Even if Nat *had* been upset enough with him to have decided to cut off all financial support, was that the sort of thing the dean pulled you out of class for? No, of course it wasn't. Lou's classes for this semester were paid for. Now that he really thought about it, getting pulled out of a college classroom was the kind of thing that only happened if you were in some sort of trouble.

And suddenly, following Dr. Steinberg down that tile-floored hallway felt like a very long walk.

"I think there's an open room up here where we can talk," said Dr. Steinberg.

Lou thought back to his impulsive trip down here on Wednesday night, driving like a bat out of hell and feeling a bit like one, too. He thought back to getting terrifically, colossally sauced that evening—*woo-woo*—and the room spinning around him. He thought about the mystery bed he'd woken up in the next morning, in a part of campus he'd never been to before. But mostly, he thought about his split lip and the fella he'd laid out with one punch. Until now, he hadn't worried much about who'd been on the receiving end of that slug. Or what had happened to him afterward. He tried to remember the details and realized he didn't recall seeing the guy get up.

"Okay, right in here," said Dr. Steinberg, and gestured toward an open doorway.

It was a classroom nearly identical to the one where Dr. Brunner was currently continuing his lecture, now with one open seat. The room was the size of a small auditorium, with stadium-style seating that went up and back some fifty rows deep.

Behind Lou, Dr. Steinberg pulled the door shut. The sound of it closing echoed through the auditorium, and Lou felt a bit like he'd just stepped into the batter's box in the top of the ninth with two outs, down by too many runs to stand a hope, no chance left to be the hero, only a chance to keep yourself alive long enough not to be the last guy to go down.

"Take a seat," said Dr. Steinberg.

"Do I have to?" said Lou flatly.

Dr. Steinberg's frown deepened yet again. "I think you should."

Lou wasn't normally one to back down, but he also wasn't one to be obstinate just for the sake of it. He selected a chair in the front row.

Dr. Steinberg leaned back against the podium from which professors in the Department of Business Administration lectured about topics like credit interest, intangible assets, and other things that Lou couldn't wait to never hear about again. Then Dr. Steinberg put a hand over his mouth and let out a long sigh that escaped through his fingers like air brakes on a big rig.

"Louis," said Dr. Steinberg.

"Lou," Lou corrected.

"Sorry," said Dr. Steinberg. "Lou. . . . Lou, I don't feel right about being the one to tell you this, but I don't know who the 'right' person would be, given the circumstances. And it wouldn't be fair to keep you in the dark until that person were to show up. We just received a call at the main office. I contacted your academic advisor, who informed me of your schedule, and I came right over, personally, as quickly as I could. Lou, your father had a heart attack this morning. He was on the golf course, alone. By the time somebody found him, it was too late."

Lou felt numb. "Too late?" he said.

"I'm sorry, son," said Dr. Steinberg. "Your dad is dead."

Chapter Thirty-Seven

Latonia City, Pennsylvania
December 2019

THERE ARE TIMES when the exact wording of a piece of terrible news is etched in one's heart forever, as immutable and ugly as a block-lettered name scored in the bark of an old tree, and the mind requires no great leap to return to the instant when the news was given, bringing into sharp detail the sights, smells, and thoughts of that never-forgotten moment. But for Owen, all he would remember was that the news came in the form of a frantic phone call from Kayla when he'd been climbing into the car, about to leave his parents' house—just a few minutes after reading a note his grandfather had written on a playbill as a boy.

Owen didn't remember much of the drive from Silvern Row, either. One moment, he was answering the call. The next, he was pulling into Ruth Lee's driveway—no, *his* driveway—to find a fire truck in the front yard and a small fleet of volunteer firefighter vehicles with blue lights spinning atop their roofs or on their dashboards.

Kayla had told him over the phone that everyone had made it out. He would believe it when he saw it.

It struck him how many people were there—a small crowd, most of whom appeared to be just standing and watching. He saw no flames, no billowing clouds of smoke as he might have expected. Surely that was a good sign. But everywhere hung a brown-yellow haze, turning the view of the house and the front yard into a sepia-tone photo. The odor was deep in his nostrils before he even threw the Ford Focus into park. It was not the sort of burning smell with which he was familiar. Not like a fireplace; more like a burn barrel. But dirtier. More chemical. He reached to unbuckle his seatbelt, realized he hadn't buckled it, and fumbled with the door handle several times before he managed to get it open.

Kayla saw him before he saw her. Emma was in her arms as she came running to him out of the crowd.

His girls. His beautiful, wonderful girls.

Owen threw his arms around them. Gripped a fistful of the back of Kayla's shirt. Pulled Emma's head against his chest and buried his face in her dark, curly hair.

"I love you," he said as tears spilled from his eyes, into their hair. "God, I love you. Thank you, Jesus."

"Owen," Kayla cried into his shoulder.

"Where's your mom?" he said.

"She's fine," said Kayla. "She's here. Oh, God, Owen."

He could taste the brownish, chemical-smelling haze in the air and felt an involuntary spasm at the back of his throat. He swallowed against it.

"We're okay," he said, speaking as much to himself as to anyone else. "We're all okay. That's all that matters."

"Dada," said Emma.

"Emma," said Owen, kissing her on the head. "Emma, my sweet girl." He turned to Kayla. "What happened?"

"We don't know yet," she said, wiping her face. "Mom and Emma and I went to the store. When we came back, the smoke alarms were going off and we could smell something burning. Mom was determined to go in and get the dogs. She opened the door, and when they didn't come out, she was going to try to crawl in under the smoke. I practically had to drag her away from the door. The fumes were so bad that just being close made me dizzy. I don't know how bad it is."

Scanning the crowd, Owen saw Ruth Lee talking to a firefighter. A hose ran from the largest truck, across the yard, past Owen's old rusty bike leaned against the siding, and in through the front door.

As Owen watched, a firefighter in full gear stepped out through the hazy doorway. Balanced in his outstretched arms was a blackened ball of fur. Kayla turned Emma away.

The firefighter made his way to the front lawn, where he kneeled and laid the body of Wilma, the beagle of indeterminate age, out in the grass.

Ruth Lee went to Wilma, got down on her knees, and began to pet her. Then Ruth Lee, whom Owen had never seen shed a tear in his life, put her head in her hands, and her shoulders shook with sobs.

"Bandit?" asked Kayla, still looking away.

Owen shook his head. "Wilma."

"We shouldn't have left," Kayla said. "If we'd been home, maybe we could have stopped it."

If you'd been home, thought Owen. *Oh, God. If you'd been home. . . .*

He couldn't finish the thought.

He pulled his girls close again, and this time it was Kayla's hair that he buried his face in. His hands trembled.

"I don't know what to do," Kayla said.

Neither do I, thought Owen.

Letting go of Kayla with one hand, he took out his phone and tried to call his dad first. It rang half a dozen times and went to voicemail.

"Hey!" someone shouted. "Hey-hey, look what we've got here!"

Owen turned toward the voice. One of the firefighters had opened the door to the attached garage, and out jumped a teddy-bear-looking puppy that came tearing across the yard.

"Here, boy!" Owen shouted, dropping down on his knees. "Bandit! Here, boy!"

Bandit leaped into Owen's arms. Kayla nuzzled his face. Emma laughed. And Bandit tasted tears as his chicken-nugget nub of a tail wiggled back and forth.

Owen decided to try calling his mom next. But before he could call, a new text message appeared on his screen.

Don't want to worry you, read the text from his mother, *but I can't get a hold of your dad, and his phone's GPS is in the same place it was when I checked forty-five minutes ago. . . . You know the golf course better than I do. Is there a reason he would stay in that spot?*

Owen's chest went cold.

Chapter Thirty-Eight

THE MACCULLOCH CURSE.

Owen had never believed in such things. And he didn't think his father ever had, either. But as he took the turn at the top of the hill and slammed the gas pedal to the floor of the Ford Focus, he couldn't help but wonder if curses, when they came to collect, didn't care whether you believed in them or not. Scoreboards didn't lie.

Callum MacCulloch. A locomotive driver who'd been relieved of his job after he'd started hearing voices, and had taken his own life by stepping in front of a moving train. He had been thirty-eight years old.

Grant MacCulloch. A factory worker who'd been killed in an accident at the Germania Oil Well Supply Company. He'd fallen from a catwalk and had died in the back of an ambulance car while it was halted at a railroad crossing. He had just turned forty.

Nat MacCulloch. An accountant turned Chamber of Commerce director who'd died of a heart attack attributed to hypertension aggravated by stress while alone on a golf course, just a few days after resigning from his position amid controversy. There had been multiple threats on his life in the weeks leading up to that day, resulting in rumors—never investigated and thus never substantiated, but also never disproven—of foul play being involved. At fifty-three years old, he'd been the longest-lived MacCulloch male in generations.

Lou MacCulloch. A high school art teacher who, at the current age of fifty-seven, had lived the longest of any of them. So far.

And Louis Owen MacCulloch, who had gone by his middle name, Owen, all his life to avoid confusion. A thirty-two-year-old copy editor at the *Oildom Morning–Herald*, currently racing toward the golf course where the GPS location of his father's phone last placed him.

After receiving his mother's text message, Owen had realized that he had a few options: Call someone and ask them to go looking for his father, or drive to the golf course and look for himself.

"I don't want you to go alone," Kayla said. "I'll come with you. Do you want me to drive?"

She is an angel, Owen thought.

"Right now, I think your mom needs you," Owen said. "I can do this myself." But then he hesitated.

"We are fine," Kayla said, sensing his apprehension at the idea of leaving them, "but your dad might need you."

Owen pulled off the main road and onto the narrow state road that led to a little country golf course. The one whose owners allowed their regular customers to walk on whenever they liked during the cold winter months, as long as they didn't mind golfing without flags on the greens, and as long as it meant the occasional twenty slipped under the door of the clubhouse—the course Lou frequented despite the fact that, frankly, he wasn't all that good at golf. And the same golf course where his father, Nat, had been found dead thirty-seven years prior.

Owen had called his mother shortly after leaving Ruth Lee's house to tell her about the fire. Now, Deb was heading over there to be with Ruth Lee, Kayla, and Emma. As for her husband's missing-in-action status on the golf course, Deb seemed to think he must have just dropped his phone somewhere. It didn't seem to have occurred to her that any other explanation could account for his stagnant GPS location. She'd even tried to convince Owen not to drive out to find him.

"You can't leave your house right now," Deb had protested. "Your dad will show up any minute."

"I'm sure you're right, Mom," Owen had said, though he wasn't. "But it will make me feel better to check."

The entrance to the golf course was a dirt lane off the state road, but Owen bypassed it; a little further along, this road intersected the course between Holes 4 and 5, and he knew it would be faster for him to park beside the cart-crossing and walk to Hole 6 from there. The shock of the housefire had nearly worn off by now, replaced by memories of being in the room at the hospital the day they'd told his father about his high blood sugar. Owen thought about how Lou had shrugged it off as one more little plastic bottle with his name on it. He thought about their fight months ago, on the very same golf course. And he thought about how his father *never* drove a cart when he played eighteen holes. Instead, he always walked the course, despite the way he'd been huffing and puffing the last time they'd gone out together.

Owen pulled off to the side of the road beside a yellow sign with a black outline of a golf cart on it, shifted the Focus into park, and removed the keys. He opened the door.

For a moment, he almost couldn't bring himself to step out of the car. It was so quiet out here. The sunny 35-degree day was now overcast, and the temperature had dropped maybe as low as 30 or 25. In an hour, the sun would be down. He took a deep breath, trying to calm his racing heart and prepare himself for what he was about to find. Then he stepped out of the car.

He didn't run. He walked quickly. It was the kind of walk he'd often utilized on this same course in the past to keep up with his father, who always got impatient if you didn't hustle. His philosophy was that anything that was worth doing was also worth hustling for. Owen hadn't always felt like hustling. Golf was supposed to be fun and relaxing, after all. But he was hustling now.

He hurried over the wide, dipping fairway of Hole 5. He shielded his face against the winter-bare gnarls of bushes as he veered off the fairway and cut the corner of Number 5's sharp dogleg left. This brought him out on the other side, back onto the fairway with some scrapes on his forearms.

Behind the green was a copse of trees with a path leading into a more thickly wooded area, where the final holes of the Front 9 meandered their way back to the clubhouse. By the time Owen made it to the back of the green and reached the trees, he couldn't stand to merely hustle anymore—he took off running down the wooded path toward Hole 6.

"Looks like he's on the 6th green right now," his mother had said.

He sprinted down the Hole 6 fairway. It was a narrow one. A hook or a slice would have put you into the trees on either side. And there was a water hazard. Too small to be called a pond. More like a very wide ditch. At the moment, it was frozen over.

He could see the green now. And there was something lying on the ground.

It was just beyond the green. Difficult to tell what it was from here, but it looked like a piece of blue fabric sticking out from behind a large oak at the corner of the cart path.

Owen's throat was dry and his lungs were already burning, but he ran even faster. So fast that he tripped and nearly toppled forward but managed to regain his footing.

Please, God, Owen prayed.

Perhaps, ideally, he ought to have been uttering a more specific invocation. But his mind was too jumbled—his wits too shaken after having had his life turned upside down at least once and now perhaps twice in the past hour—to think of any other words to say as he ran.

Please, God. Please, God.

By the time he reached the green, he had shifted to repeating it aloud.

"Please, God. Please, God."

He bypassed the green and hurried to the cart path. There, his feet faltered. The piece of fabric on the ground appeared to be a shirtsleeve.

He didn't want to take another step. It was that old denial thing again—the naïveté of his consciousness that seemed convinced that if he turned around now, nothing bad would have happened. Like a bad dream, maybe he could just wake up from it if he tried really hard.

He stepped forward. And he blinked in confusion. The shirtsleeve, he could now see, was not connected to a shirt. Because it wasn't a shirtsleeve at all. It was a small blue towel with a metal clip on it like a keyring, the kind that golfers attached to their bags to wipe clean the heads of their clubs. And it was clear, judging by the dirt and bits of leaves stuck in its fibers, that it had been there a long time. Beside it, with feet curled and neck twisted back strangely, lay the dead body of a small bird. A common American robin.

Owen looked around. Based on the GPS location, this was where he'd expected to find . . . something. But he saw nothing other than somebody's old, lost rag. He'd nearly resolved to take off in a sprint to Hole 7 and repeat the whole affair when an idea occurred to him. He reached into his pocket, pulled out his phone, and called his father's number.

A buzzing sound—the vibrating of a phone. Coming from nearby.

He turned in place, trying to pinpoint the source. It wasn't coming from ahead, toward Hole 7. And it wasn't coming from the woods, either. It was coming from behind him, on the green he had bypassed.

Backtracking, he followed the buzzing to the back edge of the green. There, in the inch-and-a-half-tall grass where the fringe ended and the rough began, lying face-down, was Lou MacCulloch's cell phone.

Owen picked it up. For some reason, he thought it prudent to swipe his finger across the screen to choose to ignore his own incoming call. In doing so, he saw that his missed call was one of many.

"There's that damn thing."

Owen wheeled toward the voice. Down beside the cart path, Lou stood looking up at his son with his hands on his hips in annoyance. He wore a heavy winter coat, jeans, dark aviator sunglasses, and a Nike hat, and there was a crooked smile on his face—a fancy-seeing-you-here sort of look.

"Must've fallen out of my bag," said Lou. "I've been retracing my steps for half an hour at least. Didn't expect to find you with it, though."

Owen started walking toward his dad, gradually becoming aware of the rapid pace of his heartbeat and how hard he was panting from his run. As he got closer, Lou's fancy-seeing-you-here expression melted away, and he took off his sunglasses. "What's wrong?" he asked.

Owen kept walking. He stopped in front of Lou.

"You're all right?" Owen asked.

Lou looked himself over. "Of course I'm all right," he said.

The MacCullochs were not huggers. But Owen stepped forward and wrapped his arms around his father.

"I'm sorry, Dad."

Lou stood frozen in place for a moment. He returned the embrace cautiously, adding a polite pat on Owen's shoulder. "I'm sorry, too. What's going on?"

"There was a fire at our house," said Owen.

Lou pulled away. "The girls?" he said.

"They're fine," said Owen. "Everyone's safe. Except poor Wilma. But our house. . . ."

It was just like Lou MacCulloch to say nothing in response. But for once, Owen didn't take the bait. And after a few moments, Lou grabbed Owen and pulled him into a second hug. There was something different about this one, though. He'd returned Owen's initial embrace in an obligatory way. Now, his arms wrapped all the way around, and his hands grabbed tightly to Owen's shoulders.

"You're all right," he said into Owen's ear. "And your girls are all right. Nothing else matters."

"But our house," Owen repeated.

"Forget the house," said Lou. "You will get through this. You. . . . We will get through this. Do you understand me? *We* will get through this."

Chapter Thirty-Nine

OWEN DIDN'T SLEEP that night, as he'd known he wouldn't. On a normal evening, he'd have been at work at the paper. Instead, he spent the first part of the night being led through the house by firefighters with flashlights. The house had been saved. But the consensus was that it would be a long time before it was livable again.

It appeared that an electrical fire had started in the basement, not all that uncommon in houses with old wiring. The firefighters told Owen there hadn't been many flames, really, but the melting wires had caused the home to quickly fill with invisible, odorless carbon monoxide. If it had happened in the middle of the night, while everyone had been home, Owen's family might never have woken up.

Inside, a sticky layer of residue—soot, the firefighters had called it, but it was more like tar—covered everything. One of the firefighters showed Owen how, when he moved one of Emma's pink sippy cups that had been left on the kitchen counter, the place where it had been sitting was completely unaffected, leaving a negative image of the cup's location in the soot. Then the same firefighter used his flashlight to point to where Wilma had been lying on the kitchen floor. Her body had left a cookie-cutter-perfect beagle outline in the soot—a reverse snow angel, complete with a comma-shaped tail, where the linoleum floor was still clean and white. The rest of the floor was black. Ruth Lee took some comfort in the fact that Wilma hadn't been burned. It had been the fumes. For the old mostly-beagle, it would have been like drifting off to sleep.

Through everything, Owen's father was there with him. Not hovering over his shoulder. Not taking charge. Most of the time not even saying a word. Just there.

Finally, around the same time that Owen would have normally been getting off work at the paper, Lou drove him to the house on Silvern Row. The house his father had grown up in, and that his grandfather had grown up in before him. That sort of thing didn't happen much nowadays. It was kind of neat, when Owen thought about it.

His first priority was to check on his girls. Deb had set them up in the master bedroom. There, he found three generations of women in the same bed, sleeping the hard, deep sleep of exhaustion. A sleeping bag and pillow were prepared for Owen on the floor.

He lay there for a while, staring at the ceiling and listening to Ruth Lee, Kayla, and Emma breathing, breathing, breathing. And thinking how grateful he was for those sounds. When it became clear that sleep wasn't going to come, he got up and went out to the kitchen. It was 4:03 a.m., and Lou was standing with his arms crossed, leaning with his rear end against the counter. Owen took up a similar position nearby. Lou had already put on a pot of coffee.

When the coffee maker grumbled, then groaned, then hissed, Lou poured them each a cup. Bandit the Corgi puppy wandered in and sat, looking at them expectantly at first. But when it became clear that the humans were not going to do anything interesting, he lay down, sighed heavily, and went to sleep.

For a long time, Owen and Lou remained silent, staring into their respective cups, as if by looking hard enough they might find their answers somewhere within those molecules of water filtered through beans from a faraway place. After a while, the kitchen windows began to lighten. And that was how the night of the fire became the morning after it. It was how time would be measured from then on. Just as the Christian calendar measured time in reference to the lifespan of a noteworthy Carpenter, so would the MacCullochs measure everything from then on in reference to a singular event. *Anno ignis.*

Owen got another cup of coffee.

"What's going through your head?" asked Lou. For a man who wasn't much of a talker, he didn't beat around the bush when he got the notion to say something.

"That I've got to get my family out of this town," said Owen. "Before anything else happens."

"If you're talking about what I think you're talking about," said Lou, "it's a bunch of bull, and you know it."

"That's what I've always thought," said Owen. "But look at what happened to your dad. And his dad. And *his* dad. . . . And now this. How is that not a curse?"

Lou didn't even have to think about the answer: "Because you didn't lose anyone in it."

He let those words hang in the kitchen air, alongside the motes of dust caught in the first sunbeams streaming through the window.

"That girl you said you work with at the *Herald*," said Lou. "Felicia. Did I tell you I knew her mother?"

"No," said Owen.

Lou nodded. "Once, when I was driving home from Pitt, I found her walking along the side of 322, alone in the cold and the rain, no coat. Fifteen years old. I picked her up and gave her a ride. She was beaten up pretty badly. Turns out, she was in the car with her father, and they got into an argument, and he threw her out of the vehicle and just drove off. Left her there, bleeding on the side of the road, and kept driving. I found out, a couple of days after, that her dad wrecked his car later that same night. He was drunk, going too fast, and took his Chevy off the road and straight into a telephone pole. The guy didn't get a scratch. 'Drunkards have the devil's luck,' as your grandmother once told me. But the whole passenger side of his car was nearly sheared off by the impact. Right where that girl would have been sitting if she hadn't been walking along 322 with no coat and a black eye."

Owen was only partially listening. Instead, he found himself thinking again of the place on the kitchen floor where Wilma had been lying. The white dog-shaped form, surrounded by black. A shape as clear as a coloring book picture. He thought about what the firefighters had told him, how high concentrations of carbon monoxide could kill so quickly that the poor dog may never have even known she was in danger. How a human being asleep at the time of exposure can easily continue sleeping through the initial symptoms and die without ever waking up. How people in their beds could slip away, never even realizing anything was wrong. And he thought about his daughter's crib in the bedroom upstairs. And what sort of morning this would have been if the fire had occurred a few hours later, while he'd been at work and his wife and child and mother-in-law had been asleep.

Owen's father went to the corner of the kitchen. There, the old playbill that the contractors had exhumed from the wall of the basement during their repairs sat on the countertop. He placed his palm on it, resting his fingers beside his long-dead father's handwritten note—the words of a ten-year-old boy making promises about a grand future.

"Obviously your grandfather did not become a world-famous trumpet player," said Lou. He gave a quiet chuckle. "To tell you the truth, I never thought he was very good. And I never played baseball at the pro level the way I wanted to. Hell, *most* people don't achieve the dreams they have when they're kids, but I don't. . . . I don't think it means we're failures. It just means that dreams change. And the dreams that don't change, well, they take longer than you expect them to. Longer than some of us are given on this earth. Nat MacCulloch was no Gid Rust, but look at what he did instead. The businesses he helped during the hard times. The hospital. This house. The legacy he left for me. Look at this family. I've got a wife and a son. A wonderful daughter-in-law. A beautiful granddaughter. All sleeping safely under my roof, even after what happened. . . ." He shook his head. "Son, no man with so many blessings could be cursed."

Lou paused to sip his coffee, then continued.

"Your grandfather was a good man, but he lived believing—and I think he was convinced, at some level— that he would either die young like his dad, or live long enough to lose his mind like people said his grandfather did. That was the story he told himself. He was a troubled person, but he never backed down from doing what he thought was right, even when a very vocal minority of this community wanted to tar and feather him and run him out of town. . . . There were rumors about some sort of foul play surrounding his death. But that's just a bunch of small-town gossip. For a long time, I was convinced that it was the stress *I* put him through that finally proved too much for him. But the truth is, he was likely living with undiagnosed heart disease and, possibly, like me, diabetes. And in spite of it, he still outlived his father by fifteen or twenty years. Grading on a curve, I'd say he did all right. All my generation wanted to do was get out from under the shadows of our fathers and the things they built here. But maybe if we stop expecting this place to be what it once was, and instead start building something of our own, maybe it can become . . . I don't know. Something new. Something even better. In small ways, you can already see it happening. If you think the answer is to get your family out of this town, I respect your decision, but I hope you'll reconsider because there's no other place like it."

As Lou spoke, he never moved his hand from the eighty-year-old playbill. He ran his thumb over his father's handwriting, then finally stepped away and looked up at Owen.

"What happened last night was awful," Lou said. "It *is* awful. And I know it must feel like everything is wrong and nothing will ever be right again and the pain will never go away. But pain is the blessing of living. If you still feel it, it means you're still alive."

Owen took those words and stored them away, intending to return to them another time. "But it's not supposed to be this way," he said.

"How *is* it supposed to be, then?" said Lou.

"I don't know," Owen breathed. "Easier?"

"Well," said Lou, "it's not. It's damned hard. It's also good. Even when it's bad, it's good."

Owen turned to look out the window. From somewhere on the other side of the house, he heard the soft baby-noises of Emma stirring—awake with the dawn as usual. There had never been a more beautiful sound.

"When you think about it," said Lou, as Bandit woke up and followed the sounds of Emma out of the kitchen and through the house, "even the difficulties this family has gone through came from great victories. Your great-great-grandfather's victory was bringing his son to this country and starting a new life for him here. Your great-grandfather's victory was establishing a strong foundation in a flourishing city for his son—so much so that that son went from a dirt-poor boy from the wrong side of the tracks, literally, to the director of the city's Chamber of Commerce. Your grandfather's victory was getting our new hospital built so that when someone in our area needed emergency care—the kind of care his dad wasn't able to get the day he needed it—they could get it."

There was something about the way Lou concluded that last statement that didn't feel like a conclusion at all. As if he had been planning to say more but had cut himself short. In the past, Owen wouldn't have pressed the matter, wouldn't have "pried." But he'd had enough of that style of family communication. So he asked, "What's your victory, Dad?"

Lou finished his coffee in one large gulp, patted Owen on the shoulder, and walked away.

Chapter Forty

IN THE DAYS that followed, things happened that Owen expected to happen. The sort of standard logistical measures that must follow an accident. But there were also surprises, good and bad.

He found himself grateful, for instance, that their home insurance policy would cover so much and take care of his family while the house was being made livable again. That said, some of the red tape he had to cut through to get to that point stunk of bureaucracy. And finding out how many of your possessions could be ruined just by soot—that was no fun either.

The nice surprises were things like the care packages, which began to arrive right on the heels of the first sunrise after the fire. There were household essentials. There were clothes, towels, shampoos, and soap. But there were also things like children's books for Emma, and a baby doll, and a stuffed Curious George that was an exact duplicate of the one she wouldn't get back until it was professionally cleaned and returned to them. It became commonplace to find home-cooked meals in Tupperware containers left outside the front door, with helpful reheating instructions on sticky notes. Some of Kayla's coworkers got together and gave her five sets of scrubs (layered atop a bottle of Moscato at the bottom of the box). And letters arrived in the mail from some of Lou's art students.

Davewhite and a few of Owen's other coworkers at the *Herald* sent him a package containing a can of dark roast coffee and a book called *Archaeological Sites of the Oil Region.* The card read, "To Mr. Archaeologist, with love from your Herald family." And not only was Mae Baughman's name on the card, but a few days after the fire, an article ran in the "On This Day" section of the paper from 1987, about the ground-breaking ceremony for the region's new state-of-the-art medical center, how it ushered in a bright new future for Latonia City, Cornplanter, and the entire county, and how Lou MacCulloch had been on-hand in memory of his late father, Nat, the man who had worked so hard to make this vision a reality.

As for Dave Albaugh, he came to the MacCulloch home personally to visit, and to tell Owen to take "as much time as he needed." Felicia from reception visited, too, bringing boxes of take-out, Christmas presents, and a crayon drawing done by her oldest son: a picture of a beagle of indeterminate age wearing angel's wings.

Well-wishers came like moths to a back porch lamp. Owen's in-laws—the Woodford side of the family as well as the Harts—extended multiple offers to Ruth Lee and to Owen, Kayla, and Emma to put them up in their homes until they got back on their feet. Ruth Lee took advantage of *all* these offers and embarked on a sort of extended family-visiting excursion, staying with a whole host of loved ones over a period of several weeks. But Owen, Kayla, and Emma stayed at the MacCulloch house. Owen and Kayla were closer than they had ever been, and the only downside of living with his parents was finding enough alone time with his wife at a time in their lives when their need for alone time had never been greater.

There were calls and text messages from family members and friends whom Owen hadn't spoken to in years. All of them wanted to know how they could help. It was not a fun time, those first few days after the fire, but it may have been the most loved Owen had ever felt in his life.

Two weeks after the fire, Owen was in the kitchen when he called up Dave to tell him he was ready to return to work the following week, and to apologize for the inconvenience of his absence.

"We'll be glad to have you back," Dave said, "but it was no inconvenience. Mae agreed to stay on a little longer to cover for you until you're ready."

"Cover for me?" said Owen.

"Sure. I hired a new girl, smart kid right out of college, to take over the ads and most of the copyediting. I'd still like you to oversee the copyediting desk. But if you're up to it, I'd like you to take over Mae's position. You'll have assignments, of course, but I'd also like to see some original ideas. Maybe you could start with something from one of those history articles on your corkboard."

"I could probably come up with something," Owen said.

"No more six-to-midnight shifts!" said Dave. "I'll see you at ten o'clock on Monday morning."

"Your Mr. Archaeologist will be there," said Owen.

"Mr. Journalist," Dave corrected, and hung up.

"Is that something you want to do?" Lou asked Owen later, over another late-night coffee in the kitchen. By now, this had become something of a tradition: Owen and Lou drinking coffee, standing in the kitchen while Bandit snored on the linoleum.

"I think it's something I'd like to try," said Owen.

His gaze wandered to Gideon Rust's playbill with Nat MacCulloch's writing on it, which was now preserved under framed glass and hanging on the kitchen wall.

"It's a shame they're going to tear down the Derrick," said Owen.

"I don't think it's a sure thing just yet," said Lou, "but it's prime real estate, and there's been a battle to have it torn down for years."

"Huh," said Owen, who suddenly had an idea of the kind of story he might like to write.

"You ever hear about the time your grandfather saw Gid Rust at the Derrick?" asked Lou.

"You mean that actually happened?" said Owen. "He and his friends really snuck into the theater?"

Lou made a face. "Where'd you hear that?"

"Dave Albaugh's dad told me about it," said Owen. "He said when he and your dad were kids, they snuck into the Derrick Theatre to see Gideon Rust."

Lou chuckled. "Dick always was a character. Nah, this was when your grandfather was an adult. It would have been sometime in the 1960s."

"But look at the date on the playbill," said Owen, pointing. "He wrote that he was going to sneak in and see him that night. July 1939."

"Well, yeah," admitted Lou. "It also says he's going to be the greatest trumpet player in the world. I'm not saying it *couldn't* have happened. If it did, Dad never told me about it. But, come to think of it, I did hear a similar story once. It was Ruth Lee's older brother, Art Hart, who told it to me. I'd always assumed it was just a tall tale. Guess I can't say one way or the other what happened in 1939, but I *know* he saw him play there in the 60s. And he certainly didn't sneak in. He was a member of the Latonia Arts Council at the time and helped set the show up."

"Huh," said Owen. "So Grandpa really did see Gid Rust at the Derrick Theatre."

"Oh, he didn't just see him," said Lou. "He met him."

Chapter Forty-One

Latonia City, Pennsylvania
August 1964

NAT SWALLOWED HARD—again—against his dry throat.

The woman he was following did not lead him to the door that he knew was the entry to a small office with a window and a fire escape. It was almost a shame that she didn't, because wouldn't that have been poetic? Instead, she led him a bit farther down the hall, to a different room, where she stopped and knocked.

For a few moments, the knock was met with no reply, and Nat thought he could smell smoke of a variety that was not usually imbibed through a traditional tobacco pipe. Then a scratchy voice from behind the door called out, "Yeah?"

"It's Miss Franklin," said the woman, the third-generation owner and operator of the Derrick Theatre. "I was wondering if you might have time to meet someone."

"Oh yeah?" the voice said.

"I hope you don't mind," said Miss Franklin. "He's a big fan of yours. He was in the front row for tonight's show."

"Sure, sure, okay," said the scratchy voice. "Let him in."

With that, Miss Franklin opened the door and motioned Nat to enter.

Nat stepped in, and there *he* was.

The first time Nat had seen him, he'd been overweight but not fat, tall but not towering, with hair that was thin but not entirely balding. Now, he was, if anything, underweight. His back was bent, reducing his height a bit. And with the exception of a tiny bit of hair at the back of his head, his scalp was shiny and smooth. He had removed his suit jacket and sweat-soaked shirt, and he sat, alone, on a metal chair in his trousers and undershirt. A second chair sat directly in front of him, where his trumpet stood on end, with a white handkerchief lying beside it.

Gideon Rust looked up at Nat and smiled broadly. "Hey, Mack," he said in his raspy voice.

Gid called everybody Mack.

"This is Nat MacCulloch," said Miss Franklin. "He's a founding member of our city's Arts Council and was part of setting up tonight's show."

Nat wanted to step forward and shake Gid's hand, but he worried this would be too presumptuous, so he just nodded respectfully and said, "It's an honor to meet you, Mr. Story. May I call you 'Louis,' Sir?"

The smile on the face of Louis Gideon "Rust" Story grew even broader. "You know, not many people know my real name."

Miss Franklin flashed Nat a smile, then stepped out of the room to give them some privacy.

"I'm, uh, a bit of a student of jazz history," said Nat. "And a dedicated reader of your album liner notes."

"Guess you must have been reading for a long time, then," said Gid. "I don't think I've said anything about my real name, even in a liner note, since the 40s."

"Oh, I've been a fan since before that, Mr. Story," said Nat.

"That a fact? Well, I'll tell you what. If you paid for a front-row seat, you can just as well call me Lou, okay?"

At this, Nat found himself giggling like a kid. "Okay, Lou."

It was then that Nat noted the small dots of blood on Gid's undershirt. He had split his lip during the encore. From what Nat understood, that happened to him quite a lot. These days, Gid Rust, who was considered one of the inventors of jazz music, was pretty old to be touring so relentlessly. In *Rust Story: The Life and Music of Gid the Great*, which Nat had read twice since its publication three years prior, the author claimed that Gid had "never really learned to hold a trumpet to his lips the right way," and as a result, frequently split his upper lip from his intense, high-register playing, sometimes requiring medical attention. The resulting buildup of scar tissue had to be frequently shaved from his upper lip by physicians to keep him in playing shape. The condition also reportedly kept him in constant pain. Up close, the scars on Gid's lips were far worse than Nat would have expected, one of which had been freshly reopened tonight.

It was strange to see this once vibrant man looking so old. Almost frail. A lot had changed since the days when a young Louis Gideon Story, playing a secondhand cornet in the brothels of New Orleans, first began combining ragtime and blues into a style of music that would come to be known as jazz. He was now old enough to have been confronted with one of the most tragic hardships an artist can endure: living long enough to see himself fall out of favor. With the emergence of bop, which pushed the bounds of musical complexity, jazz had evolved from dance music into a serious art form. And a byproduct of this transformation was that Gid's brand of jazz and his vibrant style of showmanship were seen as middlebrow at best. He was widely criticized by the new generation of jazz musicians, who thought of him as too accommodating to audiences, even bordering on subservient. You wouldn't have caught Miles Davis or Dizzy Gillespie goofing around onstage or pulling faces to make the crowd laugh. But in every interview Nat had ever read, Gid maintained that his persona was not about being accommodating, but about being his authentic self, with a zest for life, and just putting on a good show. But Nat was only a fan. He couldn't have understood the underlying issues at play, and he didn't claim to.

"So, what'd you think of the show?" said Gid.

He made a face and touched his throat tenderly as he said it. It sounded as if it pained him to speak. Gid Rust's distinctive growl of a voice had grown increasingly gravelly over the years. A magazine article published in the late 50s claimed that this was due to nodules on Gid's vocal cords, which were actually quite problematic and threatening to his health. He'd even undergone a series of throat surgeries in an attempt to remove the nodules, but the results had been unsuccessful, leading to recurring infections that had further compromised his health and occasionally got bad enough to interrupt his touring.

If it pained the man to even speak, Nat couldn't imagine what it had felt like to belt out eight choruses of "Dinah" tonight.

"The show was phenomenal," said Nat. "Even better than the last time I saw you."

"Oh yeah? When'd you see me last?"

"Last time you were here, Sir," said Nat. "1939. That was a great show, too."

Lou shook his head in wonder. "You know, you may not believe it, but I remember that show well. I've played everywhere, man. All over the North. New York City. Chicago, especially. Played in Paris, France, all the time—this was back before the war. Played more places than I can count down South where the white folks would pay fifty dollars a head just to see me blow my horn but wouldn't let me use the bathroom in the same building. Did broadcasts with Frankie and Bing out west. Had a few parts in a couple of pictures. But even though I must've played a thousand theaters all around the world, I *remember* this place."

"The Derrick is a wonderful theater," said Nat. "The older I get, the more I realize how lucky the city is to have this place. A beautiful waterfront venue like this, right on the Allegheny."

"Nah, it wasn't the building. It was the people. Something about the crowd. That's what sticks with you.

A wonderful crowd. It was the same tonight. This place has got good folks. They've treated me right."

Nat couldn't help but wonder if part of what had made that 1939 show memorable for Gid was the brief disruption near the end of the night, when a few half-pint show-crashers had been chased out of the projectionist's room and down the second-floor fire escape. He even started to open his mouth to mention this, but instead, he just said, "It—it's such a thrill to meet you, Mr. Story. I just wanted to thank you for everything you've done for me. I practically idolized you as a kid, and your music got me through some not-so-good times."

"Thank you," said Gid, smiling. "That's kind of you to say."

"I, uh," stammered Nat. "I even bought a used cornet as a kid and tried to learn your version of 'Dinah.' It drove my sisters crazy. My dream was to be a great trumpet player like you. I would make-believe I was onstage with Gid the Great, right here at the Derrick."

Gid lit up, laughing and smiling wider than ever. "You still do any playing nowadays?"

"A little," said Nat, although the truth was that he practiced every night without fail. "I'm an accountant by trade, so the music thing never really happened. But I still wanted to thank you."

Gid nodded and stroked a dark, stubbled cheek. Then he craned his neck toward the door. "Hey, Miss Franklin?"

Nat grimaced, realizing he'd been rambling. He had overstayed his welcome.

"Yes, Mr. Rust?" said Miss Franklin, leaning back inside the doorway.

"Would it be a major inconvenience to turn the stage lights back on for a few minutes?" asked Gid.

"Of course not, Mr. Rust." And Miss Franklin hurried off down the hallway to make it happen.

Gid stood from his chair and grabbed his trumpet. He flashed a smile at Nat and gestured toward the door. "You feel like swinging a number or two?"

Nat felt his mouth hanging open. "I didn't bring my horn," was all he could think to say.

"That ain't no problem, you can borrow one of mine," said Gid. "What do you say?"

Nat stared. "I say . . . golden aces! God, yes, Mr. Story! I would love that!"

Gid threw his head back, laughing loud and long. He clapped Nat on the back and started for the door. "Then come on, Mack, let's blow."

Nat was here, thought Nat MacCulloch as he followed Gid down the hallway, *on the day Gideon Rust came to play at the Derrick. Nat is going to sneak into the Derrick Theatre to see him tonight. Nat will someday play trumpet with Rust and will be the most famous trumpet player in the world.*

Nat smiled.

Two out of three wasn't half bad.

Chapter Forty-Two

Latonia City, Pennsylvania
January 2020

THE FIRST PHASE of the project was done. Through a combination of electric sanders, metal-edged scrapers, and good-old-fashioned elbow grease, the old paint had been removed to reveal a blank surface beneath. It was the first week of the new year, and it was seven o'clock on a Friday. On any other day, Owen would have been home by now—he didn't work past six anymore. But today was an exception. He wasn't working. He was volunteering his time. And he wasn't just a participant in this work initiative. He'd set the whole thing up himself.

He had spent weeks reaching out to local businesses and individuals, asking if they would be willing to donate paint, supplies, tools, or their time to help renovate the lobby of the *Oildom News–Herald*, whose hyphenated name, Owen had recently learned, was a holdover from the 1869 merger of Oildom Centre's *Oildom Daily News* and the *Lay's Bend Herald*, at the same time that the two towns on the opposite sides of the Allegheny River were incorporated into Latonia City, almost 150 years prior. Who would have thought?

The community response to Owen's work day initiative had been greater than he ever could have hoped for. The *Herald* had received more donations than they needed, enough that Owen was certain they could have comfortably hired a team of contractors to do the work for them. But there was something special about getting the staff to take an active role in the job. Each of them had a personal stake in this lobby's transformation now and could take ownership of the results. With any luck, they would have enough funds left over to have the keystone mosaic floor professionally cleaned.

While the night staff was just beginning their shift, most of the day shift had stayed to help with the current phase of the project. The team was spread out across the lobby, with tarps laid out carefully beneath them to protect the magnificent floor. Dave Albaugh was there, and even his father Dick had made an appearance to serve as an enthusiastic delegator. Felicia had managed to find a sitter for her kids and was currently locked in conversation with Davewhite, who was regaling her with the latest chronicle in the saga of Mary Anne the ginger cat, who, on New Year's Eve day, had brought Davewhite the gift of a small mouse and dropped it on his pillowcase beside his head while he was half asleep; Mary Anne had, however, neglected to kill it first, and Davewhite was not too proud to describe how he'd nearly streaked his tighty-whities scrambling to escape from the rodent as it went scurrying beneath his bedsheets. He summed it all up by concluding, "Yeah, 2019 was a doozy of a year for everybody, I think. I'm sure 2020 will be smooth sailing."

Kayla was there, too. And so was Lou. And so was Owen, of course, as the organizer of the project. He had personally taken down the NO SMOKING sign, and he did not intend to put it back up again.

Presently, he wedged the business end of a flathead screwdriver into the lid of a paint bucket, pried it open, and stuck a wooden stirrer in to begin mixing. Right about now, the new copy editor under his tutelage would be in the back offices, looking over the articles he had written, which would run the next morning.

So far, none of Owen's articles had received as great a response as the very first story he'd written: a piece on the Derrick Theatre and the dozens of noteworthy entertainment acts that had graced its stage over the years, including that world-famous pioneer of jazz, Gideon Rust. It had been an innocent, informative human-interest story featuring a bit of local history, although he may have also included a sentence or two about the current initiative by a few wealthy citizens to have the Derrick torn down, and how its destruction would mark the end of an era for Latonia City.

A renewed surge of interest in the building had been spurred by Owen's article, and the Derrick Theatre had even been submitted as a nominee for the National Register of Historic Places. If it was accepted, everything about the building's future would change.

It occurred to Owen that he hadn't been entirely unbiased in writing that first article. A journalist was supposed to be impartial, but it would have been obvious to *any* reader that the writer, Owen, didn't want to see the building torn down. Did that make Owen a hypocrite? Was he no better than Mae Baughman, knowingly influencing her readership? Time would tell, he supposed.

When the color was mixed, Owen set the stirrer to the side, poured a bit into the metal tray in front of him, and moved his roller back and forth until it was soaked. Then he climbed the small stepladder and began to apply the first coat of paint to the spot where, just a few days prior, peeling paint had hung in a roll like snakeskin. He had a funny feeling that he was being watched, and when he turned, he caught his father smiling at him. Lou looked away, but Owen wasn't fooled.

Owen applied some more paint to the roller. There was work to be done.

Epilogue

Latonia City, Pennsylvania
July 1988

LOU DIDN'T GET IT. This kid just *would. Not. Sleep.*

He had tried over and over again, every way he could think of. But this boy just did not want to close his eyes. Lou was at his wits' end. And he couldn't rightly be mad about it because the kid wasn't even being unpleasant. Not cranky. Not sad. Not crying. Just awake.

Looking down at his son's wide, energy-filled eyes, Lou wished *he* was still able to feel this wide awake once in a while. But these days, he was tired. He was always tired—why hadn't anybody told him that being a parent made you so *tired*?

After trying every chair, couch, loveseat, and bed in the house, Lou had retreated to the back porch swing, where the air of a muggy midsummer's night parted around him like a damp curtain. He instantly felt sweaty and regretted the decision to come out here, even before taking his seat on the swing. But as soon as he did, he realized he'd made the right choice. The child looked up from Lou's arms, and those eyes—always so present and bright and full of life and attention—took on a different look. His eyelids drooped a little before snapping back open.

"You're fighting it," he whispered to baby Owen. "I don't know why you always fight it, but you do."

Owen stretched, placing one fat-fingered hand on Lou's arm.

"My dad never had to rock *me* to sleep, you know," said Lou. "Men of his generation didn't really do that sort of thing. Your grandma was the one who did all the work while Grandpa smoked his pipe in the next room and read the paper. What a life." Lou threw a cautious glance over the back of the swing toward the house to ensure that Deb wasn't listening from the door. "Not that I'm complaining, of course," he said.

The blink of a lightning bug in Lou's peripheral vision drew his attention back toward the yard—the backyard of a small rented house just a few miles from the home he'd grown up in and where his father had grown up before him. The grass was getting tall and in need of mowing.

Lou certainly hadn't expected to still be here, in this little town, at the age of twenty-nine, worrying about things like mowing the lawn. Such an apparent lack of forward momentum had the distinct whiff of failure about it, and there were times when Lou felt his spirit pulse in desperation for an escape.

Can't afford it right now, he reminded himself as another lightning bug lit up above the tall grass, *but this is only a season. A couple more years, maybe.*

That was what he told himself. But there were also times when the desperation diminished to such an extent that he almost forgot about it. Almost misplaced it. In those moments, he felt something he couldn't quite describe. He felt almost . . . content. Like maybe this place, this life, wasn't so bad.

It was easy to forget what you were supposed to want, especially on a warm, lazy summer's night with lightning bugs floating over the backyard.

"I'll have to teach you to catch lightning bugs," Lou told Owen in a whisper. "Not that it's hard. You'll be a natural. Probably better than me. Probably better than me at lots of things. Hell—er, sorry—*heck*, you'll probably be better than me at playing ball, too. Stronger. Smarter. You'll get out of here and go places and do things I'll only ever dream of. And I hope. . . . I hope you and I have a better relationship than I had with my dad. Because one of the things I regret the most is that, after all the times he was patient with me when I acted like a fool, I didn't return the favor the one time he needed it."

Lou had always thought of his old man as something of a supporting character in his own story. But maybe he'd had it backward all this time. Or, more likely, the truth was somewhere in the middle. It didn't much matter either way. The real story kept moving. And it would keep on moving long after he was gone.

When Lou looked down, Owen's eyes were closed.

"Finally," whispered Lou.

He rested his hand over Owen's. To his surprise, even in sleep, the set of tiny, fat fingers clamped down on his thumb. The grip was strong. It felt more like an innate, biological reflex than a conscious decision on the boy's part, but Lou didn't mind.

"I can't promise you life will be easy," Lou whispered to his sleeping son. "But there's good in it. You're proof enough of that. I've done so much wrong. Spent so long trying to win—thinking I needed to hit big goals, plant a flag, announce my victory. That stuff seemed important for some reason. I don't know what happened, exactly, but somehow. . . . Somehow, none of it feels quite as important as it used to. Maybe, all this time, all I needed was you."

As the lightning bugs silently winked on and off across the yard, Lou closed his eyes, thought of nothing, and fell asleep with his victory in his arms.

About the Author

COREY MCCULLOUGH has worked as an independent ghostwriter, copy editor, proofreader, and archaeological field technician. He lives in western Pennsylvania with his wife Vanessa and their three children. His favorite pastimes are reading, writing, spending time with his best friend (Vanessa), and, most of all, being a dad.

Instagram @cbenmcc
facebook.com/mcculloughwrites
patreon.com/coreymccullough

About This Book

THE BOOK YOU JUST READ was written and released by an independent author.

Independent authors retain creative freedom and control of their work at the cost of many of the resources available to major publishing houses.

If you would like to support this independent author please consider leaving a customer review wherever books are sold.

Visit www.patreon.com/coreymccullough to support this author in exchange for exclusive content.

Thank you for supporting independent art.

Books by Corey McCullough

Rust on the Allegheny: A Novel
<u>The Fallen Tetralogy</u>
The Fallen Odyssey: A Parallel Universe Fantasy Novel
The Fallen Aeneid: Book 2 of The Fallen Odyssey
Shadows of the Fallen: Book 3 of The Fallen Odyssey
The Fallen Anabasis (coming soon)
<u>Rogues Galaxy Series</u>
A Knife in the Dark: A Science Fiction Noir Thriller
A Knife in the Dark: Alloyheart

Get a free ebook copy of *The Fallen Odyssey* at
thefallenodyssey.com/free

Books available at thefallenodyssey.com/products

Products available at etsy.com/shop/mcculloughauthor

Patrons-only stories at patreon.com/coreymccullough

Made in United States
North Haven, CT
19 November 2021

11292615R00188